"It's good to be back here again."

Sharon couldn't be sure if Mac meant the ranch or right there on the porch with her. She only knew what she wanted him to mean, and how dangerous that kind of thinking could be.

She stood up abruptly. "It's been a long day. I think I'll go to bed."

To her dismay, he rose, too, barring her way to the door. He was too close again. Her heart pounded so hard that he must surely have heard it.

"Don't let me run you off," he said, with just a trace of resentment.

She raised her eyebrows at him. "You're not. I'm just tired, that's all."

He shook his head slowly, his gaze speculative. "It's almost as if you're afraid of me."

She wondered if he noticed her guilty start. "Why in the world would I be afraid of you?"

"Maybe because of what happened that night."

Dear Reader,

We've got six drop-dead-gorgeous and utterly irresistible heroes for you this month, starting with Marilyn Pappano's latest contribution to our HEARTBREAKERS program. Dillon Boone, in *Survive the Night*, is a man on the run—right into Ashley Benedict's arms. The only problem is, will they survive long enough to fulfill their promises of forever?

Our ROMANTIC TRADITIONS title is Judith Duncan's *Driven to Distraction*, a sexy take on the younger man/older woman theme. I promise you that Tony Parnelli will drive right into your heart. *A Cowboy's Heart*, Doreen Roberts' newest, features a one-time rodeo rider who's just come face-to-face with a woman—and a secret—from his past. Kay David's *Baby of the Bride* is a marriage-of-convenience story with an adorable little girl at its center—and a groom you'll fall for in a big, bad way. *Blackwood's Woman*, by Beverly Barton, is the last in her miniseries, THE PROTECTORS. And in J.T. Blackwood she's created yet another hero to remember. Finally, Margaret Watson returns with her second book, *An Honorable Man*. Watch as hero Luke McKinley is forced to confront the one woman he would like never to see again—the one woman who is fated to be his.

Enjoy them all, and come back next month for more great romantic reading—here in Silhouette Intimate Moments.

Yours,

Leslie Wainger
Senior Editor and Editorial Coordinator

Please address questions and book requests to:
Silhouette Reader Service
U.S.: 3010 Walden Ave., P.O. Box 1325, Buffalo, NY 14269
Canadian: P.O. Box 609, Fort Erie, Ont. L2A 5X3

A COWBOY'S HEART

DOREEN ROBERTS

Published by Silhouette Books

America's Publisher of Contemporary Romance

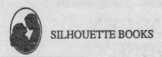 SILHOUETTE BOOKS

ISBN 0-373-07705-X

A COWBOY'S HEART

Copyright © 1996 by Doreen Roberts

Printed in U.S.A.

DOREEN ROBERTS

has an ambition to visit every one of the United States. She recently added several to her list when she drove across the country to spend a year on the East Coast. She's thinking about setting her future books in each of the states she has visited. She has now returned to settle down in Oregon with her new husband, and to get back to doing what she loves most—writing books about adventurous people who just happen to fall in love.

To my patient and dedicated editor,
Karen Taylor Richman, for all her hard work
and efforts on my behalf.
And to Bill, my lifeline. What would I do without you?

Chapter 1

The road looked hauntingly familiar as he drove down from the pass through Oregon's Cascade Mountains. The rolling meadows spread out before him, misted by the warmth of the early-morning sun. Beyond them he could see the lower ridge of the mountain range, a hazy purple against a cloud-dotted sky.

He had driven this road so many times when he was just a young kid. He'd learned to drive on this road. Randall Douglass had taught him to drive the horse trailers to the brokers, and sometimes directly to the stock contractors themselves.

That's how he'd first come in contact with the rodeo. It had eventually become his life. And now it was over, his career ended by an enraged bull who had almost killed him. Now he was on his way back to the past, where it had all begun so many years ago.

His pulse quickened as he rounded the curve. There it was, lying low in the wide valley between the mountains, looking much the same as it had seventeen years ago. The Double S Ranch.

The actual house was hidden by a circle of firs, but he could see the outbuildings and the white fenced corrals. It wasn't a large spread. Mostly horses, a handful of cattle, just enough to make a comfortable living for the Douglass family.

He could feel his heart beginning to thump. The memory that had haunted him for so long seemed much stronger and clearer now that he was so close. Not for the first time, he wondered if he'd made a mistake by coming back.

He left the pickup at the end of the driveway. He needed the walk to settle his mind and prepare himself for the meeting with Randall Douglass. After what had happened, he wasn't at all sure how welcome he'd be, or if Randall would even listen to the proposition he was prepared to offer.

Halfway down the long, winding path between the rows of towering firs, he wished he'd driven up to the house after all. His leg hurt like hell, so much so that the limp he fought so hard to disguise became impossible to avoid.

Sunlight dappled the paved road, the shadows flickering back and forth as the wind shifted the frothy branches. It was a warm morning for late April in Oregon. Right about now he should have been heading east to Montana for his first big ride of the season.

The bittersweet pang of regret was mercifully swift. He had resigned himself to his enforced retirement, though he couldn't escape the occasional ache of nostalgia for the good old days, when he was younger and walked on two good legs.

He'd ridden hard, and he'd beaten the toughest of them. Now those days were behind him—for good. Byron McAllister, known to his adoring fans as "Mac," the celebrated rodeo star and national champion, had taken his last ride.

Mac's lip curled in a cynical smile. All he had left of those glorious days, apart from the healthy bank account he'd accumulated, were his silver trophy belt buckles, a pair of scuffed boots and his black hat. In a few months his name would be forgotten, erased by some flashy young stud showing off his superiority in front of an adoring crowd.

Soon his own memories would fade, too, drifting across time and space like tumbleweed blown across the prairies by the ceaseless wind.

All except one.

Randall Douglass had picked him up off the streets and given him a home when he was barely sixteen. For seven years he'd been treated like a son, until the night he'd let his emotions rule his head in the arms of Randall's daughter.

He had kept alive the memory of his betrayal for one reason only—to remind himself that he was not invincible. For seventeen years that memory had helped him keep a cool head, especially on a hot night with an eager body in his arms.

True, there had been a time or two when he'd yielded to the temptation, but it had been his show all the way, his senses always under control.

Mac tilted his head back as the noisy chattering of a squirrel disturbed the peace. Looking up into the thick, dark branches of the firs, he could see the tiny creature balanced on a flimsy bough that dipped beneath its weight.

Birds twittered and whistled, sheltered by the foliage that looked pretty much the same as it had all those years ago. The breeze rustled the branches, and the pungent fragrance reminded him sharply of the days he had spent at the Double S Ranch.

Sharon Douglass had just turned eighteen the last time he'd seen her. Someone had told him several years ago that she'd divorced her husband and gone back to the Double S to help her father.

He hadn't even known she'd been married. He'd taken small comfort in the realization that what he'd done hadn't ruined things for her in that respect.

He wondered what she looked like now. She'd been no more than eleven when he'd first met her. Raised by her widowed father since she was five, she'd been a tough little kid.

He could see her now—her long hair, the color of buttermilk, streaming behind her as she'd raced bareback across the meadow clinging to Whitefire's mane.

That girl could ride a horse the way an eagle's feather rode the wind. She was the one who'd taught him how to break a horse without breaking its spirit. She'd taught him to throw a lasso and snag a colt at fifty paces, and how to tell if a mare was pregnant before its body swelled.

Those had been happy days—the happiest of his life, until Sharon's eighteenth birthday and that sultry summer night he'd lost his head.

He'd lit out the next morning, devastated by his loss of control. He'd owed Randall Douglass his life, and he'd betrayed both the rancher and his daughter. He'd never been able to forgive himself for that one night of stolen passion.

He'd taken only what was his on his back, the same way he'd arrived. He'd joined the rodeo circuit ten days later. With a relentless need to drive his betrayal out of his mind, he'd pitted his wits and strength against the broncs and bulls with a grim determination that had rocketed him all the way to the top.

Even then he hadn't been satisfied. There were some who'd said that Mac McAllister was out to kill himself in the arena. And finally he almost had.

The sudden sound of an engine bursting to life disturbed Mac's troubled thoughts. The house lay around the bend, still hidden from view by the fragrant green branches of the firs. Whoever had started the car was in a hurry, judging by the squeal of tires.

Even as the thought occurred to him, the flash of red through the trees warned him the vehicle was almost upon him. As the sports car hurtled around the bend, he lunged sideways.

He'd forgotten about his bum leg. With his weight full on the damaged bones, the limb gave way, sending him sprawling in the dust. He just had time to glimpse the white face of the driver before the car roared past him in a flurry of noise, hot air and the acrid smell of the exhaust.

Pain shot up his leg, taking his breath away, and for a moment he wondered if he'd broken it again. He lay where he was for a moment, listening to the fading sound of the engine, until all he could hear was the chirping of sparrows and the harsh, solitary cry of a frightened blue jay.

After a while, however, he was able to sit up and gingerly run his hands over the mended fractures. Apart from a few sore spots, the leg seemed undamaged. Carefully he climbed to his feet and dusted his hands down his light blue wind jacket and jeans.

He tested his weight until he was satisfied, then squaring his shoulders, he marched purposefully, and as evenly as he could manage, toward the house.

He'd heard rumors some time ago that the Double S was in trouble. Randall raised and broke horses, mostly for the rodeo, and bad news traveled fast on the circuit.

After the fall that had nearly killed him and put an end to his career on the circuit, he'd decided to offer his services free of charge. At least until he figured out what he was going to do with the rest of his life.

He owed Randall a huge debt, and this was his big chance to repay it. Then maybe he could finally put the past behind him and get on with his life.

At the moment his future was unpredictable. All he knew was horses and what he'd learned about running a business during the seven years he'd lived at the Double S.

He wasn't real worried, though. He was used to meeting problems head-on. He'd blazed a new trail enough times in the past, and he'd do it again. Right now he had a purpose, and that would take care of today. He'd worry about tomorrow when he got there.

He still had his health and strength, and his leg was getting stronger every day. It had taken months for him to feel secure enough to go back to work, but now he was pretty confident he could handle it.

His self-admitted stubbornness and his iron will had helped him get through the ordeal of his recovery. Once he had settled his debt with Randall Douglass, those same qualities would put him on the road in a new direction, as they had before. And this time there would be no Sharon Douglass to haunt his dreams.

Sharon stared moodily out of the living-room window as the sports car disappeared down the driveway. These days it was almost impossible to have a conversation with her son without ending up in an argument.

Now that Tim had turned sixteen, she'd hoped that his newly acquired driving license and the freedom it afforded would help to ease the tension between them. Instead, it had simply made it easier for Tim to storm out of the house at the slightest provocation and disappear for a few hours, leaving her seething with helpless frustration.

A slight movement at the edge of the circular driveway caught her eye. She watched the squirrel dart easily up the smooth, straight trunk of a fir, then bounce from limb to limb until it vanished into the mass of green branches.

The tiny animal reminded her of her son. Restless, unpredictable and nearly always out of sight. His moodiness had begun to transfer itself to her own temperament, and lately she didn't seem able to control the irritation and intolerance that sparked so many arguments.

If only Tim had grown up with a father's guidance and control, his adolescence might have been easier to bear. Her own father had done his best, but Randall Douglass had been too absorbed in the running of the Double S to give much of his failing energy to his grandson.

For a moment she allowed the flash of resentment to fester. She'd had to do it all, and most of the time alone. Life could be very cruel and unfair at times.

The next moment she washed the bitterness from her mind. The choice had been hers. She had made her decision a long time ago, and there was no going back.

She was about to turn away from the window when the frantic barking of the dogs caught her attention. For a moment she thought it was Tim walking back to the house, and her heart skipped in apprehension as she wondered what had happened to the car.

Then, as the figure drew closer, she could see he was taller and much older than Tim. He was wearing a black hat pulled low over his face, and his features were hidden from her. Although he appeared to be limping slightly, he was heading toward the house at a pretty fast clip.

He was probably looking for work, Sharon thought as the man paused a few yards from the front steps. Jerry, her chief trainer and foreman, would be out in the corral, working with the horses. She'd send the guy out to him, though she doubted if Jerry would hire him. They were already overbudget on their payroll.

The two retrievers bounded into view, their hackles raised, their throats growling a warning. They knew better than to attack without a command, but even so, Sharon watched anxiously as the stranger turned to face them.

He held out his hand, and after a moment or two the dogs quit growling, though they kept a respectful distance and watched the man warily as he dropped his hand and turned back to the house.

Watching him, too, Sharon was caught by the sudden stillness of his body as he looked about him. She saw him raise a hand and tip his hat back on his head, revealing his face for the first time. A shaft of shocked recognition rocked her on her feet. It couldn't be, and yet...

She found it impossible to breathe as she watched the tall, lean figure move closer to the steps. A tiny moan escaped from her dry lips when he lifted his chin to look up at the gabled roof. He was staring straight at the window of what was once his bedroom. The unthinkable had happened. Mac McAllister had returned to the Double S.

She seemed unable to move, to think, to function on any level. Questions plunged and scattered throughout her mind. In a cold daze she watched as the man she had never been able to forget slowly mounted the steps and then disappeared from view beneath the porch. A second later the doorbell pealed, echoing its shrill summons throughout the house.

The sound shattered her frozen state, and for a moment or two she floundered in panic. She was alone in the house. Maybe if she didn't answer, he'd go away. Almost at once she knew that hope was futile. Mac never gave up...on anything. He'd simply go off in search of the men, and he'd find them easily enough. Sooner or later she would have to face him. Better to get it over with now, and get rid of him, before Tim came back.

That thought galvanized her into action. Almost unconsciously her hand went to her hair as she hurried to the door. Against her will she formed a mental vision of how she would look to Mac, after all these years.

She had been eighteen then, too thin and careless about her looks. Now, at thirty-five, she wore light makeup and was a few pounds heavier.

The years had taught her how to tame her wild blond hair, and she wore it caught at the nape with a dark brown ribbon. The cream shirt she wore blended perfectly with her coffee-colored pants, and a pair of golden horseshoes, a gift from her father, gleamed in her ears.

In spite of her best efforts to compose herself, her heart pounded heavily as she reached the front door. The bell pealed again, three short, impatient jabs, sending a jolt throughout her body. Wondering if she would have any voice left to speak, she slowly opened the door.

She knew right away that he hadn't expected to see her there. It gave her a spasm of satisfaction to see his eyes widen and his jaw tense. Mac had always been an expert at disguising his feelings. Even that slight change in his features told her that she'd shaken him.

His reaction gave her the edge, since she had already braced herself for the confrontation. "Well, this is a surprise," she said smoothly as Mac continued to stare at her in silence. "To what do we owe this distinct pleasure?"

She could tell from the slight lift of his dark eyebrow that he'd noted the sarcasm. "I came to see Randall," he said with just a trace of resentment underlying his deep voice.

Deeper than she remembered, Sharon thought, immediately angry with herself for the telltale flush she could feel on her cheeks. So he didn't know. Remembering how close Mac had been to her father, she felt a tinge of sympathy for him. "You'd better come in," she said quietly.

The second he stepped inside the hallway, she regretted the invitation. He was taller than she remembered. His body still retained much of the hard, lean strength of his youth, judging from what she could see of it. His shoulders, however, had broadened, and the once-smooth skin of his harshly chiseled face now bore the brunt of too much sun and wind.

Deep creases lined the corners of his steel blue eyes, and an occasional thread of silver gleamed in the thick, dark hair at his temples. His mouth, once curved and teasing, was clamped in a hard, uncompromising line.

Only the stubborn set of his jaw with its hint of shadow reminded her vividly of the young man she had once adored with all the passion of a first and only love.

She watched him sweep off his hat with a flamboyant gesture that was wholly unfamiliar. "You've changed," he said abruptly, as if echoing her thoughts.

"I've grown up." The words, flung over her shoulder as she led him into the den, sounded harsher than she'd intended. When she looked at him again, his expression told her he was once more in command of himself, as always.

He stood in the center of the room, his gaze touching on the familiar surroundings. Little had changed in that respect at least, she thought as she watched him skim over the green, deep-seated couch and the soft leather armchair that her father had coveted.

The writing desk still stood in the same corner, and the bookshelves that lined the walls were crammed with trophies and souvenirs, just as they had been when Mac had first arrived at the ranch as a bedraggled teenager so many years ago.

He'd be forty now, she realized with a shock. Somehow, on the rare occasions she'd allowed herself to think about him, she'd always envisioned him as he'd been when he'd left—twenty-three years old, with a shock of unruly black hair and a grin that could always melt her knees.

"Randall's out in the corral with the horses, I guess," Mac said gruffly.

Startled, she realized he'd caught her staring at him. Turning away from him, she said unsteadily, "I'm sorry, Mac. My father died three months ago."

The long pause that followed her announcement unnerved her. She wasn't sure she could look at him without giving away some of the devastation she'd gone through watching her father struggle for life.

Just when the silence became unbearable, Mac said quietly, "How'd it happen?"

She took a moment to collect herself, and picked up the small framed photograph of Randall Douglass that stood on top of the desk. Gazing down on the image of her father, she tried to draw strength from it as her mind inevitably went back to that dreadful day.

"He fell," she said, her voice hushed in the quiet room. "We don't know exactly what happened. The doctor thinks it might have been a stroke. He hadn't felt well for some time. In any case, his spine was broken. His horse came back without him. I knew, as soon as I saw that damn horse—" Her voice broke.

Out of the corner of her eye, she saw Mac sharply raise his chin.

"He was in terrible pain," she went on, determined not to give in to the grief again, "but he fought like a wildcat to live. It took him five days to die."

Across the room Mac swore. "He was too damn young to die," he muttered.

Sharon swallowed hard, her eyes stinging with the effort to hold back her tears. "It was a blessing he did. He would have been paralyzed from the neck down. To my father, that would have been a living hell. As you well know, he was always such an active man, and lived for his horses. To be confined to the house, without any hope of recovery, would have destroyed his soul."

She risked a glance at Mac, who stood staring down at the leather armchair as if he could see Randall Douglass still sitting there. After a moment he lifted his head and looked at her. "If ever a man lived to be under an open sky, it was your father. You can bet your braces that somewhere on an open plain, his spirit is still riding the range.''

The unexpected sentiment was almost her undoing. She nodded, afraid to trust her voice. Carefully she replaced the photograph, and prayed that Mac would leave before she made a fool of herself in front of him.

To her dismay, he sat down in the armchair and placed his hat on his lap, apparently prepared to stay awhile. The window of the den looked out on the fields at the back of the house. She wouldn't be able to see Tim if he decided to return. She had to get rid of Mac before her son came back.

Over the years she had managed to convince herself that Tim was never likely to meet Mac McAllister. Although her son's fondest dream was to join the rodeo, she was determined to send him to university.

Tim was a bright, intelligent boy, with the keen, logical mind of his grandfather and his mother's eloquent tongue. He was cut out to be a lawyer, and had shown some interest in the field. Sharon was not about to let him waste his life pursuing some wild dream of the rodeo.

It was a hard life, a lonely life, with little stability and no roots. She'd heard too much about broken bones and broken spirits, the never-ending risk of permanent injury for little more than a meager living. Except for the very few who made it to the top. As Mac had.

Suddenly remembering his limp, she wondered if he'd taken a bad fall. She'd heard his name mentioned occasionally, but she hadn't been to a competition in years. Now that she thought about it, he should be out on the circuit by now.

Glancing down at him, she was disturbed to find him watching her with an intent look in his eyes that warned her she was giving away too much with her expressions. She never had been able to hide her feelings the way Mac could.

"I'm surprised you hadn't heard about Dad's accident," she said, smoothing out her face. "The news must have been all over the circuit."

"I've been out of action since last season." His instinctive glance at his leg told the story.

"I'm sorry," Sharon murmured. "It must have been a bad fall."

"It was. Enough to put me out of the running for good."

She closed her eyes briefly, glad that he wasn't watching her. His voice had held no evidence of the anguish he must have felt. She could only imagine his initial reaction to that news. "I'm sorry," she said again.

Mac shrugged. "I had a good shot at it. Longer than some."

There didn't seem any answer to that, and once more she wished he would go.

"I heard you'd got married," Mac said, leaning back to cross one booted foot over the other.

This time she fought to disguise her apprehension. She didn't want him wondering why she was so anxious to be rid of him. Mac was smart; he might very well figure things out, especially if Tim came back before he left.

"I did. Soon after you left, in fact. It didn't last."

"Anyone I know?"

She hesitated, then decided there was no point in keeping it from him. "I don't know if you remember Will Carlson. He managed the race track out near Falls Bend."

If Mac was surprised at that, he gave no indication of it. Instead, he nodded, his lips pursed. "Yep, I remember. Big guy, had a loud laugh."

Sharon grimaced. "That about sums him up."

"Any kids?"

She could tell he was merely making polite conversation, but she couldn't help wondering if he'd seen the guilty start she hadn't been able to evade. "One. A son. Tim is ... in high school."

Mac's face changed. "I think I saw him. Driving a red sports car with his foot slammed to the floor?"

She nodded, wondering how closely he had seen her son. "That was Tim." It was time to change the subject, she decided, and added lightly, "How about you?"

If she hadn't known him so well, she might have missed the slight twitch of his jaw muscle. "I was always moving around too much," he said. "Never in one place long enough to get involved."

She didn't answer, reluctant to pursue that particular line of conversation.

After a moment or two Mac shifted in his chair. "So, how's the ranch doing?"

She knew he must have heard the rumors about the problems at the Double S. They had been in deep trouble since last summer. Randall Douglass seemed to have lost his ability to manage his affairs at least a year before he died.

He had set impossible schedules and demanded ludicrous standards. He'd been impatient with excuses and had ignored the numerous complaints.

Unhappy with the situation, his ranch hands had threatened to leave. Randall had solved that problem by raising their salaries, above what the ranch could afford.

Sharon had done her best to intervene, but her father's stubborn independence had prevented him from listening to any advice, from her or anyone else. At times it had been difficult to recognize the tense, irritable man as the gentle-mannered father who had raised her single-handedly.

She knew now what he had been too proud to tell her. His health was failing, and the headaches that had driven him crazy for so long finally ended in his death.

Since then the problems had escalated. The ranch hands made no secret of the fact they resented a woman being their boss, and to make matters worse, her father's death had affected her relationship with Tim.

Without the steadying influence of his grandfather, her son had become belligerent, rebellious, more determined than ever to throw away his life on the rodeo. The arguments between them had intensified, becoming more and more frequent, until it seemed as if they were constantly fighting with each other.

Realizing that Mac was watching her curiously as he waited for an answer, she gathered her scattered thoughts. She wasn't about to discuss her problems with him. She wasn't sure why he had bothered to come back after all these years—she didn't want to know.

He had left that summer day so long ago, without a word to her or her father, who had treated Mac like the son he'd never had. She would never forgive him for that.

"The ranch is doing just fine," she lied, looking him straight in the eye. "Things got a little unsettled before my father died, but now we have the problems straightened out and everything is running smoothly now."

"I'm glad to hear it."

She knew by his tone of voice that she'd surprised him. She glanced at the wall clock, feeling guilty that she hadn't at least offered him something to drink.

He looked a little tired, and had obviously walked up the long driveway, though she couldn't imagine why. Unless he had hitched a ride to the ranch.

The sudden thought hit her like a sledgehammer. Surely he hadn't expected to stay awhile at the ranch? But then, maybe he had, if he'd thought that Randall was still alive. She would have to find a way to get rid of him.

Deliberately she looked at the clock again. "I'm sorry to cut this visit short," she said with just the right amount of regret in her voice, "but I have an appointment for lunch in town. I have to get ready now."

He gave her a long look, and for a second or two she felt like a teenager again, experiencing all the strange emotions that had confused her whenever he was near.

Abruptly she turned away from that intense scrutiny. "I'm sorry my father wasn't here to see you. I know he would have wished you well."

"I'm sorry, too."

She heard the chair creak as he stood. Although she was several feet away from him, she detected a faint waft of cologne—earthy and spicy, like the man who wore it.

Annoyed with the frivolous thought, she turned to face him again and made her voice deliberately cool. "It was . . . nice seeing you again, Mac."

"You, too." He hesitated, not quite able to meet her eyes.

She guessed what was coming and tried desperately to forestall him. "I hope—"

He cut her off, decisively, as if determined to speak the words that must have been awkward for him. "Sharon, I reckon I should apologize for what happened that last night."

She resisted the urge to pretend she didn't understand what he was talking about. The subject had been hovering between them ever since he'd entered the house. She lifted her chin a fraction and said evenly, "It was a long time ago, Mac. We were very young."

"That's no excuse."

Deliberately she lifted her shoulders in a casual shrug. "I've forgotten about it. I suggest you do the same."

After a long moment he gave her a slow nod of agreement. "I'm sorry about your father," he said, changing the subject. "He was a good man. I reckon you must miss him a lot."

"I do."

After a pause that seemed to go on too long, Mac made a move toward the door. "I guess I'll be getting along, then."

She didn't look at him as she led him into the hallway. Before she reached the front door, however, she heard the sound she had been dreading.

The roar of Tim's sports car seemed to resound all through the house as he pulled up with a squeal of brakes. The car had been a birthday present from his grandfather, bought after his death with what was left of the insurance money. Tim seemed to live in it nowadays.

Hastily Sharon pulled the door open as Mac said behind her, "Sounds as if your son is back."

Before she could answer, Tim had slammed the car door and bounded up the steps. "Hi," he said, apparently catching sight of Mac standing behind her. "I saw your pickup parked down the road. I was hoping you'd still be here."

"Hi yourself," Mac said easily.

Sharon felt as if every nerve in her body had been scraped raw. She saw Tim look expectantly at her, apparently waiting for her to introduce him. It was the very last thing she wanted to do.

Mac's silence unnerved her, and she couldn't think what to say. She could only look helplessly at her son and wait for him to say something.

Finally, after a quick look of impatience for her, Tim brushed by her and held out his hand. "I'm Tim Carlson," he said, his voice high with excitement. "I'm sorry I nearly creamed you in the driveway. I was in a hurry."

"So I gathered."

Sharon watched Mac take her son's hand in his and give it a firm shake. "No harm done," he added, flashing a grin she remembered only too well.

"I thought you looked familiar when I tore by you," Tim said, dragging off the windcheater she'd bought for him on his birthday.

"I realized who you were a few minutes ago." He dropped his coat on the stairs. "I couldn't believe that I'd actually nearly mowed down one of my rodeo idols, the great Mac McAllister."

Sharon's gasp at the news that Tim had come close to hitting Mac went unnoticed as the two regarded each other—Mac with discomfort, Tim with undisguised awe.

"You are Mac McAllister, aren't you?" Tim said anxiously when Mac didn't answer him right away.

"I am, but I don't know about 'the great' bit. I'm not sure I deserve that handle."

"Trust me," Tim said, grinning in relief. "You're not going, are you? I mean, you can't leave now, I've got tons of questions I want to ask you." He looked pleadingly at his mother. "Tell him he's gotta stay. He's the first real rodeo champ I've met."

At least that explained why Tim had returned earlier than usual, Sharon thought, regarding her son's anxious expression. She shouldn't have been surprised that he'd recognized Mac. She was well aware that Tim knew everything about everyone on the circuit, although she had refused to discuss the subject with him.

"I'm sure Mr. McAllister has better things to do than spend his time listening to your endless questions," she said, warning Tim with her eyes. He knew very well how she felt about the rodeo. He had to know she would be opposed to him spending time with one of the riders, champion or not.

She hoped her expression of disapproval would be enough to dampen his enthusiasm. She could hardly tell Tim the real reason she didn't want her son within a hundred miles of Mac McAllister.

It was a futile hope, of course.

"I'm not in any hurry," Mac said, "but your mother has a lunch appointment in town. And it's 'Mac.' No one ever calls me Mr. McAllister."

"Well, she can go, Mac," Tim said airily. "I can take care of you. I'll get you a beer." He was backing down the hallway as he spoke. "Mom won't let me drink beer, but I'll have a soda while we talk. I won't be a minute, so don't go away, okay?"

"He seems like a good kid," Mac said, looking after Tim with a look of wry amusement.

"He can be a little wild at times," Sharon admitted, "but on the whole he's pretty good."

"Would you mind if I stayed for a while? I'd like to talk to him. He kind of reminds me of myself at that age."

The remark put her even more on edge. *Yes, she minded.* She minded very much. Allowing the two of them to talk together could open up all kinds of explosive danger. Not only would Mac be adding fuel to the flames of Tim's ridiculous ambitions, but there was a very real chance that he could uncover the one secret he must never know.

There didn't seem to be much she could do about it, however. To refuse to let him stay would not only be incredibly rude, but it might very well trigger suspicions in Mac's mind.

True, after the way he had left, she was perfectly entitled to feel reluctant in offering him her hospitality. But that had been so long ago, it would seem silly to bear a grudge, unless she had a deep personal reason for her resentment. And that was something she couldn't afford to let him know.

Meeting his glance, she did her best to relax. "No, of course I don't mind. As a matter of fact, the lunch date isn't that important. Under the circumstances, I'm sure my friend won't mind if I postpone it."

His eyebrow twitched at that, but she rushed on, waving her hand at the door of the den. "Why don't you go back and wait for your beer. I'm sure Tim will be back in a minute. I'll just call my friend and explain, then I'll join you.''

He gave her a brief nod. ''Sounds good.''

She sent one last desperate look at him, then fled up the stairs. She didn't wait to see if he went back into the den. All she wanted was a moment of solitude to collect her thoughts and soothe her shattered nerves.

As she reached the top of the stairs, she heard Tim coming back along the hallway. She heard his voice as he went into the den, though she couldn't hear the words.

Her stomach ached with tension as she hurried into the bedroom. Sinking onto the bed, she drew in a long breath. She couldn't leave them alone for long. Just long enough to make the imaginary telephone call, and then she would have to go back down there. The longer she left them alone together, the greater the chance of something slipping out.

She wasn't exactly sure how Tim would be able to reveal her secret; she was beyond rationalizing at this point. All she knew, above a shadow of a doubt, was that Mac must never know that Tim was not Will's son.

Nor could Tim ever know that his real father was actually a rodeo champion by the name of Mac McAllister.

Chapter 2

Seated in the leather chair, Mac accepted the beer from the excited teenager and flipped open the top. He would have liked more time to catch his breath, he thought as Tim flung himself down on the couch.

It had been a shock to see Sharon standing in the doorway. He hadn't expected her to open the front door. When he'd lived at the Double S, there had been a housekeeper to do that.

There was something else he hadn't expected. Something that had shaken him right down to his boots. The moment he'd looked into those earth brown eyes, he'd felt it. The same wild, driving need that she'd aroused in him so long ago.

Over the years he'd managed to convince himself that the hunger he'd felt that night had been nothing more than a combination of the raging hormones of youth and too much champagne.

He should never have given in to Sharon when she'd begged him to take her out to celebrate her eighteenth birthday. For months he'd done his best not to notice the shapely curves that had gradually turned her from tomboy to woman.

Sharon hadn't helped matters one bit. She'd been out-and-out flirting with him that evening, brushing up against him and murmuring provocative remarks that had fired his blood and set his heart hammering. If she hadn't demanded a birthday kiss from him, it might never have happened.

The moment he'd taken a handful of that soft, fragrant hair and covered her pouting lips with his eager mouth, he'd lost his senses. She wasn't his first woman. She was, for sure, the first and only woman to sear his mind with her hot kisses and bold hands.

Driven almost to the edge of insanity by her frenzied caresses and urgent whispers, his passion had finally exploded. He'd been helpless to stop what had happened, even though he'd been well aware that he was the first man to touch her.

He'd always prided himself on his self-control. It was that ruthless domination of his emotions that had patterned his life, shaped his temperament.

Even during the worst of the beatings he'd received from his abusive father, he had never uttered so much as a whimper. He would never allow himself to show weakness at the hands of a bully.

When he'd received the news that his older brother had been blown to bits in Vietnam, he hadn't spoken a word for five days, terrified that he would break down and cry like a baby.

But he'd almost cried the night he'd stolen Sharon Douglass's virginity.

"Are you okay? Did you get hurt when you fell in the driveway?"

With a start Mac realized that Tim had been waiting for an answer to a question he hadn't heard. Shaking his head, he took a long draft of beer and swallowed it. "Sorry. Just thinking about the old days, I guess. It's been a long time. Sitting here in this room brings back a lot of memories."

Tim's eyes widened in shock. "You've been here before? When? Did you know my grandfather? He died a few months ago, you know."

"Yeah," Mac said slowly. "I know." So she hadn't mentioned him. Nor, apparently, had the old man. His name was probably lower than horse shit after he'd taken off without a word. No wonder neither Sharon nor her father had talked about him.

He didn't need a crystal ball to tell him that Sharon had not been happy to see him. The tension between them had been hot enough to burn his hands. He'd seen right through that story about the lunch date. She'd done her level best to get rid of him.

Not that he could blame her. He had been all ready to leave, anyhow, seeing as how the ranch was doing okay. He didn't need any reminders of what he'd done, and looking at her brought it all back far too clearly.

He couldn't help noticing that the curves that had driven him crazy in his youth had filled out and softened. It was the same face that looked back at him, but that, too, had lost the rebellious look of the tempestuous teenager.

Sharon Douglass, or Carlson, as she was probably called, had matured into an elegant, self-possessed woman, which made her all the more seductive, since he knew only too well the fires that blazed beneath that cool exterior.

He'd been all set to put as much distance between him and the Double S as possible, but then Tim had come charging up to the house.

Looking at the boy, with his long, lanky build, light blue eyes and his mussed brown hair, he was reminded of himself at that age. Right about the time he'd literally landed at the feet of Randall Douglass one wet, windy night.

Intrigued by the rancher's grandson, he'd been easily persuaded to change his mind about leaving.

"I used to work here," Mac said as Tim waited expectantly. "A long time ago. I was your grandfather's head trainer by the time I left."

"But then you left to join the rodeo."

"That's right." If the boy was waiting for him to tell him why, Mac thought grimly, he was going to be disappointed.

"Is Mac your real name?"

"Short for McAllister." Mac paused, then added reluctantly, "It says on my birth certificate that my name's Byron, but no one's ever called me that and lived."

Tim grinned. "What's it like, being in rodeo?"

"Dangerous, dirty and sometimes extremely painful," Sharon said from the doorway.

Tim's head shot around as if he'd been caught with his hand in the cookie jar. "I was just asking," he said a little too defensively.

"Perhaps Mac will tell us how he came to smash up his leg so badly he had to quit," Sharon said smoothly.

Mac watched her walk gracefully across the room and sit down at the writing desk. The look on her face confirmed what he'd already guessed. She didn't want her son talking about rodeo. He didn't know the reason why, but he could guess. The excitement in Tim's eyes was easy to read.

"Your mother's right," he said, "it can be dangerous, and it's downright dirty. Anyone would have to be a little short on brains to ride rodeo for a living."

"But you did it," Tim breathed, his eyes glowing with admiration. "And you made it all the way to the top. National champion five years in a row."

"Until he fell," Sharon said deliberately. "Tell him about it, Mac."

Mac shrugged. "Not much to tell. I was riding a bull, and he was a mean one. He didn't just try to throw me, he slammed me up against the fence so hard he broke my leg. Just for good measure, when I hit the ground he stomped all over me before they ran him off."

"Ouch," Tim muttered, wincing.

"Tell him all of it," Sharon said from across the room.

Mac met her fierce gaze, and for a moment he was back in the stables, facing her across the broad back of Whitefire. She'd been all of fifteen. He could barely see her eyes above the horse that day, but he remembered so well the fire that had burned in them.

One day, she'd told him recklessly, *you will not be able to turn away from me, Mac McAllister. One day you'll see me as a woman, instead of the little kid who used to follow you around. One day you'll want me as much as I want you.*

He'd been so shocked he hadn't been able to answer her at first. Then he'd done his best to laugh it off, telling her she'd been listening to too many love songs. He'd always been able to tease her out of her moods before, but this day he could see that he'd hurt her.

She'd flung her brush at him and stalked off, and hadn't spoken to him again for the best part of a week. Things had never been quite the same between them after that.

Aware of the sudden silence in the room, Mac realized he'd been staring into Sharon's eyes for the past few seconds. Snatching his gaze away, he looked back at Tim, who was watching him with stark curiosity on his face.

"My left leg was broken in two places," Mac said evenly. "My left arm was fractured and my collarbone jerked out of its socket. My right leg got pretty smashed up. They had to do some work on that."

"And that's not the first time you've broken bones," Sharon ruthlessly persisted.

He was getting the message loud and clear. She was doing her best to disillusion her son. Judging by Tim's face, it wasn't working. The kid had it bad.

"I've broken one now and again," Mac admitted, "but nothing really serious until now."

"Wow," Tim said, throwing a leg over the arm of the couch, "that's cool. Man, I'd give anything to ride rodeo. Mom won't even talk about it."

"And for good reason." Sharon stood, glancing meaningfully at the clock. "I won't encourage him to waste his time dreaming about something that's never going to happen. Tim could be a brilliant lawyer, or anything else he put his mind to, for that matter. I know he is far too sensible to throw his life away on such a ridiculous profession."

"It's not ridiculous," Tim protested. "Ask Mac. He did great until he had a bit of bad luck."

"And you could do great as a lawyer." Sharon laid a hand on her son's shoulder. "And you won't have to risk your life every day to do it."

Mac could tell by Tim's rebellious expression that this was an old, and probably constant, argument. Telling himself he had better get out of there before he got drawn into the battle, he got slowly to his feet.

It was time to leave. He couldn't seem to look at Sharon without remembering how his pulse used to race whenever he was near her. His only regret was that he hadn't been able to pay back his debt to his old friend. Now it would always lie on his conscience.

"I reckon I'd better move along," he said as Tim jumped up with a look of dismay.

"You're not leaving," he exclaimed while Mac tried not to notice Sharon's look of relief.

"Yep, I guess I've stayed long enough." Mac sent Sharon a brief nod. "I'm glad things are going okay. I should have known the ranch is in good hands."

"Do you want to see it again?" Tim asked eagerly. "I can show it to you. I bet there have been lots of changes since you were here."

"Tim," Sharon said quickly, "don't you have your homework to do?"

"It's Saturday," Tim said, sounding surprised. "You know I always do it on Sundays."

"Well, I don't think we should keep Mac any longer. I'm sure he has plenty of things he has to do."

"Aw, Mom..." Tim whined.

"I'd like to take a look around, if you don't mind," Mac said, staring thoughtfully at her. She'd sounded kind of desperate. Almost as if she had something to hide.

As if she'd read his thoughts, Sharon uttered a light laugh. "Oh, all right, if it's that important to you. I'll come with you."

She started to walk across the room, but just then the phone rang and she paused, obviously deciding whether or not to answer it.

Tim grabbed it up, however, muttering an impatient "Hello?" After a moment's pause, he held out the receiver to his mother.

"It's for you. I think it's that creepy Bud Everett."

Mac wondered if this was the "friend" she'd talked about, and was immediately annoyed with himself for the twinge of resentment. Whatever Sharon Douglass did in her private life was none of his business.

Right now, he was curious to know why she didn't want him looking over the ranch. Maybe she'd lied to him about things going well. If so, he wanted to know.

"Come on," Tim said, giving Mac a friendly shove, "he'll keep her talking all afternoon. I can't wait to show you off to the guys. She can catch up with us later."

Mac glanced at Sharon, who lifted her shoulders in resignation, then flapped a hand at them to go ahead. Feeling more disappointed than was comfortable, Mac followed Tim out of the room.

The boy had been right, Mac thought as he stood at the edge of the corral a few minutes later. There had been a lot of changes. And none of them good. The buildings looked run-down, and the stables were low on stock, from what he could tell.

It wasn't just the general air of neglect about the place. The men seemed to have a bad attitude, as well. Most of them were lazing around, apparently taking a long lunch break, while the foreman, who Tim introduced as Jerry, was openly hostile, especially when Tim mentioned that Mac had once been Randall Douglass's head trainer.

"Yeah," Jerry muttered at the news, "well, now I'm head trainer. And foreman. So if you're looking for a job, you're outta luck."

"I wish you were coming back to work here," Tim said later as they stood watching the horses quietly grazing. "Things sure haven't been too good since Gramps died."

"In what way?" Mac asked casually. He leaned his elbows on the top railing of the gate, pretending to be absorbed in the horses. Beyond them the meadow sloped up to a small rise. On the other side, the Douglass property rolled gently out toward the hazy purple ridge of the mountains in the distance.

Bordered on one side by the dense forest, and a wide, fast-running creek on the other, the land was a perfect spot for raising horses. Randall Douglass had sacrificed and sweated blood to make a success of the Double S. Knowing the rancher as well as he did, Mac knew that Randall would turn over in his grave if his daughter lost the property now.

"Oh, I dunno," Tim said, staring moodily at the distant mountains. "Things like the stock not being delivered when they're promised. Or the wrong horses being delivered. Some of them are not properly trained. The money just isn't coming in the way it used to.''

''You got any ideas whose fault that is?''

''Maybe. It's like the men don't care anymore. None of them. It wasn't that great when Gramps was alive, not the last year anyway, mostly because he was ill. I guess he let things slide, but it's even worse now.''

''How do the men like having your mother for a boss?''

''They don't.'' Tim uttered a mirthless laugh. ''That's a lot of the problem right there. Jerry really freaks out about it sometimes. He hates being bossed around by a woman. I heard him say so. He's not much of a boss himself, anyway. None of the men listen to him. They just do what they like, and he never says anything to them.''

Mac straightened and turned to lean his back against the fence. From there he could see the back of the house, basking in the warmth of the afternoon sunshine. Two stories high, it nestled in the clearing of trees, long and sleek like a sleeping cat.

Shadows danced across the shake roof, thrown by the branches shifting in the breeze. Huge latticed windows gleamed in the white walls and dormers, their dark green frames matching the firs that sheltered them.

The flower beds lining the white picket fence blazed with deep red and pink azaleas, already blooming in the premature spring weather, while the white camellias each side of the back door had already lost the best of their blossom.

At least there things looked much the same, Mac thought, though the house could use a coat of paint. ''What does your mom say about all this?'' he asked when Tim remained silent.

The boy shrugged, looking unhappy. ''Not much. Actually we don't talk about it much. We don't talk about anything much anymore. She won't listen to anything I say.''

"About what?"

"About anything. She's always too busy doing something else. And I can't say anything about the rodeo without her doing her nut over it. She won't let me even talk about it anymore."

"I think she's afraid you'll give up a chance to make something of your life," Mac said quietly.

"But it's my life." Tim turned pale blue eyes on him that looked vaguely familiar. "When Mom and I first talked about getting a degree, it seemed kind of cool, thinking about living and working in a big city after spending all my life on the ranch. All I could think about at first was getting away from here. It's pretty boring, you know."

"I suppose it could be to some," Mac said dryly.

"The more I thought about it, though, the more I knew it wasn't what I wanted. I don't want to be stuck in a law office all day, or in a stuffy courtroom." He tilted his face to the sun and let out a huge sigh. "Like I told Mom, I have a right to choose what I want to do with my life. It's not as if I'm planning a career in dealing drugs or something. And believe me, I've been offered the chance more than once."

"I bet you have."

"I just want a chance to try it, that's all." Tim lowered his chin and scowled at his sneaker as he dug the toe of it into the ground. "I might not like it, or I might not be good at it, but I want the chance to try. It's all I can think about. It's all I want to do. I don't even have any girlfriends. Not steady ones, anyway."

Mac smiled. "Well, I'm sure your mom is worried about the ranch right now. Give her time to get things straightened out here, and she'll more'n likely listen to your problems then."

"I doubt it," Tim said gloomily.

Watching his face, Mac felt a stab of sympathy for the boy. He knew what it was like to desperately want something he couldn't have. "We'd better be getting back to the house," he said. "Your mom is probably wondering where we are. She hasn't come out to join us, so I guess she's waiting for us to get back."

"She's probably still talking to Bud," Tim muttered. "That guy is the worst bore I ever met."

Mac didn't answer. He was too absorbed in his own thoughts. It was pretty obvious from what he'd seen and what Tim had told him that the rumors were true. The ranch was obviously heading for real trouble.

Rodeo managers and brokers depended on prompt service. Delays were costly, and they would soon go elsewhere if their demands were not met. No matter what Sharon said, she needed help.

Apparently she couldn't afford both a trainer and a foreman. He could help her out for a while as trainer, until the ranch got back on its feet.

Even as he made the decision, he could hear the warning bells going off in his head. He was doing this for Randall, he told himself stubbornly as he trudged back to the house with Tim chattering at his side. He would just have to do his best to stay out of Sharon's way.

She'd made it painfully clear that she wanted nothing to do with him, anyway. After what he'd done, she probably hated him, and who could blame her. For the sake of the ranch, he hoped they could get along. He'd do what he had to do, then he'd get out and never look back again.

The biggest problem was getting her to agree. She was never going to accept his help; that much was plain. He would have to be as diplomatic as possible—a tall order for someone who was used to being blunt about what he wanted.

Sharon met them at the top of the steps, her face rigid with disapproval. Mac couldn't ignore his spasm of resentment. He didn't know what the hell she was worried about. There wasn't anything he could say to Tim about rodeo that the boy didn't already know. Tim had his mother's strong will, and Mac could see trouble ahead, without any help from him.

"I was beginning to worry about you," Sharon said, her glance flicking across Mac's face and down to her son.

"We were just talking about the ranch," Tim said a little huffily.

"Well, I need you to run down to the store for me," Sharon said, glancing at her watch. "I just noticed we're all out of coffee, and you know how Jerry complains if we don't have the coffeepot going all day."

"Okay," Tim muttered. Hunching his shoulders, he looked up at Mac. "It was sure nice meeting you, Mac. I hope you'll come back and see us again real soon."

Grasping Tim's proffered hand, Mac gave it a firm shake. "I'll keep in touch."

Tim nodded, then ran lightly down the steps and leapt into the sports car.

Mac waited until the roar of the engine had faded into the trees before turning back to Sharon. She was staring down the driveway with a worried expression that made him forget his own resentment. Maybe she cared a little too much for her son, but it was far better than not caring at all.

"He'll be okay," he said awkwardly.

"I'm sure he will." Once more her cool gaze rested on his face. "As long as he forgets this ridiculous idea of his about joining the rodeo."

Ignoring what promised to be dangerous ground, Mac said easily, "I had a good look around the place. It seems to me you could use an extra hand around here. If you remember, I used to be a pretty good trainer, thanks to your dad's teaching. I was wondering if you could use some help?"

"Thanks for the offer, but I already have a trainer," Sharon said shortly.

"Yeah, I met him." Mac paused, framing his words carefully. "Seems like a good foreman, too. Only I reckon it must be tough for him, trying to work both jobs. Tim says that Jerry's having a little trouble getting the stock out on time."

"Tim tends to exaggerate." She uttered a laugh that sounded forced. "You know how boys that age can be."

Mac nodded. "All the same, I figure there's room for another pair of hands. To be honest, I'm not offering help, I'm asking for it. I wouldn't need much—maybe a bed in the bunkhouse and meals. I'd be happy enough with that, just until I found another job. It isn't easy for a beat-up cowboy with a bum leg to find work nowadays."

He saw a flicker of sympathy in her dark eyes, and gritted his teeth. He'd never had to beg for anything in his life, and he resented having to do it now. But he had to make her think she was doing him the favor, not the other way around.

He saw the refusal in her face before she uttered the words. "I'm sorry, Mac. Perhaps if you try at the Bar M ranch. I could put in a good word for you."

He shook his head, a little too fast. "Thanks, but I reckon I can find my own work. Anyway, I'll be in town for a few days. I'm staying at the Longhorn Tavern on Market, if you should happen to change your mind."

"I don't think that's likely." She backed up through the doorway and started to close the door. "Goodbye, Mac. I hope you find a good position somewhere."

Stubborn as ever, he thought as he trudged back down the driveway. She never would admit when she was in trouble. As independent as all get-out. He remembered well how mad at him she used to get if he tried to help or advise her.

There was the time he'd tried to tell her that she'd never make a calf horse out of the colt she'd treated as a pet.

"You can't baby them," he'd told her. "A good calf horse has to fear you a little. You gotta have their respect."

She'd yelled at him for ten minutes, reminding him that she was the one who'd taught him all about horses, not the other way around.

He'd been woken up a few nights later by the sound of the front door closing. He'd seen Sharon heading for the stables, and he'd followed her, curious to know what she was doing out there in the middle of the night.

He'd watched in grudging admiration as she'd spent the best part of an hour trying to coax Whitefire to back up, a move that was tough for a horse to learn, since it went against its basic instincts. He could only guess how many nights she'd struggled out there in the moonlight before she'd finally given up the battle.

Reaching his pickup, Mac climbed wearily into the front seat. He didn't know how he was going to persuade her to let him help her out this time. Maybe it was just as well, he told himself as he gunned the noisy engine. Maybe Old Man Douglass was looking down on him, warning him to stay clear of his daughter.

Mac scowled, scanning the road warily for the red sports car before pulling out. Although he hadn't said as much, he wondered if her refusal to hire him was because of what he'd done to her. He hadn't believed for one second her assurance that she'd forgotten about that night. It was there in her eyes, in the way she held herself so damn tense all the time, as if afraid he'd make another move on her.

He'd stick around for a few days, he decided as he headed back toward town, just in case Sharon should change her mind. If not, he'd just have to tell himself that he'd done the best he could, and leave it at that.

He could only hope that the gesture was enough to bury the past once and for all.

* * *

Sharon stood at the living room window, gazing absently out at the driveway. It hadn't been easy to turn down Mac's offer. It would have solved a good many problems for her, as far as the troubles at the ranch were concerned.

She was only too aware that if things didn't improve, it was only a matter of time before she'd run out of money. She'd have to start selling off the stock, and once she did that, she might as well say goodbye to the business. She couldn't afford a professional trainer, and while Jerry did his best, he didn't have the expertise that Mac had.

Impatient with herself, she moved away from the window. It was impossible, of course. She had been a nervous wreck all the time Mac had been alone with Tim.

Her relationship with her son had deteriorated rapidly after her father's death. No matter how hard she tried to communicate with Tim, attempting to talk about his friends, his efforts to play the guitar, his life at school, his interest in baseball, he remained sullen and uncooperative.

All he wanted to talk about was his crazy dream of the rodeo, and nothing else seemed to matter to him anymore. Whenever she attempted to introduce a different subject, Tim bluntly announced that he had to visit a friend and promptly left the house.

The shock of finding out the truth about his father could very well put an even greater wedge between her and her son. Not to mention the fact that if Tim knew his real father was a rodeo champion, it would only add fuel to his desire to ride the circuit.

The sound of the sports car roaring up the driveway shattered her thoughts. Why did Mac have to come back now? she thought fiercely as she waited for Tim to come into the house. She had put that part of her life behind her, and if she hadn't been able to forget the stormy, emotional roller-coaster days of falling in love with him, she had at least come to terms with the memories.

Now that she'd seen him again, looking more rugged, more experienced and even more devastating than when she had last seen him, the fires she thought had been banked long ago had begun to smolder once more.

"Damn," she muttered out loud as the front door slammed. "Damn you, Mac McAllister. Why couldn't you have stayed in the past, where you belong?"

"I got the coffee," Tim announced as he bounded into the room. "I got some more beer, too. Just in case Mac comes back soon."

"He won't be coming back, so just forget the idea," Sharon said, taking the grocery sack from him.

"Why not?" Tim's face darkened with suspicion. "What did you say to him? You told him not to come back, didn't you? You don't want him here because he was in rodeo."

"He came here looking for a job," Sharon said evenly. "I told him we didn't need him. That's all."

"Why didn't you tell me he lived here once?"

She had no answer to that, and after a moment Tim swore under his breath and swung around to head for the door.

Reaching it, he looked back at her. "You didn't tell me because you were afraid I'd go to see him, that's why."

She took a step forward, holding out her hand to him in mute appeal. "Tim, I didn't talk about Mac because the subject never came up. He worked here a very long time ago, long before he became a rodeo champion. For a long time I didn't know what had happened to him after he'd left."

She might as well have saved her breath. With a scowl on his face Tim rushed out of the room. The front door slammed, and a few seconds later his car engine roared to life, then faded into the distance.

She was shaking, Sharon realized. Though whether it was a result of her argument with Tim or the memories that had been savagely reawakened, she wasn't sure. All she knew for certain was that both she and Tim would be better off if they never set eyes on Mac McAllister again.

The rest of the weekend passed in a blur as Sharon struggled to balance the accounts, trying hard not to think about Mac being in town less than three miles away. By Monday afternoon she felt drained of all energy.

Faced with the task of telling the men she could pay them only half of their salary for the month, she braced herself for the ordeal.

She decided to tackle Jerry first, who was out in a corral, halter-breaking one of the horses.

"This'n here's gonna make a fiesty bronc," Jerry told her after she'd watched him give up his struggle to control the rearing animal. "Every now and again we get a real mean one, and he's one of the meanest."

Seated on the top rail of the fence, he looked down at her from his perch. His swarthy face was flushed and sweaty, in spite of the bushy gray clouds that cooled the sky, and when he grinned he revealed two large gaps in the top row of his teeth.

A battered hat sat on the back of his head, covering what was left of his sandy hair, and his eyes, damaged by the sun, constantly watered. He was forever swiping at them with the back of his sleeve.

"That should please the contractors," Sharon said, watching the frisky sorrel canter around the paddock.

"Yep, I reckon it will." Jerry coughed, then made a guttural noise in his throat and spit. "Should fetch a few dollars. A real outlaw, that's what this'n is, all right. Recognized it right away, the minute I tried to get that halter on him. No one's ever gonna tame that one, that's for sure."

The horse thundered past them, head tossing, mane flying and steam blowing from its nostrils beneath the white blaze.

"That's what makes a great bronc," Jerry drawled, as if Sharon didn't already know. "It's that mean spirit, just like a man that's gone bad. 'Cept there's usually a good reason for a man to turn criminal, where's a horse has it born in him."

Still watching the horse, Sharon envisioned Mac astride the spirited animal. If anyone could tame him, Mac could. In the next instance she dismissed the thought, angry at herself for allowing it into her mind.

Jerry was right. Broncs were like the criminal element of society, unpredictable and often dangerous, but excellent stock for bareback riding.

Unlike the wild horse, the broncs could usually be tamed to a degree, though never fully trained. They showed their anger much the way a barroom brawler showed his, by fighting, bucking and kicking until exhausted.

The best anyone could hope to do was get a halter on one, and maybe even a saddle. But no one would ever ride him. Not even Mac McAllister.

A shout from behind her disturbed her thoughts, and Sharon turned her head to see Tim marching toward her across the field, looking even more irritable than he had all weekend.

With a sinking heart Sharon watched him approach, and wondered what could have gone wrong now. She didn't have to wait long to find out.

"Someone smashed up my car," Tim said the minute he was within earshot.

Sharon let out a gasp of dismay. "Are you hurt? What happened?"

Tim halted in front of her. "I'm not hurt. I wasn't in it at the time. They sure made a mess of my lights, though."

"Who's they?" Sharon demanded while Jerry muttered something about pesky kids being horsewhipped.

"I don't know." Tim stared down at the ground as he kicked at a clump of grass. "I came out of my last class, and Mike told me that someone had smashed up my car. I thought he was fooling until I saw it. There was glass everywhere. My taillights are gone, as well as my side mirrors. It looks as if someone took a baseball bat to them."

"Oh, honey, I'm so sorry." Sharon automatically put an arm around Tim's shoulders. She knew better than anyone how Tim felt about his car. She was the only one to see him struggle to hold back the tears when he'd first spotted it waiting for him in the driveway, covered in white ribbons.

He hadn't expected it, of course. Knowing that Randall had planned for years to buy a car for his grandson's sixteenth birthday, Sharon had ignored the mounting bills and taken the rest of the insurance money to buy the car she'd seen in the poster pinned up on Tim's wall.

When Tim had learned that the car was from his grandfather, he'd almost broken down again.

"Young bastards don't have no respect for anything these days," Jerry muttered. "That's what happens when you give them everything they want. Bunch o' spoilt brats if you ask me. Need to work for what they get. It sure would teach them a thing or two."

Aware that the dig was aimed at her, Sharon chose to ignore it.

"I don't know who would want to do something like that," Tim said, "but I'd sure like to get my hands on him."

"Don't worry, we'll get to the bottom of this." Walking across the yard with her son, Sharon realized she still hadn't told Jerry she would have to shortchange the men.

She could feel the faint depression that had been weighing on her since her father had died deepening. Nothing had gone right since then. It was if Randall Douglass had left a curse on the ranch.

Maybe he wanted her to get rid of it, she thought despondently. Maybe it was his way of relieving her of all the worry. If only she had someone she could trust enough to talk to about it. But there was no one. Her father was dead, and Tim was so far removed from her these days, she couldn't talk to him about anything.

They had always been the only two people with whom she could discuss her problems. Except for Mac, and he was the very last person she wanted to talk to about anything.

Feeling more alone than she had ever felt in her life before, Sharon accompanied a brooding Tim back to the house.

Chapter 3

Back inside the house, Sharon waited for Tim to go up to his room to do his homework, then picked up the phone. Hoping the principal would still be there, she punched out the number of Tim's high school.

Fred Stillman rarely spoke at length on any subject, believing that actions speak louder than words. He was, however, conscientious and dedicated, and if anyone could get to the bottom of the attack on Tim's car, the principal was most likely the man.

His soft voice answered her after the second ring. Speaking quickly, she repeated what Tim had told her. "Tim doesn't have any idea at all of who might have done this," she finished, "and as you can imagine, he is extremely upset by it."

"I am so sorry, Mrs. Carlson," the principal murmured. "I can understand how you and Tim must feel. I'm afraid this sort of mischief happens a lot, for a variety of reasons. It's always difficult to apprehend the culprits, but

I can assure you the matter will be investigated to the best of our abilities. I'll be in touch."

Sharon thanked him and replaced the receiver, feeling vaguely dissatisfied. She was still worrying at the problem when Tim came down an hour or so later.

"Are you hungry?" she asked him when he slumped down on the green couch in the den.

He shook his head, and stared moodily at his feet.

"I called the principal," she said, wishing she had better news for him. "He said he'd look into it and try to find out who did this."

Tim shrugged. "He won't find anything. They never do."

"The car is insured."

"Yeah, after the deductible."

Sharon sat down next to him. "I know I said you had to be responsible for any repairs, but in this case I think I can help out."

"You don't have to. I'll manage."

Looking at his dejected face, she searched her mind for a way to cheer him up. "I have an idea," she announced, rising to her feet. "I'll take you out to dinner. My treat. Anywhere you want to go."

He looked up at that. "Just the two of us?"

"Yes," she said, smiling. "Just the two of us."

Looking at him across the table in the cozy little Italian restaurant he'd chosen, she was glad she'd suggested the outing.

They had been seated in a corner of the room, beneath a huge painting of an Italian seaside village. The miniature oil lamp and vase of silk flowers added a festive note to the table, which was covered in a red-and-white-checked tablecloth.

All around the room baskets of wax fruit stood next to empty bottles of Chianti in straw containers, and the appetizing smell of Italian herbs and spices tempted their appetites with visions of tasty pasta and exotic sauces.

Even Tim seemed more relaxed, and was actually laughing about something that had happened at school that day.

Sharon rolled her spaghetti on her fork and chuckled with him as he described the look on his science teacher's face when the skull he'd been about to pass around the class suddenly fell apart in his hands.

"He looked as if he'd just murdered somebody," Tim said, his face glowing with amusement. "Everyone just cracked up."

Happy that he seemed to have recovered his good spirits, Sharon felt herself relaxing with him for the first time in weeks. "What about baseball?" she asked as Tim pushed his empty plate away with a sigh of satisfaction. "You haven't said much about it lately."

"I didn't make the team this year, that's why," Tim said, picking up his soda. "I didn't say anything before because I figured you'd be disappointed in me."

"Oh, Tim, of course not." She leaned forward and patted his hand. "I'm proud of you no matter what you do. You know that."

"Anything except rodeo, that is."

She watched the closed expression creep across his face with a feeling of dread. Before she could answer, Tim added, "I bet Mac feels lost now that he's out of rodeo. I wish he could have come to work for us. I think he's a neat guy."

"He is," Sharon murmured without thinking.

Tim's expression cleared, and he leaned his elbows on the table, fixing her with an intent stare that reminded her so vividly of Mac she had to look away. "Tell me about him," he demanded. "When did you first meet him? How did he come to be working for Gramps?"

She hesitated, reluctant to talk about the past or Mac McAllister. She knew full well that Tim's interest was focused more on what Mac had done for a living than on the man himself.

On the other hand, for the first time since her father had died, she and Tim were communicating again. If she refused to answer his questions now, she could lose what little ground she had made up.

Leaning back in her chair, she caught the waitress's eye. "Do you want dessert?" she asked as the woman approached.

Tim shook his head, looking disappointed. He obviously thought she had deliberately changed the subject.

"I'll have the tiramisu, and another glass of wine," Sharon told the waitress. "And please bring a soda for my son."

The woman nodded and left, while Sharon looked back at Tim, who sat staring into his empty glass. "I first met Mac when I was eleven years old," she said quietly.

Tim's head shot up, his eagerness shining in his eyes. "How old was he then?"

"He'd just turned sixteen." She twirled her empty wineglass in her fingers and steeled herself to let her mind go back to that stormy night in late fall.

"He'd run away from home, because his father beat him whenever he was drunk, which was pretty much all the time, from what Mac told us."

"Did he just come knocking on the door for a job?"

"Not quite." Sharon smiled. "Mac was a city boy, and knew nothing about ranching. Your grandfather was in town that night, having dinner with some business associates. It was cold, windy and raining hard. Gramps left the restaurant and was on his way back to his truck when he passed a bar. The door opened, and someone was flung out onto the street."

Tim's eyes widened. "Mac?"

Sharon nodded. "Apparently he'd demanded a beer, and the barman wouldn't serve him because he was underage. Mac started arguing and ended up flat on his back on the street at your grandfather's feet."

"All right! So Gramps offered him a job?"

"Not right away." Sharon paused as the waitress returned, carrying the drinks. She waited until the woman had left again before adding, "Gramps brought Mac home to the house. I'd gone to bed, but I heard them talking and crept down the stairs to see who it was. I saw this tall, skinny boy, soaked to the skin and covered in mud, his hair all over the place and the most defiant look on his face I'd ever seen. I liked him right away."

Tim laughed. "I would've, too. Did he see you?"

"I don't know. I never asked him. Mac didn't talk to me for a long time. He didn't talk to anyone much except your grandfather. Probably because he showed Mac the first kindness he'd had from an adult. Mac idolized him."

And she'd idolized Mac, her treacherous mind added.

"So when did Gramps give Mac a job?" Tim demanded eagerly.

Collecting her thoughts, Sharon smiled at his fascinated expression. "The next morning. He gave Mac a bed for the night, and the next morning Mac got up before anyone else and went out to the stables. Gramps found him talking to the horses. He figured that with a little work, Mac would make a pretty good ranch hand."

"And he did," Tim said, grabbing up his glass. He took several gulps, then put the glass down again. "Did Gramps teach him to ride?"

"Among other things." Sharon smiled. "It wasn't easy, from what I heard. Mac was pretty raw and inexperienced, and after living on the streets he was one tough, know-it-all kid. But he loved horses and he loved the life. Gramps taught Mac everything he knows about horses and ranching."

She lifted her own glass and took a sip of wine. "Well, maybe not quite all. I was the one who taught him how to break a horse and how to rope a calf."

She regretted the confession the minute it was out.

Tim looked stunned as he stared at her. "*You* taught him? Then how come you never taught me any of that stuff? How come you wouldn't even let me learn?"

Because she anticipated the very problems she was having now with her son, Sharon thought ruefully. Once Mac had learned the basics of rodeo competition, he was hooked. And eventually his obsession with it had taken him away from her. She was not going to let that happen to Tim.

"There just wasn't time for all that," she lied as Tim continued to stare at her accusingly. "By the time you were old enough to learn, your father and I were divorced. After that I was busy helping Dad with the ranch, and he barely had time to keep up with it all."

"Someone else could have taught me."

"I wouldn't trust anyone else."

She was relieved when he dropped the subject.

"I'd sure like to talk to Mac again," he said after a moment's pause. "I wish he still worked at the ranch." He looked at her with a wistful expression. "Why did he leave in the first place?"

She had been expecting the question all night. Now that it was there between them, she wasn't sure how to answer it. She had often asked herself that question in the desolate days after Mac had left.

After Tim was born, she had struggled to suppress the memory of that last night, unable to deal with the shame and the guilt that still lay heavily on her even now, after close to seventeen years.

At eighteen she had been young and reckless, used to getting her own way. That night she'd been heady with her first taste of champagne, and so desperately in love with the boy she had watched grow into a man.

Frustrated by his apparent indifference to her, longing to know the secrets she'd heard whispered in the school hallways, she had deliberately set out to seduce him. She'd succeeded. Little had she foreseen the consequences.

She had blown apart several theories that night. First and foremost, she'd found out that making love was not the wondrous ecstasy it was cracked up to be. It had been painful and confusing.

She had discovered what happens to a man when he's fully aroused. Mac's passion had frightened her when she'd realized that he was helpless to stop what was happening even if she'd changed her mind.

She had also disproved the theory that a girl couldn't get pregnant on her first time.

When she'd learned that Mac had left, she'd wanted to die. Only then had she realized the true depths of her feelings for him. Yet that night had meant nothing to him. He had cared so little for her that he'd gone after his dream without a word to her or her father, more than likely afraid she would hold him back.

The next few weeks had been hard. Suspecting she was pregnant and fearful of what her father would say if he'd known the truth, she had let him think that Mac had been the instigator and had taken advantage of her momentary weakness. Randall Douglass had wanted to hunt Mac down, but she'd been adamant.

She wanted nothing from Mac, she'd told her father. Mac had practically ignored her ever since he'd first arrived at the ranch, except for that one night. And that had been her doing. She had thrown herself at him, and he'd taken what was offered, as any man would.

Knowing him as well as she did, she was certain he would have offered to marry her if he had known about the baby. She couldn't bear the thought of being tied to a man who had been forced by his own integrity to stay with her. Neither of them could find happiness that way.

Things were never the same between her and her father after that. He was disappointed in her, and although he did his best to hide it, she was constantly aware of his disillusion.

A week after the doctor had confirmed her pregnancy, Will Carlson had proposed, promising that he'd care for the baby as his own. Realizing that her father must have told Will, hoping for just such an outcome, she'd accepted. She knew that Will cared for her. If she couldn't be happy, she might as well be secure. That way, she'd decided, she could help her father and give her son the best that life could offer.

She'd cried when Timothy was born. He'd reminded her so much of Mac, with his light blue eyes and dark fuzz of hair. She'd done her best to raise him the way she thought Mac would have wanted. Nothing was too good for her son.

"Mom? You okay? What are you thinking about?"

Sharon started, wondering how long she'd been lost in the past. "Oh, just remembering."

"So why did Mac leave?" Tim repeated.

Sharon shrugged. "I guess he got tired of working on the ranch. He just picked up and left one morning, without a word of thanks to your grandfather for everything he'd done for him."

"Man, that was a bit low."

"Very," Sharon said firmly. She felt bad about running Mac down in front of Tim, but she was determined to discourage her son from pursuing any contact with the man who had unwittingly fathered him.

"Well, I guess he felt the same way I do. About the rodeo, I mean," Tim said, giving her a sly look.

"I guess he did." She took another sip of wine, then set the glass down. "Not that it did him much good. Look at him now. Forty years old and looking for a job, with nothing to show for all those years except a few scars and a bad limp."

"But his leg is getting better," Tim said defensively. "He told me. He said he was ready to ride again."

"Ride, maybe," Sharon said quietly. "But he'll never earn his living with the rodeo again. There's too much competition out there, too many young kids eager and more than capable of taking his place. People don't have much time for losers, only winners. Mac is doing the right thing by quitting while he's still a champion."

"I could be a winner. I know I could. I could make champion, too."

In spite of her unwillingness to talk about his passion, she was even more reluctant to lose this rare moment of communication between them. She resisted the urge to change the conversation, as she had done so many times in the past.

"I'm sure you could," she said evenly. "I've never disputed that. You have the same wonderful command of horses that your grandfather saw in Mac. But just because you can do something well doesn't necessarily mean that you should give up a promising future for a life that is dangerous, unpredictable and insecure."

"Lots of men do," Tim argued.

"And no doubt it's the right thing for them. But those men are a special breed, they're not like most men. They're tough, rugged, wild...like the horses they ride. It's a rough life, Tim. You have to be a certain kind of man to live it."

"Like Mac?"

"Yes," Sharon said quietly. "Like Mac. To be successful in rodeo takes more than being able to ride well and handle horses. It takes guts, stamina and a complete disregard for the conventional way of life. I just don't think you would be happy living that way."

Tim didn't answer, and deciding it was time to get off a dangerous subject, Sharon picked up the check and gathered up her purse. "We'd better get back to the house. Tomorrow's a school day."

To her relief, Tim offered no resistance to the suggestion. He seemed preoccupied as they drove back to the ranch, but as he paused at the foot of the stairs to say good-night, he added offhandedly, "Thanks for dinner, Mom. It was real nice."

Warmed by his words, she smiled at him. "I enjoyed it, too. We'll do it again soon."

"Okay." He lifted his hand in an achingly familiar gesture, then raced up the stairs.

It was just as well, she thought, watching him go, that she hadn't accepted Mac's offer. Sooner or later Mac would start to wonder about things. Tim's age, for one thing. Although she'd married Will within weeks of Mac leaving, if he took the trouble to work things out, he could easily guess. Unless he thought she'd gone immediately into another man's arms.

Assuring herself that she'd done the right thing in turning Mac away, she still had trouble fighting the ache that persisted throughout the restless night.

The next morning, after Tim had left for school, Sharon went out to the corral again, determined to tell Jerry the bad news. She would let him tell the others, she decided. He could handle the ranch hands better than she could.

This time Jerry wasn't in the corral. A few minutes later she found him in the stables. He was sitting on an upturned bucket in front of the stalls, a cigarette dangling from his lips, and a copy of *Playboy* open on his lap.

He jumped to his feet when he saw her, guiltily stuffing the magazine into a back pocket of his jeans. "I was just taking a short break," he said, giving her a belligerent look that dared her to complain.

Sharon did her best to curb her irritation. It wasn't the first time she'd caught him with a cigarette in there, in spite of her insistence the men stick to the rules.

"You know I don't like anyone smoking in the stables," she said, keeping her voice as even as she could manage. "It's so dangerous with all this dry straw around."

Jerry dropped his cigarette stub and ground it into the dirt with the heel of his boot. "I lit it outside," he muttered.

Deciding to let that go for the moment, Sharon stuck her thumbs into the pockets of her jeans. "Well, I'm afraid I have some bad news for you," she said, wondering uneasily how he was going to take it.

Jerry looked at her through half-closed eyes. "Oh, and what's that?"

"I'm afraid I'm a little short this month. I'm going to have to put you and the men on half pay, and try to make it up next month or the month after. With the rodeo season starting up again, we should be bringing in more money soon."

She tensed, as Jerry moved closer to her. The leery expression on his face disturbed her.

"You can't pay me what I'm owed. Is that what you're saying?"

She nodded, determined not to let him see her sudden apprehension. "That's about it, at the moment. I'm sorry. I was hoping you'd give me a break and be willing to wait a month or two for the rest." It wasn't the first time he'd been asked to wait for his money. It was the first time she'd been the one doing the asking.

"After gettin' on at me all these weeks to step up the work, you're tellin' me you can't pay me?" Jerry said, making it sound as if he'd never heard of such an outrage.

"I can give you half now and the other half later," Sharon said firmly. "I'd appreciate it if you'd explain things to the rest of the men."

"Oh, I'll explain things, all right," Jerry said, grinning unpleasantly. "I can tell you right now, though, they ain't gonna be any too happy, ma'am. That's for sure."

"I don't suppose they are," Sharon said, shifting away from him. "I'm not too happy about the situation myself."

"Well, I'll tell you what you could do." Jerry lifted an arm and drew his sleeve across his eyes. He blinked at her and took another step toward her. "We can take it out in kind."

She hoped he hadn't seen her flicker of apprehension. "I beg your pardon?" she said frostily.

He was close enough now that she could smell the sweat on him. For a second she felt a strong urge to run, then her temper kicked in and she stood her ground, eyes blazing as he eyed her up and down with ugly audacity. If he so much as touched her, she'd kick him where it would hurt him most, she thought fiercely.

"You know what I mean," Jerry said, baring his teeth. "You be real nice to me, and I forget the money."

For a moment she was too shocked to answer. She hadn't really believed he would come right out and say it. He'd been working for the Double S for four years, and although she'd been uncomfortably aware of him staring at her now and then, he'd never made a pass until now. No doubt because he was afraid that Randall Douglass would have his hide if he tried.

Sharon dropped her hands and pulled her back straight. Well, he wasn't dealing with Randall Douglass now. He was dealing with her. And she was going to let him know it.

"I'll be damned if I'll let any one of my employees speak to me like that," she said, keeping her voice low in spite of her fury. "You are fired, Jerry Samuels. You pick up your things and you get out of here by tonight. If you're still here in the morning, I'll call the sheriff."

Jerry's expression turned nasty. "I was only foolin', ma'am. That's the trouble with dang women, they can't never take a joke."

"I can take a joke with the best of them. What I won't take is your insolence and your sleazy attempts to humiliate me. You have until 7:00 p.m. to get out of here."

"You can't kick me out just like that," Jerry blustered, his face turning red.

Sharon gave him a grim smile. "That's just where you're wrong. I own the Double S now, and I can fire whoever I like."

"The guys ain't gonna like this," Jerry warned, swiping at his eyes with his sleeve again.

"The men will mind their own business if they want to keep their jobs." Turning her back on him, she headed for the door.

"What about the money you owe me?" Jerry yelled after her.

"I'll make out a check right away," she said without looking back. "You can pick it up at the house before you leave."

Outside in the warmth of the sun, she drew in a long breath of clean air. She couldn't feel sorry about losing Jerry. His disruptive influence on the rest of the men had caused enough unrest. Maybe now that he was leaving, the rest of her crew would settle down and get things running smoothly again.

Still trembling from the unpleasant experience, Sharon hurried back to the house to write the check.

There went the feed bill, she thought ruefully as she sealed the envelope in the den a few minutes later. It was worth it, though, to be rid of the troublemaker.

Laying the envelope down on the desk, she gazed pensively through the window. From there she could see the line of thick firs that bordered the land behind the corrals. Heavy gray clouds scudded across the sky, promising more of the April showers that had plagued the meadows earlier in the month.

She would have to decide on whom to promote to foreman, she thought, creasing her brow in concentration. Out of the crew she had left, only a couple of them were passable trainers.

If only Tim hadn't shown such an interest in rodeo, she might have taught him that side of the business. But she refused to let him anywhere near the rough stock.

That was how Mac had started, weeding out the occasional bronc from the trainable horses, and trying his darnedest to tame the outlaw. He'd broken his first bone when he was seventeen, trying to stay on the back of a bucking bronc for longer than a second or two.

Tim had finally gotten tired of pleading with her to let him learn to break in the horses. He'd given up any interest in the business entirely, contenting himself with occasionally riding the friskiest horse in the stables. Since he'd had the sports car, he hadn't ridden at all.

Maybe he'd agree to help out a little until things improved financially, Sharon thought as she waited for Tim to come home from school that afternoon. She could use the extra hand, and she'd even offer to pay him for his time, now that she had one less salary to worry about.

She was all set to talk to him about it when he burst into the house a short while later. Before she could say anything, however, he asked in a voice rising with excitement, "What's up with the men?"

Frowning, she shook her head. "What're you talking about?"

"The men." Tim waved a hand at the window. "Go look for yourself. They're all sitting on the fences. They look like they're holding a conference or something."

With a sinking heart, Sharon looked out of the window. It looked as if all her crew was out there, gathered around the main corral. She could smell trouble at once.

"I had to fire Jerry this morning," she told Tim as she crossed the room to the door. "You'd better come with me. I may need your help."

"I'm not going out there. It's got nothing to do with me." He brushed past her, heading for the stairs.

"It has everything to do with you," Sharon said as she followed him out into the hallway. "This is a family business. It pays for your keep and it will pay for your education. The least you can do is give me a hand with it now and again."

Tim, already halfway up the stairs, paused to look over the banisters at her. "Yeah? Well, I've told you a million times, I don't need the business or the education."

"And I've told you a million times you can't be successful in life if you don't go to college."

"You didn't go."

"Exactly. Which is why I want you to go. I want something better for you."

"Like being a stuffy lawyer."

"If that's what you want. If not, you can at least consider your options."

Tim snorted and yanked a thumb over his shoulder. "I don't know why you don't sell the place. Then you wouldn't have jerks like that to deal with."

"There won't be any place left to sell," Sharon said grimly, "if we don't settle this problem with the men right now."

"Then we won't have anything left to argue about, will we?" With that he bounded up the stairs before she could say any more.

Scowling with frustration, Sharon marched out to the corral, where several of the men sat with their backs to her, talking idly among themselves.

"Is this a private conversation, or can anyone join in?" Sharon asked lightly as she approached them.

Barney, the closest man to her, turned his head. He was a thick-set man with a full white mustache and bushy gray brows. He gave her a stony look from beneath the wide brim of his hat.

"Reckon you ought to know what we've been saying," he said grudgingly as the other men fell silent.

"Then you'd better tell me." She waited while Barney looked slowly around the group.

After a lengthy pause he mumbled, "We're staging a sit-down strike, on account of Jerry losing his job."

The wind had changed, bringing cool air in from the mountains. Shivering a little, Sharon folded her arms and stared in contempt at each of the men in turn. "Really. Don't you think you are all being just a little bit childish?"

Barney shifted his position, looking uncomfortable. "This here's a protest, ma'am," he muttered. "We're entitled, I reckon."

"You're entitled to what? Wasting time gossiping about something that is none of your business, while the work gets even further behind schedule? We are in enough trouble now, without all of you going out of your way to make matters worse."

Barney tipped his hat back and scratched his forehead. "Well, it's like this, ma'am. The men don't like seeing Jerry treated that way. I guess we're all worried it could be one of us next, seeing as how the ranch ain't doing so well. Jerry told us you can't pay us a full wage this month."

Sharon lifted her chin and raised her voice to carry across the paddock. "I intend to make up the money next month, when we start selling to the rodeos. Any one of you is welcome to walk out of here if you don't like the way things are run. You won't be nearly as well paid elsewhere as you are here, I can assure you.''

She paused, waiting a moment or two for a response. When no one said anything, she added, ''Incidentally a good many of the problems are in your own hands. If you'd all pull your weight instead of bitching about the work, we wouldn't have half of the problems we do.''

''We can't pull our weight if we don't have a good man to lead us,'' Barney said stubbornly.

Murmurs of agreement from the others rippled around the paddock.

''I don't consider Jerry that much of a loss,'' Sharon said clearly. ''He deserved to be fired, no matter what he told you. And that goes for the rest of you, as well. Any man who is not back at work in ten minutes will be fired along with him. So make your choice.''

Head held high, she stalked back to the house, her fingers crossed so tight she cut off the circulation.

Entering the quiet den a few minutes later, she felt like bawling. If only her father were there to handle things. Men listened to another man a good deal more readily than they'd listen to a woman.

She was well aware of the resentment among the hands at having to take direct orders from her. As long as she was out of sight and someone else was giving the orders, they could forget they had a woman for a boss.

The problem was, without a competent foreman she was forced to get out there herself. That, coupled with her problems with Tim, was just too much for her to handle.

Glancing cautiously out of the window, she was relieved to see that the men had apparently returned to work. She'd won this round. Though the way things were going, there promised to be more confrontations ahead.

She needed someone to take over, she thought wearily. Someone who wouldn't take any lip from the men. Someone who was an expert at ranching and knew all there was to know about raising and training horses. Someone she could rely on and trust, knowing that the business was in good hands.

Someone, her common sense told her, like Mac McAllister.

She didn't sleep much that night, tormented by the doubts and fears that would not let her rest. She needed Mac desperately if she was going to pull the Double S out of the hole it was in.

He needed the job. He'd offered to work for her for room and board. It was an excellent chance to take advantage of his expertise without it costing her an arm and a leg.

With Mac's help she was quite sure she could pull things together and get out of the red as far as the business was concerned.

The men would be paid on time, and paid well. With Mac in charge they would be more willing to work, and he would see that it was done properly. He was the answer to her prayers.

On the other hand, he could very well bring her world down on her head. What if he suspected Tim of being his son? What could she say to him if he asked for the truth? How would she explain to Tim without losing him completely?

There was also Mac's past occupation to consider. The presence of an ex–rodeo champion was bound to be an added incentive for Tim to follow his dream.

Pummeling the pillow, Sharon fought with her indecision. All she had to do was keep quiet about it, she assured herself. After Tim had lost the first dark fuzz on his head, his hair had grown in lighter.

He'd inherited her fair skin and his blunt features from his grandfather. His eyes and his lean, lanky build were all that resembled Mac physically.

As long as she kept quiet, Mac would never know for sure, she told herself.

Sharon stared up at the shadows on the ceiling. If she explained to Mac how opposed she was to Tim's goal and all the reasons why, he would most likely cooperate. In fact, it might even work in her favor. Tim obviously looked up to Mac. It was quite possible that Mac could manage to discourage Tim enough to put an end to his crazy ambition.

Flinging the covers aside, she slid her legs out of bed. She needed some warm milk to help her sleep if she was going to look her best the next day.

The plain facts were, she needed Mac McAllister. She had spent the past seventeen years trying to make up to her father for disappointing him. She wasn't about to let him down now because she was frightened to take a risk.

Nothing mattered to her at the moment as much as saving the ranch, for both her father's sake and for Tim's future. Mac was the one person in the world who could help her do it. Tomorrow morning she would go to him and offer him the job.

Trying to ignore the quivering sensation in the pit of her stomach, she crept down to the kitchen to get her milk.

It was time to leave town, Mac decided as he showered the next morning in the tiny bathroom. His elbow cracked against the side of the shower wall, making him wince. The Longhorn Tavern boasted six rooms, all of them hardly big enough to swing a possum around in. He was getting tired of being cramped up in the place.

The smell of stale cigarette smoke was getting to him, and the constant thump of the bass beating out a country tune downstairs had given him a headache for the best part of last night.

Dressed in just his jeans, Mac leaned forward and stared into the speckled mirror, rubbing his scratchy chin with his fingers. Three days was long enough for Sharon Douglass to change her mind, he reckoned. He should have known that the years couldn't soften the stubborn streak she'd inherited from her father.

She was running the ranch into the ground, and she'd be the last darn woman on earth to admit it. She'd see it go under before she came begging for help.

Mac sighed and reached for his razor. It was really too bad. He would have given anything for the chance to repay his debt to Randall. He would never really be free of the guilt now. It was an unresolved issue, and would most likely torment him to the end of his days.

Flicking on the razor, Mac drew it across his chin. On the other hand, he told himself, given the way he still felt about the lady, maybe it was just as well he was done with her and the Double S.

She still got under his skin. He felt it every time she laid those velvet brown eyes on him. She was the only woman in the world who had made him forget what he was doing. The only time he'd ever lost control.

He'd been helpless under her searching, eager fingers. He couldn't get enough of her that night, powerless to heed the warnings clanging in the back of his head.

He'd wanted her so badly.

No, he'd desired her—craved her, until the hot, throbbing sensations had flooded his mind, blacking out everything except her warm, writhing body beneath his.

His entire being had thundered with the force of his hunger. He'd driven into her, aware of her muffled cry of pain yet unable to comprehend anything beyond his own desperate need.

Afterward, when he'd finally cooled down, he'd realized what he'd done. By that time, of course, it was too late.

Softly Mac swore. Just thinking about it made him uncomfortable again. Making an effort to empty his mind of the memory, he laid the razor against his jaw. As he did so, he heard a sharp rap on the door.

The coffee and Danish he'd ordered had finally arrived, he thought, switching off the razor. It would have to hold him until he could get a decent meal somewhere down the road.

The room at the tavern had been necessary, just in case Sharon had come looking for him. He hadn't wanted her to know he could afford anything better.

He crossed the room in two long strides and pulled the door open. It wasn't the coffee and Danish after all. Standing in front of him was the woman who'd disrupted his thoughts, and his body, just a minute or so earlier. In fact, he still throbbed with the memory.

He couldn't help wondering, as Sharon's startled gaze swept down his bare chest to his belt buckle, if she would be able to tell that he'd been thinking about her just seconds ago.

Chapter 4

She wore jeans and a soft denim shirt that opened beneath her creamy throat. She'd done something with her eyes, making them look smoky and mysterious.

He eyed her hair, tied back with a blue ribbon, and wished he could see it tumbling around her shoulders the way it had that last summer, before he'd given in to his selfish desires and ruined everything.

"I—I'm sorry," Sharon stammered as she snatched her gaze back to his face. "I didn't mean to interrupt your shower."

"You didn't." He stood back to let her in, striving to calm his sudden turmoil at seeing her again. This was the second time he'd set eyes on her unexpectedly. He'd have to have better control of his reactions if her reasons for coming were what he hoped.

Damn her, he thought irritably. She brought out the worst in him. She always had.

She stood hovering in the doorway as if she were scared to come inside the room.

"Are you going to come in," he asked lightly, "or would you rather talk to me in the hallway?"

She gave a furtive glance down the corridor and shivered. "No, of course not." Stepping inside, she flattened herself against the wall as he closed the door.

He hadn't realized until that moment how really small the room was. The bed took up most of the space, while a flimsy table under the window and an inadequate dresser filled up the rest of it. On the wall a bad seascape hung crookedly, and the room smelled of nicotine, even though he'd left the window open.

Well aware how tacky the place looked, he almost felt sorry for her. "Sit down," he said gruffly, knowing full well that there was nowhere to sit except on the edge of the bed.

Sharon eyed the rumpled bedspread and sheet with a look of horror that would have made him laugh under any other circumstances. Right now he was too aware of her lingering perfume and the triangle of smooth skin in the neckline of her shirt.

"I won't keep you," she said, and sat down gingerly on the very edge of the bed, as close to the foot as she could be without falling off.

"Take your time." Mac glanced at his watch lying on the dresser. "I'm waiting for coffee. They're not too swift in this place."

She nodded, looking around her as if she expected bugs to come crawling out of the walls. "It's . . . a little primitive," she said carefully.

"Paradise compared to some of the places I've slept in," Mac said in all truthfulness.

She looked at him then, a glimmer of sympathy in her eyes. "I can imagine," she said dryly.

"You get used to it after a while." He rubbed his chin. "Mind if I finish shaving? I hate not finishing a job."

"Sure."

She seemed to relax her shoulders a little, and satisfied, he stepped inside the bathroom and picked up the razor. "You can talk while I'm doing this," he said, switching on the quiet motor. "I know you must be wanting to get out of here."

Over the faint buzz of the razor he heard her say, "I had to fire Jerry yesterday. I came to offer you the job. That's if you still want it."

Well, at least she didn't waste any time beating around the bush, Mac thought as he carefully guided the razor down his jaw. Here, at long last, was his chance to pay back Randall and his daughter. He'd anticipated the offer as soon as he'd seen her in the doorway, so he found it hard to understand now why he should suddenly get cold feet.

Maybe he hadn't really expected her to come begging. Things had to be really serious at the ranch for her to back down like that. The Sharon he used to know would never have backed down on anything. Even if she'd been given positive proof she was mistaken, she'd never admit it.

Or maybe the reason he was feeling so insecure all of a sudden was because of the effect she had on him. It would be damn difficult seeing her every day with all that electricity sizzling back and forth between them. He would just have to do his level best to ignore her—that was all. Stay out of her way as much as was humanly possible.

"What happened?" he asked, concentrating on the tender spot in the middle of his throat.

"He was . . . insolent."

He knew by the way she'd hesitated that the bastard had made a pass at her. Obviously she'd handled it, but he couldn't stop the flash of anger that told him he was a little too concerned about it.

The cold finger of doubt lasted only a second. Once he'd managed to get everything running smoothly at the Double S, he told himself firmly, he'd find a new foreman, train the man himself if need be, then get the hell out of there.

He laid the razor down and reached for his after-shave, tipping some into his hand. Rubbing the lotion between his palms, he pulled in a long breath. "Well, lady," he said softly, "I reckon you've found yourself a new foreman."

Seated on the edge of the bed outside, Sharon heard his answer with mixed feelings. Now that it was settled, all the misgivings had come crashing back. It hadn't helped her peace of mind when he'd opened the door just now, giving her a close-up view of his bare chest and hard, flat stomach.

She'd been right about his build. He looked just as sleek and sinewy as he had as a young boy, except he'd filled out in the shoulders and arms, building muscles that testified to his long, tough battles with the broncs and bulls.

How well she remembered the patch of dark hair curling down his broad chest, and the soft feel of it beneath her hand.

Abruptly she clamped down on the memories before she remembered too much more. It was imperative that she forget anything before this moment if she wanted the arrangement to work.

"You can move in tomorrow, if you like," she said, her breath catching as Mac came out of the bathroom. She paused a moment to steady her voice, then added, "There's plenty of room in the bunkhouse. Room and board and half the salary I paid Jerry."

"Sounds good to me."

She avoided looking straight at him. "There's just one favor I'd like to ask."

"Okay, shoot."

He leaned past her to open the dresser drawer, and she froze. His bare shoulder was inches from her face. She could smell the soap on his skin and the light fragrance of his after-shave. Clenching her fingers, she forced her mind away from the urge to stroke her fingers over his shoulder.

From the corner of her eye she saw him take out a dark gray shirt from the drawer. Straightening, he shook the garment out and unbuttoned it with practiced fingers.

Conscious of the intimacy of the tiny room, she wished now that she'd waited until they were in the roomy den of her house before discussing her problems with Tim.

Mac, however, was gazing down at her with an expectant look on his face, and there was nothing for it now but to answer him.

"It's about Tim," she said, looking down at her knees so she wouldn't have to deal with the torment of staring into his eyes. "As I'm sure you've realized, he's obsessed with the idea of competing in rodeo. For obvious reasons I don't want him encouraged in any way. He'll be graduating next year, and after that he'll be going to college, hopefully to study for a law degree. He needs to concentrate on that and put this crazy idea right out of his head."

"And you're afraid that I'm going to be a bad influence on him," Mac said wryly.

She shrugged, reluctant to look up at him. "Tim doesn't have a father figure in his life anymore. You are his hero right now. He's a little in awe of you, and will respect anything you tell him. You could help me a great deal by discouraging him from any ambitions to be a rodeo rider."

"Act like I'm ashamed of my profession, you mean?"

She looked up at him then. "No, that's not what I mean." She could see the resentment glowering in his eyes. "I want what is best for my son. I happen to think he'd be a great deal happier as a successful lawyer than he would risking his life on the back of a dangerous animal who's doing his best to throw him off."

Mac shook his head. "For someone who raises rodeo stock for a living, you sure have a bad opinion of the business."

"Raising and training horses is one thing," Sharon said stiffly. "Riding them in a rodeo is something else entirely."

"Well, you don't have to worry. I'll be real careful to stay off the subject as much as possible when he's around. Though seeing as how I'll be training rodeo stock, that might be a little difficult."

She stood up, matching his scowl. "Just do your best. Tim knows he's not allowed to have anything to do with the unbroken stock, so it shouldn't be too much of a problem."

Mac nodded, but she could tell he didn't approve of her methods.

Not that it was any of his business, she told herself as she made her way back to her car. After all, what did he know about raising a son? She tried not to listen to the tiny voice in the back of her mind reminding her that just maybe it *was* Mac's business.

Tim was elated that afternoon when Sharon told him that Mac would be moving in the next day. "How did you find him?" he asked, dropping his schoolbag onto the kitchen table. "I thought he'd left town."

"He was staying at the Longhorn for a few days," Sharon said, pretending to be busy with the chicken casserole she was preparing for supper. "I got lucky. He was still there."

"He'll sure make them sit up around here," Tim said with boyish enthusiasm. "You watch, the old place will soon pick up now."

"I hope you're right." Sharon smiled at her son. "I only hope the men are as pleased with the arrangement as you are."

"They'll soon get used to it." Tim opened the fridge and frowned at the contents. "We'll have to get some more beer in for him. Is he going to stay here in the bunkhouse?"

"Yes," Sharon said slowly, wondering how she was going to cope with Mac living at such close quarters. "It's part of the deal."

"Oh, cool. I'll be able to talk to him, then."

He didn't mention the rodeo, but Sharon knew that's what he meant. She could only hope that Mac kept his promise and did his best to disenchant her son.

"He'll be pretty busy, so I hope you don't bother him too much," she said mildly as she sliced up the mushrooms.

"I won't." Tim came by and gave her a hearty slap on the shoulder. "You worry too much, Mom. I'm going over to Mike's to tell him we're going to have a real live rodeo champ living under our roof. He'll be so jealous he'll barf."

Wincing, Sharon watched him tear out of the door and seconds later roar down the driveway in the sports car. At least he seemed to have recovered from that trauma, she thought as she chopped celery. Though she would have liked the name of the person who had smashed the lights. She'd certainly make him pay for the damage.

Covering the casserole with a lid, Sharon set it in the oven. She still had to make up the bed in the bunkhouse for Mac. The thought made her stomach quiver. He would be just across the yard from her. She could see the bunkhouse from her bedroom window.

She'd thought about moving into her father's room after he'd died. He'd slept at the other end of the hallway. The room had been left the way it had been when he'd passed away. She still hadn't been able to bring herself to clear it out as yet.

It was the biggest room in the house, and Tim had hinted that he'd like it, too. Maybe now that Mac had returned, she could find the strength to clean out her father's room, she thought as she hurried over to the bunkhouse. Though she wasn't sure why that should make a difference.

Things were going to be quite different in a lot of ways, she told herself as she flapped a sheet open. There'd be another man to feed, for one thing.

Most of the hands lived away from the ranch, traveling in each day to work. Since she'd had to let go of Emily, the housekeeper, the three men who lived in the bunkhouse either cooked for themselves, or more likely, ate at one of the taverns in town, as Jerry had.

She could hardly expect Mac to do that, she told herself, in view of their deal. He would have to eat there at the house with her and Tim. She wondered what the rest of the men would make of that, then dismissed it. It was none of their business. After all, if Mac had stayed, he would have been living in the house.

Sharon drew a pillow case onto the pillow. *If Mac had stayed.* If he had, he would have known about Tim. Most likely he would have offered to marry her. No doubt Randall Douglass would have insisted on it.

How many times had she told herself that it was a good thing Mac had gone away, without knowing he had fathered a son? Too many to count, Sharon thought ruefully. Forced into a marriage he didn't want, there was no doubt in her mind they would have both ended up hating each other.

She plumped up the pillows and drew the sheet over them. Now he was back, treating her with the same indifference he'd shown before. Which was just as well, she told herself as she straightened the comforter. Because no matter how desperately she tried, she could not seem to be indifferent toward him.

Quite the opposite, in fact.

Thinking about that morning, remembering how close she had been to his bare shoulder, the shivery sensation she hadn't felt since she was a teenager feathered down her back.

The only thing she had going for her this time, she reminded herself, was that she was no longer a vulnerable, impulsive teenager experimenting with an explosive situation.

She was a mature adult and a mother. This time she knew how to deal with her emotions, and she would not let Mac McAllister—or anyone else, for that matter—destroy her senses again. She had paid a bitter price for that mistake, and she wasn't going to make another one.

She stood back to scrutinize the bed. Satisfied with her efforts, she left the bunkhouse and returned to the house.

The only real problem she had to deal with now, she told herself as she hurried up the steps, was to make very sure that Mac never suspected that Tim could be his son. That was something she'd have to stay on guard against. But if it meant the difference between losing the ranch and saving it, the slight risk was worth taking.

Even so, as she caught sight of herself in the hall mirror, she grimaced at her image. "Sharon Douglass Carlson," she whispered softly, "I sure as hell hope you know what you are doing."

Mac arrived the next morning, carrying surprisingly little luggage. He settled in quickly, and Sharon took him out to introduce her new foreman to the rest of the crew.

For the most part they greeted him with wary silence, except for a nod as Sharon announced their names. But they obeyed sharply enough when Mac gave out his orders, in a firm but pleasant tone that could offend no one.

Well satisfied with her decision, Sharon left Mac to do his job and headed back to the house, feeling more light-hearted than she had since long before her father had died.

Tim rushed in from school that afternoon, dropped his books and took off for the corrals before she had a chance to ask him if there was any word on the vandal who'd wrecked his car.

In fact, Tim seemed to have forgotten about the incident, though Sharon knew he planned to go into town at the weekend to get the lights and mirrors fixed.

She felt a twinge of apprehension as she watched her son rush off to find Mac. She would have to get used to the two of them being together, she thought, turning away from the den window.

She'd feel a good deal more comfortable, she told herself, if she were with them when they talked. That way she'd at least have the chance to turn the conversation away from dangerous ground.

Her first real apprehension arose during supper that night. She'd gone to a lot of trouble to prepare the shrimp salad, and spent several anxious moments making sure the steak was done just the way Tim and Mac liked it.

Sharon was the first to admit she wasn't that great a cook, having been spoilt by a live-in housekeeper until the past year or two. She was, however, proud of her efforts as she dished up the meal to her appreciative audience.

"Hey, Mom, this looks great," Tim exclaimed, sounding way too surprised.

Flushing, Sharon tried to pass off the awkward moment by informing Mac, "He rarely stays home for dinner anymore. I think he's forgotten his mother is capable of cooking a meal."

"You cook like this and I'll stay home every night," Tim assured her, picking up his fork.

Mac grinned and winked at Tim. "Looks good enough to eat, I reckon."

Sharon took her place at the end of the table feeling ridiculously pleased with herself. As much as she hated to admit it, it was wonderful to have a man appreciate her efforts. Her father had done his best after Emily had tearfully left, but Sharon had always known she was no match for the housekeeper when it came to cooking. Randall Douglass had been spoilt, and he knew it.

She risked a glance at Mac, and felt a warm shiver of pleasure as he ate his steak with obvious enjoyment. "Been a long time since I had a home-cooked meal," he said after he'd washed his food down with a swig of beer, "I'd forgotten it could taste so darn good."

"I bet you had some strange meals while you were on the road," Tim said, his eyes glued to Mac's face.

Mac shrugged. "Some. Most of 'em I'd rather forget." He gave Sharon a quick glance as if to assure her he'd remembered her request. "There's nothing to beat good old-fashioned home cooking, that's for sure."

"Did you eat in taverns all the time, like some of the men do here?"

Mac took another bite of his steak before answering. "Mostly I ate wherever I could find something edible." He swallowed another mouthful of beer, then looked straight at Tim. "How about telling me some more about yourself for a change?"

Tim pulled a face. "My life is boring compared to yours."

"I wouldn't say that." Mac speared a shrimp with his fork. "For instance, I would've killed to have a car like that at your age. Or any age, come to that."

"Oh, that." Tim shot a grateful look at his mother. "That was actually a birthday present from my grandfather. Mom bought it with the insurance money because she knew Gramps wanted me to have it. I've only had it about three weeks. It's a great car, isn't it?"

"It sure is." Mac leaned back in his chair. "So I just missed a birthday, huh?"

"Sure did." Tim grinned at him. "I turned sixteen on April ll. I got my license the same day, and when I got home there was the car sitting in the driveway. Mom had called Jerry to pick it up so it was waiting for me when I got home. Man, that was a surprise . . .''

Sharon never heard the rest of the sentence. She was watching Mac's face, her heart thumping like a bass drum. Tim had been born three weeks early. Even so, it was close enough to make Mac suspicious.

To her immense relief, he went on asking Tim questions about the car, apparently oblivious to the meaning of his birth date. Even so, she felt uneasy throughout the rest of the meal, wondering if Mac would think about it later and attempt to work things out.

If he questioned her about it, she would just have to lie about when she'd first slept with Will. What did it matter if Mac thought badly of her? He probably did anyway, seeing as how she'd thrown herself at him that night. She'd gotten what she'd deserved, and it was her own fault if she'd had to pay all these years for that one mistake.

There had been times, especially in the past few days, when the memory of that wild summer night had come back to torment her, as vividly as if it had been just a week ago instead of seventeen years.

She could remember everything. The moon had ridden high on the rise that night in a black, cloudless sky, and the grass had felt damp as Mac had pulled her down to the ground. That first kiss, after all the aching to know how his mouth would feel on hers, had confused her, excited her almost to the point where she thought she would explode.

Except for the harsh chorus of the bullfrogs from the creek and an occasional whinny from the corrals, silence had cloaked the meadows. Mac's harsh breathing, his muffled moans of protest as she'd recklessly sought the secrets of his body, had finally ignited the embers that had smoldered deep inside her for so long.

She'd been curious at first, feverishly unbuttoning Mac's shirt to slide her hands over his warm, hard chest. When

A Cowboy's Heart

she'd drawn her hand down to that forbidden part of his body, he'd sworn at her in a voice she barely recognized.

In the space of a heartbeat, he'd covered her body with his, his hands moving over her, squeezing and probing with a frenzy that was both exciting and painful.

She'd been shocked by his uncontrollable passion. Unable to fully understand what was happening, she'd tried to match his inflamed hunger, until the pain had shattered any excitement his touch had generated.

She hadn't enjoyed the experience, she told herself as she closed the dishwasher door. Not then, and not since. Making love with Will had been a tedious affair.

At the best of times she could escape what was happening by losing herself in a fantasy... other times she endured all the grunting and heaving with a stoic determination to make the best of it.

Yet every time Mac came anywhere near her now, all those adolescent emotions and sensations came back to haunt her. For the sake of her son and her own sanity, she would just have to do her best to ignore them and pretend that night had never happened.

That was easier said than done, Sharon discovered over the next few days. After having his car fixed, Tim spent the entire weekend hanging around the ranch instead of taking off to be with his friends.

It was a mixed blessing, in Sharon's eyes. It was wonderful to have him close to home for a change. On the other hand, his sudden interest in the business, and Mac in particular, spelled trouble.

She was very much afraid that in spite of Mac's apparent efforts to avoid the subject, Tim's resolve to join the rodeo was being strengthened every day.

Every evening she cooked supper for the three of them, living in dread that something Tim might have said could have triggered a suspicion in Mac's mind.

As the days passed, however, she began to relax just a little. Surely, she thought, if Mac was going to have any ideas on the subject, he would have said something by now.

Seated at the dining table one evening, she couldn't help noticing how much more affable Tim had become since Mac had arrived. Listening to the two of them exchanging good-natured banter, she was reminded of how Mac used to tease her when she was still just a kid following him around everywhere.

He called her Small Fry and kept asking her when she was going to grow up. It seemed as if she'd grown up all at once, that night he'd shown her what it was like to be a woman.

Absorbed in her thoughts, she lost the gist of the conversation until she heard Tim laugh out loud. Looking up from her plate, she saw him grinning at her.

"Where were you, Mom?" he asked, nudging Mac with his elbow. "Mac spoke to you ages ago."

Flustered, she avoided Mac's eyes. "I'm sorry, I was preoccupied. I've got a lot on my mind these days, I guess."

"I was telling you I wouldn't be here for dinner tomorrow night," Mac said as she rose to clear away the plates. "A couple of the hands invited me out to eat with them. I figured it might be a good idea to be sociable."

She fought the little flash of resentment. After all, it was none of her business what he did after hours. If he chose to go carousing with the hands, she certainly wasn't going to lose any sleep over it.

"Thanks for letting me know," she said evenly. "I'll get a key to the bunkhouse cut for you while I'm in town tomorrow so the men won't have to wait up for you. Unless you plan on being out all night?"

She had no idea what made her add that last sentence. She saw one of Mac's eyebrows rise the way it used to whenever she said anything provocative to him.

"I wasn't figuring on it," he said with just a trace of mockery in his voice. "But then, you never know your luck."

Furious with herself, she grabbed up the dishes and fled to the kitchen, cursing under her breath when she heard Tim's laughter. She had to do a lot better than that, she told herself fiercely, if she was going to survive this mess. She was beginning to wish she'd never entertained the idea of hiring Mac again.

What with the strain of worrying if he was going to find out about Tim and the constant tension whenever she was within a few yards of the man, she was becoming a nervous wreck.

She might have done better to take her chances and promote one of the other men, even though none of them seemed to want the job.

She was still squirming at the memory the next morning when she had the key cut for him. She made up her mind to stay out of his way, except for supper, when Tim was there to lighten the tension.

That's if Mac chose to have supper with them again, she thought viciously. He might have such a good time at the tavern that he might very well make it a permanent habit.

Annoyed with her ignoble thoughts, she returned to the ranch with her shopping to find a message waiting for her on her answering machine. Playing it back, she recognized the voice of Jack Marlowe, the Sage City Broker.

She called him back, and was shocked when Jack informed her he was canceling the contract for the half-dozen horses he'd ordered.

"You're already behind with the order," Jack said when she asked him why. "I've got someone else willing to deliver by next week. Can you beat that?"

"I can try," she said, wondering if Mac could perform a miracle.

"Not good enough, Sharon," Jack said in her ear. "I'm sorry. If I don't get those horses soon, I'm going to be short for the opening of the season. I'm gonna have to go with the sure thing."

He sounded genuinely regretful, and Sharon hung up, wondering desperately if there was anything Mac could do. Deciding to find out, she headed for the stables.

Barney was in there alone, sorting out the tackle. Mac was in the far paddock, he told Sharon, sounding far more friendly than he had the day she'd fired Jerry. He even helped her saddle Windsong, the chestnut that had been a consolation gift from her father after Whitefire had died.

Heading out for the meadows on Windsong, Sharon loosened the ribbon in her hair and tucked it in the pocket of her jeans. More often than not the wind snatched the ribbon and tossed it away when she rode. She either had to stop and look for the darn thing or give it up for lost. She'd learned, after the first few times, to take off the ribbon and let the wind play in her hair.

A faint haze lay across the meadows, shimmering in the midday sun. It was unseasonably warm for late spring, and a welcome change after the heavy rains of April.

Sharon pulled up at the top of the rise. From there she could see the rest of the corrals. In the distance she could see Mac, and her breath caught in her throat. He was in the training paddock with the bronc.

He had the halter in one hand and he was moving toward the sorrel, his hand outstretched in a familiar gesture that stirred Sharon's heart. He had almost touched the wary animal's nose when it suddenly snorted and stepped sideways.

Mac stepped sideways with it in a fluid movement that was a joy to see. It was hard to tell he had a limp, so smoothly had he moved.

The sorrel, annoyed to find his tormentor still in front of him, pawed the ground, then with a loud whinny, rose on his hind legs and lashed out.

Sharon cried out as Mac jumped back, stumbled and almost lost his balance. Without waiting to see what happened next, she kneed Windsong into a fast gallop and headed straight for the paddock.

Mac must have heard her coming as the chestnut's hooves thundered on the ground. He kept his gaze firmly on the sorrel, however, who was pawing the air with both hooves.

Watching him over Windsong's flying mane, Sharon's heart seemed to stop as Mac jerked on the horse's mane, bringing the sharp hooves down almost at his feet. Angrily the bronc tossed his head and snorted. Stepping sideways, he half circled Mac, who held on, keeping the sorrel's nose down.

By the time Sharon pulled up at the fence, the bronc was stomping his feet and watching Mac with a gleam in his eye that warned of a rising temper.

Sharon dismounted but kept quiet and still as Mac carefully raised the halter, talking soothingly to the restless sorrel all the time. The rope touched the horse's ear, and he shied away, whinnying loudly as he cantered off across the paddock.

Sharon let out her breath on a long sigh. She hadn't realized she'd been holding it in. She waited for Mac to climb over the fence before saying lightly, "For a moment there I was afraid you might try to ride him."

Mac shook his head. "Not that one. He's got a real mean streak. I know my limitations. I'll leave him for the young kids, their bones are more supple than mine."

"I would think that you'd stay off the broncs permanently," Sharon said, absently stroking Windsong's nose. "Haven't you broken enough bones?"

Mac shrugged, watching the sorrel with a wistful expression. "Once riding is in your blood, it's tough to let go."

"But you don't have to ride the broncs. We have enough tamed horses to ride."

He glanced down at her, his eyes steel blue beneath the brim of his hat. "Life's not worth living unless you're willing to take a risk now and then."

"I hope your life is worth enough to make you think twice about taking unnecessary chances with it."

"Maybe." He narrowed his eyes as he continued to look at her. "Were you here for a particular reason?"

She dropped her gaze, aware once more of the odd, pleasurable twinges deep in her belly that she felt whenever she was near him. "As a matter of fact, I was looking for you. I have some bad news, I'm afraid."

His look of alarm took her by surprise. "Not Tim, is it?"

"No, he's fine, as far as I know." She hadn't realized he cared that much about her son. She wasn't sure she wanted him to care that much. "It's the Sage City Brokers. The contractor has backed out of the order. He says he has a firm delivery offer from someone else. He doesn't want to take a chance on us not delivering the horses soon enough."

Mac swore, tipping back his hat to lift his face to the sun. "How many did he have ordered?"

"Six. How close are we to completing the training?"

"By next week? Not close enough." Mac leaned back against the fence and propped his elbows on the top rail. One boot crossed the other as he stared down at his feet. It was a gesture Sharon had seen often in the days when he was a carefree teenager.

Guiding her mind away from the memory, she said briskly, "How long would you say?"

He frowned. "Ten days, maybe more. Depends how much help I can get."

"If I can give you an extra hand, can you guarantee ten days?"

"Maybe if they're willing to work an hour or two overtime."

"If it's the difference between them being paid or not, they'll work," Sharon promised grimly. "I'll get back to Jack and promise him delivery in ten days."

"Why would he wait if he can get replacements in a week?"

She swung herself up onto Windsong's back and gathered up the reins. "Because," she said smugly, "I'll throw in the bronc for half price. As you well know, contractors will pay through the nose for one with a real mean temper. That bronc will go on bucking until he drops. Jack might want to come out to take a look at him, but he's sure to recognize a bargain when he sees one."

Mac took off his hat, smoothed his hair back with the flat of his hand and replaced his hat on his head. "Lady," he said softly, "you got your daddy's blood in you, that's for sure."

She grinned down at him. "That's the nicest thing you've ever said to me." Wheeling Windsong around, she gave him his head, thundering back across the meadow with a smile still playing on her face.

Mac watched her go, his insides knotting up like coils of barbed wire. Her hair was shorter now, and she rode with a saddle instead of bareback, but the image was so clear in his mind he could swear he was eighteen again, watching the half child, half woman race across the grass on the back of her beloved Whitefire.

How fast she had seemed to blossom into a full-blown woman. Almost overnight, it seemed, after years of watching her legs grow longer, her body had filled out and the freckles had gradually disappear.

He remembered exactly the night he'd realized she'd left behind forever the impetuous tomboy he'd taken so much pleasure in teasing. The night he'd finally realized that she was all woman.

It was the night of her senior prom. She'd left everything until the last minute, as usual; the dress she'd planned on wearing was too short when it arrived, and there wasn't time to have it altered.

She'd stormed up to her room saying she wasn't going to go dressed in something she'd already worn before. Both Mac and her father had pleaded with her, reminding her that her date would be expecting her to go and she couldn't let him down at the last minute. Their pleas had fallen on deaf ears.

It had been Mac who had finally hit on the right thing to say. He told her that no matter what she wore, she'd outshine every other girl in the place. It wasn't what she wore, he'd told her, it was how she wore it. And he'd never seen anyone make clothes look good the way she did.

There had been a long silence while both men had held their breath. Then Sharon's door had opened abruptly. "Leave me alone," she'd told them. "I have to get ready for a prom."

He'd seen her come down the stairs that night, and he'd wished he'd been the one taking her instead of the fidgety, freckle-faced kid who waited nervously at the bottom of the stairs.

He'd never seen anything more beautiful or more desirable in his entire life. Less than a month later he'd robbed her of the most precious thing she'd had. True, she'd wanted it every bit as much as he had. But he'd been old enough to know better. He was the one who should have had the sense to stop it while he could.

Dammit, where was his control when he'd needed it the most? How could he have let her stir him up to such a state he didn't know what he was doing? What exactly were the consequences of that night?

His pulse quickened as the forbidden thought crept into his mind once more. For days he'd refused to face his suspicions, afraid of knowing the truth. Yet always, on the fringe of his mind, the possibility hovered there.

He'd taken to watching Tim closely, comparing, striving to reassure himself that he was mistaken. Yet the more he was with the boy, the harder it was to ignore the facts. Now, in spite of his efforts to resist, he knew that sooner or later he would have to come to terms with his conscience. He had to know if he was Tim's father.

The idea scared him. He was out of his depth for once, and he didn't like it one bit. But he couldn't go on being tormented by doubts. He would have to question Sharon about it. If what he suspected was true, then he would have to deal with it. Somehow.

Chapter 5

Heading back to the ranch later, Mac wished he hadn't
agreed to go out with the guys that night. He'd thought it
was a good idea at the time, but now, faced with the prospect of getting up at the crack of dawn to concentrate on
the training, he would have preferred an early and a sober
night.

When he entered the house, Sharon met him in the hallway. "I have your key," she said, turning back to the den.
"I forgot to give it to you this morning."

His heart hammered as he followed her into the den.
Maybe now was a good time to bring up the subject of
Tim. He watched her fish the key out of her purse, his
mouth dry. He hadn't felt this nervous since the first time
he had lowered himself onto the broad back of a snorting,
mean-eyed bull.

"Did you get hold of Jack?" he asked as she handed the
key to him.

"Yes, I did. I promised him he'd get the stock a week
next Monday."

Mac nodded. "I'll see that they're there. What about the bronc?"

"He jumped at it, of course, after I'd described him. He didn't even want to come out and look at him. He said he'd take my word for it." She looked at him, then slid her gaze away. "Actually it was your word he took. He said that if anyone should know a mean bronc when he saw one, it was Mac McAllister. He was quite impressed that you were working for the Double S again."

"Just like old times." He paused, bracing himself for the moment. Then he added deliberately, "Speaking of old times, I think there's something we should discuss."

She sent him a startled look, then moved away from him, across the room to the desk where she put her purse inside a drawer. "I thought we'd agreed to forget the past," she said quietly. "It's over and done with."

"Is it?" He moved to the center of the room, cornering her. "Or is there something you haven't told me?"

Slowly she looked up at him. The expression in her eyes was wary, but she met his gaze steadily enough. "I don't know what you're talking about."

He pulled in a slow breath. "I'm talking about Tim. I want to know if he really is Will Carlson's son."

He saw her face freeze, and his pulse leapt. Then she shook her head. "Don't worry, Mac. There isn't a doubt in the world that Will is Tim's father."

For a moment he was stunned by his disappointment. Although he'd been dreading the moment of truth, he realized now that a small part of him would have liked to know that he'd fathered a strong, virile son to carry on his genes. Something of him to remain on earth after he'd gone.

Wishing now that he'd let it alone, he shrugged. "Well, I guess it's just as well."

"I'm sure you're right."

He waited through the awkward pause that followed, then muttered, "I'd better be getting along. I promised the guys I'd take them down there in the truck."

He was about to turn away when she said quickly, "Oh, before I forget. There's something I want you to have. Dad kept a journal of all the horses he'd trained, complete with hundreds of training tips and things to watch out for. He talked about writing a book one day, but never did get around to it. I'd like you to have it."

He stared at her, moved by the unexpected gesture. Only she would know how much something like that would mean to him. It was much more than he deserved.

"Heck, I don't want to take something that important away from you," he said cautiously. "What about Tim? Wouldn't he like it?"

Sharon shook her head. "He wouldn't appreciate it the way you would. Besides, he has no interest in training the horses. He told me just the other day that he plans to sell the Double S when I'm ready to give it up."

Shocked, Mac stared at her. "He's young. He'll change his mind when he grows up a bit. His values will change."

"I don't think so." She looked down at the papers on the writing desk and shuffled them around into a neat pile. "I'm afraid it's my fault. If I hadn't been so adamant about him staying away from the rough stock, he might have been more interested in the business."

She turned away from him, and reached up to a bookshelf high above her head. "Anyway," she said, her voice straining as she reached for a thick black binder, "I'll feel happier giving Dad's journal to someone who'll appreciate it as much as I know you will."

He couldn't take his eyes off her rounded body. For a moment he let his gaze travel down the green-and-white-checkered shirt to the jeans stretched taut across her hips. His fingers itched to trace those curves, holding her close enough to him to feel the rest of her pressed against his body.

He was close enough to touch her. How he longed to put his arms around her waist and bury his mouth into the hair at the back of her warm neck. He could smell her perfume, and it reminded him potently of the last time he'd held her. His skin tingled when he remembered her warm, agile body trapped beneath him.

His hunger for her was like a persistent bug that wouldn't let go. Just when he thought he'd gotten over it, it came back to hit him twice as hard.

He curled his fingers into his palms in an effort to stop the hot thoughts tumbling through his mind. Then he heard her gasp, and the heavy binder crashed to the floor.

"Sorry," she said breathlessly. "It slipped."

Instinctively he ducked to pick up the journal, at the same moment she stooped to do the same thing. For a second or two their faces were inches apart.

He could see down the neckline of her shirt. Her soft, round breasts swelled above her bra. It was only a brief glimpse, as she straightened at once, but it was enough to seriously affect his breathing.

He stood up again, the journal in his hands, and saw her flushed face. The expression in her eyes ignited an immediate throbbing response in his body.

She had gone very still, as if she were held by the invisible bonds of a powerful emotion. His pulse raced, and again he fought the urge to touch her.

"I hope you enjoy the journal," she said with just a slight tremble in her voice.

He had to get out of there, he warned himself, before he stepped over the line she'd drawn between them. "Thanks, Sharon," he said gruffly. "I'll take real good care of this journal. You have no idea what this means to me."

"I think I do," she said, avoiding his gaze. "I think Dad would have been very happy to know that I gave it to you."

That was almost his undoing. It was like telling him that Randall Douglass would have forgiven him after all. Even if his daughter hadn't been able to forget.

"I'll never let it out of my possession," he promised her. He left the room then, before he could say something he might later regret.

Lying in the darkness of her bedroom later, Sharon admitted to herself that giving Mac her father's journal had been an impulsive gesture.

She'd been shaken by the question that she'd anticipated for so long, yet had been unable to answer when Mac had finally asked it. She had lied, and her guilt had prompted her to make amends. The journal had seemed like a token of apology.

The charged moment that had followed had thoroughly unnerved her. For a moment, she'd thought he was going to put his hands on her. Darn it, she had *wanted* him to put his hands on her, and there was no doubt in her mind that he had known it.

Damn him, she thought, and flung herself on her side in her frustration. She'd never get him out of her system if he had found out that Tim was his son.

Resolutely closing her eyes, she concentrated on business matters. With the money from the Sage City Brokers, she'd be able to pay off what she owed the men. She'd also be able to order extra feed. Maybe she'd have enough to buy another stallion by the end of summer, she thought, instead of having to wait for the new colts to mature enough to weed one out from them.

The sound of Mac's truck in the driveway scattered her thoughts. She waited, heart pounding, until she heard the engine die and the door of the pickup slam. Then, as his footsteps faded away, she made a determined effort to go to sleep.

* * *

Lying on his back in the bunkhouse, Mac stared sleeplessly up at the ceiling and tried to ignore the snores of the other men. He hadn't had more than a beer or two at any one time in a good many months, so he'd been careful about drinking too much. Even so, he could feel the effects of the few he'd had.

Not enough to prevent him driving home safely, but definitely enough to make him feel mellow. That wasn't all it made him feel.

He was potently aware of Sharon sleeping alone just across the yard from him. In fact, he couldn't seem to get it out of his mind. She was driving him crazy.

It wasn't enough that his mind was tormented by memories. Every time he set eyes on her, he was vividly reminded of the way she'd practically seduced him that hot summer night.

His biggest problem was that he still wanted her. Even more so than he had back then. This time it was different. She'd changed, and he liked the woman she'd become. She was still as strong, independent and stubborn as ever. But now all that was tempered by a warm, compassionate nature that hadn't been evident when she was younger.

Maybe she'd done her best to hide it back then. Or maybe he hadn't known her as well as he'd thought. He only knew that whenever he was close to her, he couldn't go five minutes without wanting to turn the tables on her.

She was so damn cool and indifferent when she was around him, making out as though that night had never happened. Sometimes he even wondered if he'd imagined the whole thing.

He wanted, in the worst way, to take her in his arms and drive her wild with his touch until she surrendered to his demands.

He wanted to be the one to shatter that composure that hid the fiery passion he knew smoldered beneath the surface. He wanted to send her out of her mind, the way she'd tormented him all those years ago. Only this time he'd be the one who was in control.

Groaning, Mac pummeled the pillow and jammed it under his head. He had to stop thinking this way. He was setting himself up for real trouble if he allowed himself to be tormented by these crazy ideas.

The best thing he could do was concentrate on getting the job done and get out of her life before he messed up again. In the meantime he'd do his darnedest to stay out of her way.

He had to constantly remind himself of that vow over the next couple of days. The way the business was run, there was just no way of avoiding Sharon completely.

It helped that it was a weekend and Tim was hanging around. The boy served as a barrier between him and Sharon, and Mac could afford to let down his guard a little.

Even so, his body ached with tension each night as he crawled into his empty bed. It was getting tougher to get to sleep, and the lack of rest was beginning to tell on him. Even his leg was bothering him more than usual lately.

If it hadn't been for the deadline on the delivery of the stock, he might have been tempted to go into town and drink himself silly.

Sooner or later, he warned himself, something was going to crack. He could only hope that he would be able to handle it when it did.

By the end of the week the sun left behind enough warmth one evening for Sharon to enjoy a glass of wine on the porch. Tim was in his room doing his homework, and the supper dishes had been cleaned and stacked away.

Mac had announced he was going out to inspect the fences, and Sharon had been relieved to see him go. It was obvious her new foreman had something on his mind.

Uneasily she wondered if he still suspected the truth. He'd actually been sharp with Tim a couple of times, though he'd apologized for it later, saying that he wasn't sleeping well.

Tim had taken to rushing out of the house again after school, and for once Sharon hadn't been too upset by his absence. It meant he wasn't hanging around Mac all the time.

Maybe Mac was edgy because he was missing the rodeo, Sharon thought, trying to reassure herself. Although he'd been kept busy enough, life on the ranch had to seem boring to someone who was used to the excitement and variety of life on the circuit.

Sighing, she rocked gently in her chair, her gaze fixed on the crimson sunset. Streaks of yellow and orange mingled in the dark blue sky as the sun eased its way down behind the black silhouetted firs. The earthy smell of the forest drifted in on the night breeze, mingling with the fragrance of the jasmine climbing up the porch trellis.

This was the time of day she loved the most, when the quiet peace of the night settled over the land, giving nature a chance to rest.

Footsteps on the porch steps startled her out of her preoccupation. Looking up, she half expected to see Tim ambling toward her. She was unprepared for the sight of Mac, standing just a few feet away.

His shirt was open at the throat, though the long sleeves were still firmly fastened at his wrists. He had a hunting knife stuck in his wide leather belt, and his jeans were tucked into scuffed Western boots. Even without his hat, he looked every inch the cowboy—relaxed, confident and incredibly masculine.

Her breath caught, and she curled her fingers on the arms of the chair.

"Am I disturbing you?" he asked, his deep voice sounding rough edged in the quiet air.

She shook her head, managing a faint smile. "No, I'm just enjoying the sunset. Did you want something?"

"I wanted to talk to you about the fencing, but it can wait until tomorrow."

She sat up, holding the rocker still with her feet. "No, that's okay, we can discuss it now. We don't have much time to talk in the mornings." She hadn't meant it to sound intimate, yet somehow it had.

"I'm usually busy first thing." His blue eyes challenged her as he slotted his thumbs into the pockets of his jeans. "I'll be happy to make time for you, though."

Her heart skipped a beat. She got up with a swift movement that violently rocked the chair. "I'm going to get another glass of wine. Would you like a beer?"

"That sounds good, if it's not troubling you too much."

"It's no trouble. Take a seat, I'll be back in just a minute."

Her face felt hot as she opened the door of the fridge. She had to be imagining that look in his eyes. She had to stop these childish reactions every time he looked at her. He had to notice the effect he had on her.

If only she could blot out the image of him leaning over her, his eyes wild with passion, his mouth hard on hers. His intensity had scared her then. Now she was only too aware that she would welcome it.

All the old feelings had resurfaced with a vengeance. Only now she was dealing with an experienced, hard-edged man instead of the boy she had once loved.

Ashamed of her treacherous thoughts, she carried the drinks back to the porch, wishing she hadn't suggested sharing a nightcap with him.

For some reason she felt nervous as she pushed open the door to the porch with her hip. Mac was standing by the railing, staring out at the night sky.

He reached for the beer as she let the door close behind her, and thanked her without looking at her.

Settling down on the rocker again, Sharon waited for him to sit down. He chose the swing, letting it sway gently back and forth as he flipped open the top of his beer.

"Do we have a problem with the fencing?" she asked, watching him tip his head back to pour the beer down his throat.

He shook his head, waiting a moment before answering her. "The men have been working hard on them," he said finally. "They're looking pretty good. It takes time to get around to all of them."

"I know." There had been times she'd worked alongside the men, patching up holes in the fences. That was before her father had died and left her in charge of everything. The men no longer welcomed her help. She was the boss now, and they were no longer comfortable with her around.

"I was wondering if you wanted the new fencing put up on the far paddock yet," Mac said after a moment's silence. "The way that bronc is kicking into everything, it might be better to wait until after next week."

She nodded. "It's your decision. I'll leave it up to you. How's the bronc doing, anyway? Is he taking the halter yet?"

Mac shrugged. "I've managed to get it on him a couple of times. He's taking it as well as he's going to, I reckon."

"Do you think he'll make a saddle bronc?"

Mac's mouth lifted in a grim smile. "No way. It's going to be tough for anyone to go the full eight seconds on that feisty, gut-twister bareback. Anyone who tries to put a saddle on him won't live to brag about it."

Sharon raised her eyebrows. "That bad?"

"That good, if you're a stock contractor," Mac said. "We have another couple of broncs that'll be ready in a week or two. Barney tried to make a calf horse out of one, but he was too darn independent. He should make a pretty good saddle bronc, though."

"That sounds promising. Things really seem to be pulling together, thanks to you. Even the men are much more pleasant." She paused, then added lightly, "They like you."

If he was surprised by her compliment, he didn't show it. "Thanks, ma'am," he said, half mocking her, "I sure do appreciate the kind words."

She sipped her wine, feeling more than a little self-conscious. The conversation had been fairly mundane, yet she could feel the tension between them vibrating just beneath the surface. This might be a good opportunity to say good-night.

Before she could form the words, however, he startled her by asking, "How come you and Will Carlson split up?"

The question sounded casual enough. Even so, she found it impossible to answer him right away. After a moment he said quietly, "Look, it's none of my business. Sorry I asked."

She managed a laugh that sounded forced, even to her. "No, it's all right. I was just thinking how best to put it, that's all."

She took a sip of wine, then said steadily, "Will and I were married for seven years when I found out he'd been dealing with some seedy characters at the track. Apparently these men had been drugging the horses. Will had turned a blind eye and in return had been given the names of the winners. I divorced him as soon as I found out. A couple of months later he was arrested."

"He went to jail?"

"No, he got five years' probation." She sighed. "But he lost his job, of course, and eventually had to leave town. He was convinced I'd reported him, although I swore I hadn't. I would have done anything to avoid that kind of publicity."

"He didn't believe you?"

She shook her head. "His last words to me were that one day, no matter how long it took, he'd get even."

"That was how long ago?"

She thought about it. "I guess it must be around nine years or so."

"Well, if you haven't heard from him in all that time, I guess you don't have a whole lot to worry about now." Mac planted his feet in front of him, and leaned his elbows on his knees, the beer can clasped in his hands. "Most times those are empty threats anyway. I've made a few myself in my time."

"I don't even think about it now." Sharon looked out across the meadows. The sky had darkened, and already the first stars were glimmering between the clouds.

"I reckon you don't have time to think about it," Mac observed. "There's a lot to running a ranch this size. You have your hands pretty full just keeping track of everything."

"I've been doing it a long time. Dad wasn't too well the last year or two, and left more and more on my shoulders. Just as well he did, I suppose, since it prepared me to take over after he . . . died."

He must have heard the little break in her voice. "You miss him," he said softly.

"Yes," she said, "I do."

"So do I. I keep expecting to see him striding around the side of the barn any minute yelling, 'Get those damn horses into that pasture before someone breaks their fool neck.'"

She couldn't help smiling at that. "He always did have a voice that could carry from the stables to the far paddock."

"Remember the time he lost his voice? It just about drove him crazy. Not to mention everyone else."

"I remember. He rushed around everywhere waving a sheet of paper with his instructions scribbled on it."

"Yep, he sure did. Trouble was, no one could read his writing."

Sharon laughed. "Remember the time he wrote down 'Get a halter on the black bronc,' and Deke thought he'd written, 'Get a holden of the backbone?'"

Mac chuckled with her. "Sure do. Poor old Deke spent half an hour trying to grab that bronc in the middle of its back, until the old man finally made him understand what he wanted."

Exchanging a smile with him, she said wistfully, "Those were good days."

Across the porch his gaze met hers. "They sure were."

The light from the windows fell across his face, softening his harsh features as he continued to look at her. The recent days in the sun had given him back his healthy glow, and the smile relaxed the hard edge to his mouth.

He was leaning forward, his elbows still on his knees, and beneath the open neck of his shirt she could see the dark fuzz on his chest. Her stomach muscles contracted sharply as the memories once more stabbed at her.

For a long moment it seemed as if everything in the world around her had frozen in time, holding her a breathless captive of the man sitting just a few feet away from her. He hadn't changed so much, after all.

The look in his eyes, however, was all man. Unwillingly her gaze dropped to his mouth. At the same moment he said softly, "It's good to be back here again."

She couldn't be sure if he meant the ranch or right there on the porch with her. She only knew what she wanted him to mean, and how dangerous that kind of thinking could be.

She stood up abruptly, and held out her hand for the can. "It's been a long day. I think I'll go to bed."

To her dismay, he rose, too, barring her way to the door. He was too close again. Her heart pounded so hard he must surely hear it.

"Don't let me run you off," he said with just a trace of resentment.

She raised her eyebrows at him. "You're not. I'm just tired, that's all."

He shook his head slowly, his gaze speculative. "It's almost as if you're afraid of me."

She wondered if he'd noticed her guilty start. She did her best to cover it with a laugh that sounded too false. "Why in the world would I be afraid of you?"

"Maybe because of what happened that night." He moved swiftly, grabbing her arms to pull her close. His mouth was close enough for her to feel his warm breath on her lips.

Shock trembled through her as he whispered savagely, "I made a mistake. A big mistake. It's not going to happen again, Sharon, I'll make damn sure of that, so you can just quit your worrying. From now on I'll do my damn best to stay out of your way."

Before she could answer him, he let her go and strode off the porch, clattering down the steps without a backward glance. She watched his dark shape cross the grass toward the bunkhouse, her breath trembling on her dry lips.

He was right. To be too close to him spelled trouble for them both. And Tim. It would be better to stay out of his way as much as possible. Wondering just how she was going to accomplish that, Sharon opened the porch door and shut the night out behind her.

Striding past the bunkhouse, Mac headed for the open meadow. He needed to clear his head. Above him a welcome breeze stirred the branches of the firs. In all the years he'd been away from the Double S, he'd never forgotten how the firs smelled at night.

Whenever he caught the fresh, tangy fragrance, no matter where he was, the smell always reminded him of the times he used to ride into the forest late at night when his frustrations wouldn't let him sleep.

Would he have left the ranch for the rodeo eventually, he wondered, if it hadn't been for his hungering for Sharon? He'd always followed the contests, eagerly reading the latest scores in the newspaper. He'd fantasized about competing often enough, but had never really believed he would actually do it. He'd figured on staying at the ranch indefinitely.

Until that morning he'd ridden out, leaving security behind and facing the unknown once more. Hell, he'd decided he had nothing to lose after that.

He shouldn't have come back. He wouldn't have if he'd known he'd be dealing with Sharon instead of her old man. She was just as much under his skin now as she had been all those years ago. Watching her shy away from him every time he came near her damn near killed him.

He couldn't let her get to him like this. He was losing his concentration. His boss would have to grow a thicker skin if she wanted him to do his best work. He couldn't be worrying about treading on her boundaries every time he spoke to her.

There was also the question of Tim. Somehow he had a strong feeling that she wasn't being straight with him about that. If she was lying to him, he could hardly blame her, under the circumstances. But dammit, he had a right to know the truth. Sooner or later he would have to tackle her again.

Swearing under his breath, he tramped across the grass, away from all the frustrations. At least for the time being.

Sharon got up with a pounding headache the next morning, more than likely because she hadn't slept properly, she thought as she studied her strained-looking face in the mirror.

She wasn't sure who bothered her more—Tim, with his endless chatter about the rodeo, or Mac, with his probing questions and too-sharp mind.

Since it was Saturday, Tim had time for a full break-fast, something he always looked forward to at the end of the week. He sat at the kitchen table, while Sharon flipped the pancakes with a practiced hand. Pancakes were one dish she prepared well without having to think about it too hard.

"Have you ever dropped one?" he asked, watching her as she landed one neatly in the pan again.

"A couple of times. When I was learning how to cook them."

"When was that?"

She sent him a smile over her shoulder. "Emily taught me when I was a lot younger than you. Mac used to tease me, daring me to flip the pancakes real high. He wouldn't be satisfied until I dropped one, then Emily would chase him out of the kitchen."

Tim laughed. "I can't imagine anyone chasing Mac anywhere."

"Not too many people did."

"I wish I could have seen him ride in the rodeo. I bet he was really something to watch."

"I wouldn't know." She was regretting now that she'd ever brought up the subject of Mac. "What are you doing today?" she asked as she set a loaded plate in front of Tim.

"I'm going to help Mac," Tim said, stuffing a forkful of pancake into his mouth.

"Doing what?"

Tim shrugged. "Oh, I dunno. Whatever he wants me to do."

"Just be sure you don't get in his way," Sharon said, her voice growing sharp. "The trouble with Mac is that he won't say when someone's bothering him."

"I don't bother him," Tim protested. "He said himself he likes having me around. I thought you'd be happy I'm doing more around the ranch. You always nagged me about not doing enough to help."

"If you want to help, go help the other men work on the fences. Mac has his work cut out training those horses. They're due for delivery on Monday."

"I know, I know. Don't worry, I won't get in his way."

Irritated by his tone, Sharon turned on him. "For heaven's sake, Tim! How many times have I told you, don't speak with your mouth full."

"Sorry," he mumbled, and lapsed into a sulky silence that got on her nerves until he finally shoved his plate away and charged out of the room.

She spent the next hour furiously cleaning up the kitchen, then tackled the rest of the house. By the time she'd finally worked off her bad mood, it was almost lunchtime.

Deciding to go and find her son and make peace with him, she left the house and walked out to the corrals, where Mac would be halter-training the horses.

To her surprise, she found Barney working with the horses.

"He's around the back of the stables," Barney told her when she asked where Tim was. "He's with Mac, taking a look at that new saddle bronc."

She quickly stifled her flash of resentment. The horse Barney was working with seemed to be in good shape. By the looks of it, he was ready to be shipped out.

She watched Barney for a minute as he put the quarter horse through his paces. Then, with a nod of approval, she left the corral and went in search of Tim.

She found him in the paddock behind the stables. Mac was with him, and to her intense irritation, she saw one of the broncs high stepping around in the far corner of the corral.

She was even more annoyed when she crossed the grass, and saw Mac hand a saddle to Tim. They were both too absorbed to hear her approach, but she heard Mac's voice quite distinctly.

"Just because he's halter-broke," he told Tim, "that doesn't mean he's going to take kindly to having a saddle on his back. You're gonna have to watch his feet when you dump it on him. Try and get at least one girth strap tightened before he gets away from you, but don't take any chances."

Tim took the saddle into his hands just as Sharon reached the railing. Raising her voice, she demanded, "Just what the hell do you think you are doing?"

Tim turned a startled face in her direction, but Mac took his time, pausing as if to brace himself before turning to face her. His expression, as always, revealed nothing of his thoughts.

Shaking with anger, Sharon climbed over the fence and dropped to the other side. Marching toward them, she said in a tight voice, "Tim, get back to the house. I'll deal with you later."

"But Mom..."

"In the house, Tim."

"Sheez, Mom, I was only—"

"I said *now,* Tim!"

"Okay, okay." Muttering under his breath, Tim threw the saddle down on the ground and stalked off.

Sharon took a moment to calm her fury as Mac slowly bent over to retrieve the saddle. In the corner of the paddock the bronc watched them curiously.

"I thought I told you, Mac," Sharon said, striving to keep her voice even, "that Tim was to stay away from the rough stock."

"You said he wasn't to ride them. I was only teaching him how to put a saddle on a bronc."

"An untrained bronc."

"A halter-trained bronc," Mac said a little too quietly. "You said yourself that you wished he'd learn how to train the horses."

"Calf horses," Sharon said hotly. "Horses who have the temperament and stability to be trained. Not wild, unpredictable broncs who lash out at the slightest provocation. Horses whose only aim in life is to see that men don't get the better of them."

She envied him his quiet tone when he answered her.

"Saddle broncs are not as dangerous as the barebacks, you know that. That's why we can at least get a saddle on them. It's only when a man tries to ride them that they get ornery."

Feeling betrayed, she could hold her temper no longer. "Dammit, Mac, I trusted you with my son. How dare you go sneaking behind my back and encourage him to disobey me?"

For the first time she saw resentment flash in his eyes. His chin came up, but his voice remained calm as he said, "I was doing no such thing. Tim asked me to show him how we get a bronc used to a saddle. I saddled this one myself only yesterday. I didn't think there was any harm in showing him how to go about it. I figured he'd be okay. After all, he's used to handling horses."

"He's not used to handling rough stock," Sharon argued, her voice rising in spite of her best efforts to prevent it. "I told you that. The trouble with you, Mac, is that you don't listen. You never did. You think you know everything. Well, you might know how to handle horses, but you don't know anything about teenagers and you don't know my son. So from now on, I'd appreciate it if you'd mind your own business and stay out of mine."

She saw a tiny muscle start beating in Mac's jaw as he took an uneven step toward her. "Calm down, Sharon," he said quietly. "I'm sorry if we riled you, but you're making a big noise about nothing. I reckon Tim's old enough to make some decisions of his own. You can't go on protecting him like he's still a baby. Sooner or later he's gonna have to stand on his own two feet, and he'll do it a lot easier if you just give him some space.''

Her temper threatening to explode out of control, Sharon hastily backed away from him. "Stay away from Tim, Mac McAllister. He's my son, and I'll decide what is best for him. And I don't need you messing things up for me.''

She clamped her mouth shut just in time to cut off the final word. *Again.*

She scrambled over the fence, then turned to face him across the top railing. "I'm going for a short ride,'' she said, emphasizing her clipped tone. "When I come back, I want to see every one of those calf horses working out.''

"Yes, ma'am.'' He gave her a mocking bow, though she could tell he was holding down his temper. Turning her back on him, she marched back to the stables and grabbed her saddle down from its peg.

Windsong seemed as anxious as she was to be out in the fresh air, and shifted restlessly until she had the girths firmly fastened. Leading him out of the stable, she glanced up. The clouds that had been threatening all day had finally cleared off, leaving just a few wisps in a warm blue sky.

It was a good day for a ride, she assured herself. She needed to get out of there for a while, and try to calm herself down. Swinging herself up on his back, she urged Windsong forward, waiting only until she hit the meadows before giving him his head.

She knew where she was headed—the only place that would bring her some peace. Riding hard, she followed the trail through the trees until she'd left the ranch far behind.

Chapter 6

Concentrating on the necessity to duck now and again beneath low-lying branches, Sharon allowed herself to enjoy the sensations of Windsong's powerful muscles moving beneath her. By the time she came out into the familiar clearing, she was feeling a little more composed.

She slid off the horse and patted his smooth, warm neck before fastening the reins to a tree branch. Spotting a fallen log, she walked over and sank down on it.

This tiny meadow nestled in the heart of the wildwood was her special sanctuary. No one came there except her. Not even Tim. Only one other person knew it existed, as far as she knew, and Mac had only seen it once. He had never visited the clearing again, understanding that the haven was her private refuge. Everyone needs somewhere where they can be truly alone, he'd told her soon after that day. He had never mentioned the clearing again.

She shouldn't have yelled at him like that, she thought remorsefully, looking back to the argument over Tim.

Even if Mac had deliberately ignored her wishes, she knew only too well how persuasive Tim could be.

On the other hand, it was all very well for Mac to say that Tim wasn't going to ride the bronc, but she'd specifically stated that he was to stay away from the rough stock.

Tim was just as much to blame, of course. He knew she would be upset with him for disobeying her.

"Damn," she muttered out loud, and picked up a long slender switch that lay at her feet. Swatting at a tall weed, she sliced the thick stem in half.

She couldn't seem to get Mac's words out of her mind. *Tim's old enough to make some decisions of his own. You can't go on protecting him like he's still a baby. Sooner or later he's gonna have to stand on his own two feet, and he'll do it a lot easier if you just give him some space.*

Space. Her father had given her space. Plenty of it. She'd grown up headstrong and stubborn, taking everything for granted and doing pretty much what she wanted without much thought about the consequences. And she'd wrecked her life. Although she could never regret having Tim, she'd tied herself down with a baby before she was nineteen, and she'd paid for it ever since. Her dreams of travel had been shattered forever. She hadn't even seen New York, much less the magical cities of Europe that had captured her imagination as a child.

Secure in the knowledge that she was alone, Sharon let the bitter tears finally spill. She'd wanted so much out of life. Before Mac had left, the future had spread out before her, full of glorious excitement, adventure and romance.

Sniffing, Sharon sliced at another weed. Romance. That was a laugh. She'd loved Mac with all of her heart, and he'd cared nothing for her. Will had cared for her, and she hadn't been able to return his love.

Now Mac had come back into her life, tearing her apart as he'd done all those years ago.

If that was romance, she thought with another swipe at the weeds, they could keep it. True romance only happened in books and movies, anyway. Most people had to settle for whatever made them happy, and not rely on someone else to bring them happiness.

Although Tim had given her happiness. She could never regret being his mother, but she'd stopped being a hopeless romantic the morning Mac had left her nursing a broken heart. Those dreams belonged to someone else. To Sharon Douglass—and she no longer existed.

And if Sharon *Carlson* didn't get a move on, she thought guiltily as she jumped to her feet, the day would be gone before she could get her chores done.

Mounting Windsong again, she turned his head back toward the ranch. Calmer now, she felt she could deal with Tim. She would sit him down and explain once again how she felt about him messing with the rough stock.

Until this past week things had been better between them. Maybe she could find that connection again, and somehow reach her rebellious son, who reminded her so much of two young people from another world, in another time.

She relaxed on the way back, letting Windsong set his own pace. She had almost reached the meadows when she heard the first thunder of hooves beyond the ridge of trees. Uneasily she tilted her head to listen. There were several of them, and they were heading toward her.

Anxious now, she guided Windsong out of the trees and into the meadow beyond. To her dismay she saw at least a dozen quarter horses bearing down on her. Behind them she saw that Mac followed hard on their tails, accompanied by Barney and a couple of the hands.

She recognized the fleeing animals right away. They were part of the unbroken herd, and they were heading for freedom. Wheeling Windsong out of the way, she watched them thunder past her, sending clumps of grass flying from their frantic hooves. Mac caught sight of her and pulled up, his horse rearing up before he got it under control. "You'd better get back to the ranch," he told her as she stared anxiously at his set face. "Tim's had a bad scare. He's pretty upset."

"What happened?" she demanded as Mac wheeled away from her. "Is he hurt?"

"I don't think so. He's pretty shook up, though." The words were flung over his shoulder as he took off after the flying horses.

Her heart pounded as she headed back to the ranch, urging Windsong into a fast gallop. Memories of her father's horse coming back without its rider were uppermost in her mind.

She would never forgive herself if Tim was injured in some way. She was the one who had brought him back to the ranch after the divorce. It would be her fault if he was hurt by any of the horses.

She'd told him to wait in the house for her, she thought as she sailed across a wide ditch. As usual, he'd apparently disobeyed her.

Unwilling to make guesses at that point, Sharon concentrated on getting back as fast as possible. Whatever had happened, she told herself, she would deal with it. In her own way.

Arriving back at the stables, she left Windsong with one of the men, and rushed over to the house. She found Tim in the kitchen. He sat at the table, looking very sorry for himself with a wet cloth pressed to his head.

"What happened?" Sharon demanded, reaching for the cloth.

Tim jerked his head away from her touch. "It's okay, it's only a bump."

"Then let me see."

Reluctantly he let her take the cloth away, and she bit back a gasp when she saw the ugly gash on his head.

"That looks nasty," she said, trying to sound calm. "I think we should have someone look at it."

"Aw, Mom." Tim gave her a pleading look. "Mac said it would be all right. He told Josh to get an ice pack on it."

She pinched her lips together. Mac again. As usual, he was taking charge of her son. "Can you see all right?" she asked anxiously. "Are you dizzy or anything? Do you have a bad headache?"

"I'm fine, Mom, honest. It hurts a bit but it's a lot better than it was."

Sighing, she sat down opposite him, aware of her heart still thumping. "You want to tell me what happened?"

He looked down at his soda, as if unsure what to tell her.

"I want the truth, Tim."

"Okay, okay. I don't know how it happened." Tim sat back in his chair and pressed the cloth to his head again. "I had my back to the corral. All the guys were having lunch out in front of the bunkhouse, and I was fooling around with the dogs. Someone must have opened the gate and spooked the horses, because the next thing I knew they were out of the corral and all over me."

"Oh, God, Tim, you could have been killed."

He nodded, his expression serious. "I almost was. They knocked me to the ground, and I had to roll out of the way of their hooves. One of them just clipped my head before I could get clear."

Hiding her alarm at his words, Sharon rose to her feet and crossed to the fridge. She opened the freezer with fingers that shook, and reached for a tray of ice cubes. She wondered if Tim realized just how close he had come to being trampled to death by the panicked horses.

"Did Josh clean that up before he gave you the ice pack?" she asked, and frowned when Tim shook his head.

Leaving him alone for the moment, she went into the bathroom and found a bottle of disinfectant. When she came back, Tim was opening another can of soda. He seemed to have a little more color, and she forced herself to relax.

"Who do you think could have stampeded the horses?" she asked after she'd done a thorough cleaning job on the gash. Looking at it now, she had to admit it didn't seem as bad as she'd first thought. Maybe Mac was right after all.

"I don't know. Like I said, I had my back to the corral." Tim winced as she stuck a strip of tape over the cut. "I took a sandwich out for Mac, since you weren't here, and we ate lunch with the rest of the guys. They were all eating at the picnic tables. Then they all started talking about the ranch business and I got bored, so I went out to the meadow with the dogs."

"You saw all the men at the tables?"

Tim nodded. "Yep. All of them."

So someone else, someone who didn't belong there, had somehow managed to creep into the corral and unlatch the gate. Sharon took the disinfectant back to the bathroom, worrying at the thought. It would have been simple enough to spook the horses and, once they were on the run, to slip away unnoticed in the confusion afterward.

The question was why? Had this person seen Tim there in front of the corral? He would have been hard to miss, especially if he'd been playing with the dogs. Surely someone hadn't deliberately set the horses on him?

She didn't want to believe that. Yet the incident with Tim's car the other day was foremost in her mind. Was it coincidence? Or was someone deliberately trying to hurt her son? If so, who in the world would want to harm him?

She hurried back to the kitchen, where Tim was still sitting at the table nursing his soda. She sat down opposite him again, saying with a little laugh so that it didn't sound so serious, "You don't have any enemies at school, do you?"

He looked at her in obvious surprise. "Enemies? Why would I have enemies?"

Sharon shrugged. "Just about everyone can name one or two people who don't like them for some reason."

"Don't like me, maybe," Tim agreed. "But I wouldn't call them enemies."

Maybe not, Sharon thought uneasily. But the fact remained that someone had let loose a herd of stampeding horses with Tim right in their path. And she wasn't going to rest easy until she knew who that person was.

Mac and the men who were with him didn't return until after supper that evening. Hot and dusty, he stopped by the kitchen for a cold beer, and told Sharon they had managed to round up the entire herd.

"They're all safely back in the corral," he assured her, standing with his back against the sink. "I was worried we wouldn't get them back before dark."

"Thanks, Mac," Sharon said, grateful that Tim was in the kitchen to chaperon. Being alone with Mac unsettled her too much. "That would have set us back quite a lot to lose those horses."

Mac nodded. "Yeah, I know. No one seems to know how they got out, that's the problem."

Deciding this wasn't the time to discuss her fears, Sharon got up from the table. "You must be hungry," she said, opening the door of the fridge. "I'll fix you some supper."

"Don't bother. I'm taking the guys down to the tavern for a drink tonight. They worked their butts off to get that lot rounded up."

"Wish I could come," Tim said, looking despondent.

"You got a ways to go before you can go to a tavern," Mac said, giving him a friendly cuff on his shoulder. "Besides, you need a rest after the crack you took on the head."

"That's what I've been telling him," Sharon said, grateful for Mac's support. "I think he should stay home tonight."

"Aw, Mom, it's Saturday. I always go out on Saturday night."

"I know, but it wouldn't hurt to stay home this one night, would it?"

As if deciding to stay out of the argument, Mac moved to the door. "I'll see you all later, then," he said, and winked at Tim. "Don't wait up."

Tim watched the door close behind him, muttering, "I don't have anything to wait up for."

"How about giving me a game of checkers?" Sharon offered, determined to keep Tim at home that evening. It wasn't the gash on his head that worried her as much as the thought that someone might be out to hurt him, and she'd be helpless to prevent it. At least if he was home where she could see him, she'd know that he was safe.

Tim looked up at her in surprise. "You never play checkers."

"I don't anymore." Sharon cleared the rest of the dishes away and stacked them in the dishwasher. "But there was a time when I could beat your grandfather now and again."

"Yeah?" Tim got slowly to his feet. "Well, I guarantee you won't beat me."

Wiping her hands on a towel, she grinned at him. "We'll see about that."

Seated in the den later, he beat her easily, and in record time. She sat back and glanced at the clock, wondering how late Mac would be this time.

"You want another game?" Tim asked, collecting up the pieces from the game board.

"I don't think so. It would be a waste of time trying to beat you."

"Told you so," Tim said, packing the game away. "How about poker?"

She blinked at him. "You play poker?"

"Sure. Want me to show you how?"

"I know how," Sharon said grimly. "I'm just surprised you do."

He shrugged a little self-consciously. "The guys taught me."

Sharon sighed, wondering what else the guys had taught him.

After a moment of silence Tim said hesitantly, "Mac told me that you were hollering at him for showing me how to saddle a bronc."

"I was. He knows how I feel about that."

"It wasn't his fault," Tim said, beginning to sound defensive again. "I told him it would be okay with you."

Sensing an argument, Sharon bit back the reprimand. She couldn't afford an argument tonight. If Tim stomped out of the house again, she wouldn't have a minute's peace until he came back, wondering if someone were out there just waiting to hurt him.

Drawing in a breath, she said quietly, "I wish you hadn't done that."

Tim let out an explosive sigh. "Mom, when are you going to stop treating me like a little kid? If I'm old enough to work with the calf horses, why can't you trust me with the saddle broncs? Mac is a great teacher, he wouldn't let me do something he thought I couldn't handle."

It was an old argument, and one she usually refused to discuss. This time, however, she was determined to keep the peace. "All right," she said slowly. "If it means that much to you, I'll think about it. That's all I can promise right now."

Tim's face registered shock, then sheer excitement. "Really? You mean it? All *right!*"

She held up her hand, wondering what she'd let herself in for. "I said I'd think about it, that's all, so don't get too carried away and start leaping onto the back of every horse you see. If you can't be sensible about it, I won't even consider it."

"I'll be sensible. I will...I promise." He jumped up and planted a kiss on her cheek for the first time in weeks. "I'm going to call Mike now. Okay?"

"You're not going out, are you?" she asked anxiously.

"No, I'm not going out." He lifted a hand to touch his forehead. "I've got a bit of a headache. I think I'll go to bed early."

She smiled up at him. "Good idea. You'll probably feel better by the morning."

She sat for a long time after he'd gone, thinking about what had happened that day. Tim could easily have been killed in that stampede. The more she thought about it, the more it seemed likely that someone had deliberately let the horses loose.

She needed to talk to someone, she thought as the quiet hours ticked by. She couldn't face the thought of going to bed, knowing she would only lie awake in the dark worrying about the problem.

She needed to get it out in the open, and there was only one person with whom she could discuss the problem and know it wouldn't go any further. In spite of her misgivings, she needed to talk to Mac, and it would have to be alone.

It was past midnight when Mac came home. He appeared to be quite sober, and apart from a slight twitch of his eyebrow, he didn't seem too disturbed by the fact that she had obviously waited up for him.

"I need to talk to you," she said after she'd called him into the house. "Can you give me a few minutes?"

"If it's about what happened this morning," he said before she could say any more, "I guess I should apologize. I shouldn't have listened to Tim. I should have known he was trying to swing one past me."

Somewhat taken aback by this sudden turnaround, Sharon said quickly, "That's not what I wanted to talk to you about. Tim has already explained what happened, and if anything, I should apologize to you."

He gave her a long look that seemed to vibrate down her spine. "I guess we got that settled, then."

She turned away from him before he could see the sudden warmth in her face. "I guess so," she echoed coolly. "There is something else I want to talk to you about, if you have a minute."

For a moment she thought he would refuse, then he shrugged and followed her into the den. He stood in the middle of the room, watching her warily as she sat down on the couch.

"Is this going to take long?" he asked as she gestured at him to sit down in her father's chair.

"I hope not." She made herself look up at him. "I wouldn't bother you if it wasn't important."

He nodded and settled himself on the chair. "Okay, let's have it."

"It's about the stampede this afternoon," she said, uncertain of how to explain her fears without sounding melodramatic.

"Yeah, I don't know what to make of that." Mac stretched his long legs out in front of him and studied his boots. "We were all together at lunchtime. I guess someone could have left the gate open earlier, though I don't know how I could have missed seeing it."

"No one had any reason to go in that corral," Sharon said quietly. "Everyone should have been either working on the fences or with the calf horses. There was no need for anyone to go anywhere near there." She paused for a moment, and when he didn't comment, she added, "Unless someone went in there to deliberately stampede the horses.''

He looked up sharply at that. "Why would anyone want to do that?''

She shrugged. "Your guess is as good as mine.''

He shook his head and stared down at his boots again. "I have to admit, the same thought occurred to me. I was going to talk to the rest of the men some more before saying anything, though.''

Sharon's heart skipped with apprehension. Hearing Mac agree with her only intensified her fears.

He lifted his head and looked at her with an intent expression she knew well. "Got any ideas who it might be?''

"I don't know. One, I guess. I think it might be possible that Will is finally carrying out his threat. He knows, better than anyone, what it would do to me if anything happened to Tim.''

"That's tough to believe,'' Mac said, shaking his head. "No father is going to hurt his own son, no matter how mad he is at his ex-wife. Even Will Carlson can't be that sick in the head.''

For a moment she was lost for an answer. She could hardly tell him that Will wasn't Tim's father—and that he had always resented her son.

Tim was a constant reminder of what she had done. For the most part Will had ignored the little boy. He'd spent most of his time at the track, rather than deal with the living proof that his wife had loved another man and yet couldn't bring herself to love her husband.

"I don't know what else to think,'' she said at last.

"What about your ex-foreman?'' Mac suggested.

She lifted her head, startled by the idea. "Jerry? I hadn't even thought about him.''

"He could be nursing a grudge.'' Mac shifted his weight in the chair. "The guys tell me that he resented you boss-ing him around. I reckon he'd resent it a good bit more when you fired him."

"It's possible, I suppose." Sharon frowned. "If so, he was taking one heck of a chance coming back here where everyone knows him."

"He didn't strike me as being too sharp. Anyhow, I think you should consider putting a call in to the sheriff. It wouldn't do any harm to let the law know what's going on."

"No," Sharon said quickly, rising swiftly from the couch. "I don't want to do that. We don't know for certain that it was deliberate, and I don't want to worry Tim unnecessarily. Besides, he would hate it if he thought we were all watching over him all the time. He's always resented what he likes to call my interference in his life."

She watched Mac get lazily to his feet. "Things have been so much better between us lately," she added as he moved toward the door, "I'd hate to set Tim off again. Especially now, when he may need me more than he knows."

"You don't think he should be warned?"

"Not at this point, no. Not until we're sure." She met his gaze steadily. "You said yourself I was being overprotective of him. I'm trying to give him some of that space you were talking about. I even promised to think about him learning how to handle the broncs. If I start clamping down on him again now, I could lose what little headway I've made."

Mac nodded his approval. "Okay. You won't mind, though, if I keep an eye on him myself? He doesn't have to know it, of course."

She gave him a grateful smile. "I'd welcome it," she said sincerely. "It will be a relief to know I haven't got this all on my shoulders."

She had been careful to keep her distance from him. But now he moved toward her, too fast for her to step out of the way. He paused in front of her, looking down at her with a grave expression that unsettled her.

"If Tim is in danger," he said quietly, "I want to be there."

He sounded so definite her heart skipped a beat. It was almost as if he knew. Yet he couldn't. Not for sure, anyway.

"Thank you, Mac," she murmured, trying not to sound nervous.

For just a second, she saw a flicker of heat in his eyes. Part of her wanted to respond, to melt in his arms. Yet she could not forget his harsh words the other night. He wanted nothing from her. And she could give him nothing.

Keeping her voice deliberately cool, she said quietly, "Good night, Mac. Thanks for listening."

"Sure," he said briefly. "Any time." The door closed behind him, cutting off the thin thread of contact.

On the other side of the door, Mac drew in a long breath. He'd wanted so much to take her into his arms and offer the comfort and reassurance she so obviously needed. It hadn't been easy to walk out of there without touching her.

He cursed himself for his weakness when he was around her. He'd always admired her courage and fearless determination. He'd seen her struggle against seemingly insurmountable odds and come out on top—sometimes battered and exhausted, but always triumphant.

She was the kind of woman who got things done, and wouldn't quit until she'd achieved whatever it was she'd set her mind on. She was a lot like him in that respect . . . too alike, he admitted ruefully. It was hard to see her like this, so anxious and confused.

He remembered a time when they'd been able to talk so easily to each other. He'd never told anyone about his childhood, except Sharon. He'd trusted her with his deepest emotions and most sensitive feelings, and she'd respected them. She'd never let him down.

He'd been the one who'd betrayed her. He could hardly blame her now for trying so hard to keep their relationship pure business. She had to be real bitter about what had happened that night. It was quite plain to see she was never going to forgive him.

Just as soon as he felt that everything was secure at the ranch, he promised himself, he'd get out of her life again. This time for good. In the meantime he'd better keep an eye on Tim, he reminded himself, just in case there was someone out there up to some mischief.

By Monday morning the bruise on Tim's head had begun to turn a spectacular shade of purple. He assured his mother, however, that he felt much better, and was eager to go back to school.

Sharon was inclined to think that his rapid recovery was due to his need to prove he was well enough to start working with the broncs.

She regretted now her rash promise to reconsider her ban on Tim's handling the rough stock. However, she would not go back on her word. Maybe, she thought, if she gave Tim some leeway, he might be satisfied with working with the broncs and forget about his dream of being a rodeo rider.

Much to her relief, Mac informed her that he would be loading up the horses to deliver to Sage City Brokers that morning. The bronc would be delivered by the end of the week, by which time he hoped to have it halter-trained.

Sharon spent the morning going over the accounts. After all the bills were paid and the men's paychecks made out, there wasn't a whole lot left. Even so, things looked considerably brighter than they had a month ago, thanks to Mac.

That afternoon Sharon took the paychecks and went to find Mac, since he would be the one responsible for getting them to the men.

She couldn't see him in the nearby corrals, and decided to check the stables before looking farther afield for him. At first she thought the stables were empty. The only sound she could hear was the shuffling of the horses as Windsong snickered a welcome.

Smiling, Sharon walked over to the stall and gently stroked Windsong's nose. "I don't have time to take you out yet," she said softly. "Maybe later this evening, if you're a real good boy."

Turning away from the horse, she paused as a slight sound caught her ear. It seemed to have come from the loft above her head. She listened intently for a moment or two, then deciding she must have imagined it, she was about to move on when the distinct sound of footsteps froze her in her tracks.

Someone was in the loft. Someone who didn't want to be heard, judging by the way he was creeping around up there.

She fought the urge to go to find help. By the time she came back, whoever was up there could be gone and she'd never know who was trespassing on her property. It was entirely possible that the intruder was the same person who'd let the horses loose from the corral. If so, she sure as hell wanted to know who it was.

Looking around her, Sharon spotted a shovel. She eyed the sharp blade and figured it would do the job if necessary. Treading carefully, she moved across the stable. The shovel felt heavy as she grasped the handle.

She was just a few feet from the ladder, and once more she listened. Above her head something dropped to the floor, and she heard a muttered curse.

Convinced now that she had the intruder cornered, Sharon slowly crept up the ladder until her head was level with the floor. Inch by inch she moved up one more step until she could see over the edge.

The loft was in dark shadow, lit only by the sunlight filtering through the narrow, paneless window at the far end. The intruder was hunkered down with his back to her, and his hat hid his face. It was impossible to tell what he looked like from there.

Inching up the ladder, the shovel raised ready to strike, Sharon held her breath, terrified the man would turn around before she was safely in the loft. She wished now that she'd gone for help.

She could've pulled the ladder away, which would have at least slowed the man down. She'd been so anxious to find out who had tried to harm her son, she hadn't thought about the danger to herself.

Damn impulsive as always. She could almost hear Mac muttering the words. It was a little late to worry about that now. Even as she wondered if she could get back down the ladder without being heard, the man sharply turned his head.

"What the—"

"Mac!" The sudden relief turned to irritation as she dropped the shovel and stepped into the loft to face him. "What the hell are you doing creeping around up here?" she demanded. "You scared me half to death."

Mac looked just as aggravated as she felt. "Not nearly as much as you scared me, you dang idiot, coming at me with a raised shovel like that. You were lucky I didn't throw a punch and send you back down the ladder."

"How was I to know it was you?" She shoved the shovel away from her with her foot. "Any normal person would've made some noise."

"I was looking for extra tackle," Mac said grimly. "Barney said there was some up here. He also told me that the floorboards were in bad shape and to watch my step."

"Well, I'm sorry," Sharon said stiffly. She wished now that she'd never come into the stables. "I thought you were an intruder."

"And you were going to hit him over the head with a shovel, I take it," Mac said, giving her a pitying look. "It didn't enter your head, I suppose, that you could have been easily hurt if it had been someone bent on mischief? Just when are you going to stop being so damn independent and admit there are some things better left to a man?"

"When hell freezes over." She turned sharply, and as she did so, her foot went through a weak floorboard. She stumbled, and feeling herself toppling forward, put out her hands to save herself.

At the same moment Mac stepped forward and grabbed her. She came up hard against his chest, and let out a little gasp.

"Are you hurt?" he demanded, his voice still harsh.

His face was so close she could feel his breath on her forehead.

"No," she whispered. She could feel those same quivers of heat that had bothered her so much whenever he was around. Only now the sensations flared as if suddenly released from a vacuum.

He stared down at her as if he were holding a keg of dynamite. Then through the sudden roaring in her ears, she heard his savage whisper.

"Damn you, Sharon."

Before she could utter a sound, his mouth came down hard on hers. Her entire body went rigid as shock thundered through her mind. Aware of her breasts flattened against his chest, she tried to pull back, but his arms locked her tight so that she was powerless to move.

Then, as he showed no sign of letting up, she gave up the contest. Relaxing her body, she stole her arms around his neck and yielded to his mouth.

It was as if the years had never been. Once more she was torn apart by the overpowering need that engulfed her—a need that she had never been able to fully understand. Spreading out her fingers, she dragged her hands over his back, hungry for his kiss as his mouth sought hers again and again.

His hands moved over her body, warming, chilling and heating with their impatient touch. How could she have forgotten the swirling feeling that could so easily send her rocketing over the moon? Caught up in the frenzy that seemed to overwhelm her, she reached for the buttons of his shirt.

Eagerly she slid her hand inside his shirt. His flesh felt warm, the sprinkling of hair soft beneath her fingers. Dimly she heard him breathe her name as he drew her hips closer to his. Shock once more trembled through her body when she realized he was as aroused as she was.

Something nagged at the back of her mind, stilling her fingers. Tim mustn't know. Tim could never know.

She pulled back, fighting the desperate need that tormented her body with sensations that had never been appeased. She had to stop this now, before he took it too far and destroyed her sanity again.

"No," she whispered urgently. "I'm...sorry. Someone might see us."

He was breathing hard, and his eyes glittered with the same fire that still flamed inside her. Then, as she stared without speaking into his eyes, she could see the fire slowly dying.

He dropped his hands and stepped away from her, looking as if he wished she would shrivel up and disappear.

She felt like crying and had to struggle to get a hold on her emotions. Summoning up all her resolve, she retreated to the ladder. Her voice sounded a little too unsteady when she said, "No one's been up here in months.

I didn't know the floor was in that bad a shape. I'd better get someone to look at it.''

"Good idea." He stared at her, his face a mask of indifference, though she had the feeling he was still angry with her. Or maybe himself.

The thought brought her back to reality. "I'd better get going," she murmured, and turned to step onto the ladder. Suddenly remembering why she was there, she shoved her hand into the back pocket of her jeans and pulled out the paychecks.

"Here," she said, holding the checks out to him, "this is why I came in here. I was looking for you to give you the paychecks."

He took them without a word, and unable to look at him any more, she scrambled down the ladder and out into the fresh air. She didn't stop until she was safely inside the house once more. Only then, in the quiet sanctuary of the den, did she let out her breath in an explosive sigh.

At least one thing was clear. Mac wasn't entirely unaffected by her after all. In fact, if she hadn't put a stop to what was happening, he might well have finished what he'd started.

She clamped down on the fierce delight that thought gave her. No matter how much she wanted him, she told herself, she could not allow things to get out of hand again.

Mac had proved once before that he was interested only in the heat of the moment, nothing more. She had to keep a distance between them. The last thing in the world she wanted was for him to find out the truth about Tim. She could end up losing them both.

Mac stayed out in the meadows that evening, reluctant to go back to the house for dinner. Furious with himself for allowing his desire for Sharon to get the better of him again, he wasn't sure he could keep his emotions in check enough to hide the turmoil from Tim and Sharon.

She had responded to his touch with the same eagerness he remembered from their first and only time together. Cursing himself up and down, he attacked the fence with a fury that matched his temper.

He was reading too much into it, he reminded himself. She was a sensuous woman, and by all accounts had not had her needs satisfied in a long time. No wonder she responded the way she did. He'd just caught her off guard—that was all.

She'd made it pretty clear she resented what happened, which was just fine by him. The sooner he got this job done and got out of there, the more comfortable things would be for them both.

Chapter 7

Finally, when it became too dark to see properly anymore, Mac made his way back to the house. Sharon was in the kitchen when he walked in, and the tangy smell of Italian sauces reminded him how hungry he was.

He wasn't sure how he felt when she turned to greet him as if nothing had happened. "Hi, I was beginning to think you'd gone to town for supper."

He shrugged. "I guess I wasn't hungry."

She turned back to the counter, apparently accepting the lie. "Well, I saved you some lasagna, and I'm making a fresh salad, if you've found your appetite again."

He hated the way she could sound so damn unaffected by what had nearly happened between them again. He was pretty sure that if they had been somewhere private, instead of the stables, nothing in the world would have stopped him from making love to her again.

He was almost as sure that she wouldn't have been so hell-bent on resisting, either. Yet she was acting as if nothing had changed. That the moments they'd spent in each other's arms were no big deal.

Which was fine by him, he told himself. The less fuss she made about it, the better. "I could eat something now," he said gruffly. "I can get it myself."

"I'll get it." She crossed to the fridge, blocking his path. "I'll just heat up the lasagna, and the salad is almost ready. Have a beer while you're waiting."

She handed him a can, and he took it, doing his best to avoid touching her fingers. Mad at himself for letting it matter, he said abruptly, "I see Tim's car's gone again."

"Yes, he's at Mike's." She had her head down, concentrating on shredding lettuce into a bowl. "Mike's his best friend. They've been together since kindergarten."

"I hope he's not mad at me."

Sharon looked up sharply. "Why should he be?"

He flipped open the lid of the can and sat down at the end of the table. "Because he asked me this afternoon if I'd show him how to saddle a bronc. I told him I was too busy."

"Oh, I see." She went on working, dicing up a cucumber with deft fingers. After a lengthy pause she said carefully, "And were you?"

"Nope."

"Then why did you tell him that?"

"I wasn't sure you wanted me to show him."

He saw an almost imperceptible movement of her shoulders that told him she'd just relaxed them.

"I told him he could learn as long as you were the one who taught him. I'm sorry, I should have told you that."

He shrugged and said, "Okay, as long as I know. How much do you want me to show him?"

"As much as you can, without actually letting him ride. We'll see how he does before we make that decision."

He liked the sound of that "we." Apparently she'd decided to trust his judgment again.

"You might also try and talk him into trying his hand at training the calf horses," Sharon said. "His help would come in handy if we got into another bind. At least until he goes to college."

"He doesn't seem too hung up on the idea of being a lawyer," Mac said, hoping he wasn't treading on dangerous ground again.

"He hasn't given it enough thought." She emptied the vegetables into the bowl of lettuce. "At the very least I want him to go to college. Nowadays an education is essential for a good job, and just in case something happens with the ranch, I want him to be prepared."

Taking a pair of large spoons, she tossed the salad. "I'm still hoping he'll want to go on to law school," she said, "but if not, he will at least have the education he needs."

"He'll do okay." Mac lifted his beer and took a swallow. "He has Douglass blood in him. How can he fail to make a success of his life?"

"Your dinner is ready," Sharon said quickly as the microwave oven beeped behind her. "Go on into the dining room, and I'll bring it in to you."

"Have you eaten already?" he asked, rising to his feet.

She shook her head. "I guess I wasn't hungry, either. It's no fun eating alone."

He took the salad bowl from her. "Here, I'll get this. You need to eat, too, so you can sit down and eat with me."

She looked for a moment as if she would refuse, then she said in a resigned voice, "Okay. If you insist."

Seated at the table a few minutes later, he was beginning to regret the gesture. After a few casual sentences, the conversation came to a full stop, and the silence was growing more uncomfortable by the minute.

For a moment or two he was tempted to apologize for kissing her that afternoon, but then he thought better of it. It might well make matters worse if he made a big thing of it. Better to take his cue from her and pretend it had never happened.

Searching for a safe subject, he said casually, "Where is Randall buried? I'd like to go and pay my respects to him. I would have asked before, except I've been so busy with those calf horses."

She gave him a smile that didn't reach her eyes. "He's in the churchyard, next to my mother."

Mac nodded. "Yeah, I should have known that. Stupid of me."

"It's been a long time," she said gently.

"I'll go tomorrow, after work." He finished the last of the lasagna and sat back in his chair. "That's unless Tim corners me."

"He probably will, so be prepared." She leaned over to reach for his plate. "More lasagna?"

He shook his head. "Did Tim get his car fixed?"

"Yes, he did."

They were floundering again, he thought desperately. He watched her get up from the table and take the plates back to the kitchen. When she came back, he said casually, "What did Randall think about the idea of Tim being a lawyer?"

She sat down again, shrugging her shoulders. "He wanted what was best for Tim, of course, but I don't think he was happy about it. He wanted Tim to learn how to run the ranch. I think he was hoping that Tim would take over the business after he graduated." She gave him a rueful smile. "Dad never did forgive me for being a girl, you know."

Mac nodded. "I reckon that was why he always treated you like a boy when you were growing up. You were one tough little ruffian when I first met you."

He watched a warm flush creep across her face. "He did the best he could," she said, sounding defensive.

"I know he did. And I was wrong, he did a hell of a job. No one could care more about this ranch, not even Randall Douglass."

"I just hope I can keep it going." She played with her glass, twisting it around in her fingers. "I guess I need to prove myself to him one more time."

Once more he had to force himself not to touch her. "Try not to worry about Tim," he said gently. "I know it must have been tough raising a boy alone, but look on the bright side. If you hadn't split up with Will, Tim wouldn't have grown up on a ranch."

"I know. I've lived with that a long time."

He frowned, wondering what he'd missed. "Too bad your mother couldn't have been around to help you out with him. It must have been lonely for you."

"It was." Sharon pushed her chair back with an abrupt movement that warned him he'd said too much.

He watched her leave the room, wondering why the hell she was so touchy on the subject. She'd never minded talking about her mother before.

He made himself face the question he'd been avoiding for so long. What would he do if he found out he was Tim's father after all? Would it be possible to stay on at the Double S, knowing that? He loved the work and the easy companionship of the men. They were a lot different from the tough, aggressive loners he'd competed against in the rodeo.

Here there was no pressure to be the top dog. All he had to do was what he loved to do: taking a wild, unbroken colt and turning it into a hardworking partner.

He enjoyed Tim's company; he was becoming quite attached to the kid. As for Sharon, he had to admit she added spice to his days. Maybe too much, if that afternoon was any indication.

Cursing under his breath, he carried the salad bowl back to the kitchen. No matter what he did, he thought as he dumped it on the counter, it seemed he was damned.

The next afternoon Sharon decided to get out of the den for a while and work on the gardens in front of the house. The exercise and fresh air might help ease the tension that had kept her awake half the night before, she thought as she collected the tools that she needed.

She also hoped the work would help keep her mind off the fact that Tim was in the corral with Mac, learning how to put a saddle on a bronc. Something told her she would live to regret giving up on her stand.

It didn't seem feasible to expect Tim to learn how to put a saddle on the horse without insisting that he ride it. She just had to trust that Mac would keep his word, at least until she'd had a chance to discuss it with him.

"Oh, Dad," she whispered under her breath, "how I wish you were still here." Not that he had much influence, either, she added silently. He was the one who had interested Tim in bareback riding in the first place. True, it had been on a trained horse, but the thrill of it had planted the first seeds in Tim's mind about competing in the rodeo.

The trouble was, she thought as she sat back on her heels to survey the flower bed she'd just weeded, Tim was right about being good enough to ride. He had his father's knack with a horse, that certain kind of affinity that is so necessary for a good rodeo man.

She smiled, remembering how Mac used to chase her across the meadow on horseback. She'd watched her father teach him to ride, with and without the saddle. He'd learned fast, and she'd had to admit that when it came to breaking in a rampaging, snorting, bucking wild horse, no one was better.

Leaning forward, she reached for an elusive weed half-hidden behind a clump of marigolds. A shadow fell across her arm, and she looked up, blinking at the silhouetted figure standing over her.

"You're doing a great job," Mac's deep voice informed her.

"Thanks." Feeling ridiculously self-conscious, she climbed to her feet and dusted her grimy hands on her jeans. "Weeding isn't my favorite pastime."

"Somehow I knew that."

She sent him a sharp look, but his face was as unreadable as ever.

"I prefer more relaxing pursuits," she said, striving to keep the conversation light. "Such as riding, reading and good country music."

"Little has changed after all," he murmured.

"Not as far as I'm concerned, at least." She stooped to pick up the garden tools and lay them in the basket.

"Meaning I have changed?"

The tone was casual, but she detected a small gleam in his eyes that bothered her when she looked at him. "In some ways," she said in an offhand manner that she hoped would put an end to the topic.

Mac, it seemed, was just as determined to pursue it. He followed her back to the house, saying, "In what ways?"

Wishing desperately she'd never started this conversation, Sharon said a little caustically, "Older, tougher and more cynical."

"I see." He appeared to think that over. "And what are the bad points?"

She wrinkled her nose at him. "Very funny."

"I just wanted to let you know I still have a sense of humor." He took the basket from her while she opened the door with her latch key.

Wondering what had generated this somewhat whimsical mood, Sharon looked at him. "How are things going with the Sage City bronc?"

He shrugged. "He still won't take a halter. I gave him a rest today, hoping the break would put him in a better temper tomorrow."

"Will he be ready to deliver by Friday?"

"He'll be ready, if I have to wring his fool neck to do it."

Opening the door, she stepped inside the cool hallway. "And how did Tim do this afternoon?"

"Pretty well. We had a few tricky moments while he was trying to get the saddle on the bronc, but he finally made it. I made him do it again three more times before I let him off the hook."

"He managed it all right, then?"

"Yeah." Mac handed her the basket, but remained on the step as she stood by the front door. "He's a fast learner, that kid. He sure reminds me of myself at that age."

"He has his grandfather's sharp mind," Sharon said quickly.

"And his mother's stubbornness?" Was it her imagination, or had there been a challenge behind the question? She relaxed when Mac said lightly, "He wasn't about to give up on that saddle. Kind of reminded me of the way you used to take Whitefire out at night, set on teaching him to back up."

She looked up at him, startled by his words. "You knew about that?"

"Sure. I used to watch you. I couldn't believe anyone would try that hard to prove me wrong."

She felt her face flush and turned away. "Whitefire never would back up for me," she muttered.

"That horse was just about as ornery as his owner."

Determined to change the subject again, she fingered the roses she'd cut, pretending to inspect them for aphids. "Tim didn't bug you to let him ride?"

"He mentioned it, but accepted it pretty well when I told him he wasn't ready to try it yet."

She nodded. "Well, thanks, Mac. I appreciate you taking the time with him. I just hope this satisfies him, at least for a while."

"I doubt it will satisfy him for long. Like I said, he's a fast learner."

"Well, do your best."

"I'll do that, ma'am."

She ignored the hint of dryness in his tone. "Now I'd better get these roses in water before they wilt."

"And I guess I'll take a run out to the churchyard." He lifted his hand to pull his hat over his eyes. "Unless you need me for anything else right now."

She shook her head. "Take your time. The men can handle anything that might come up."

"Okay. See you later, then."

She watched him walk down the path, his limp barely noticeable now, and her heart pounded beneath her breast. *He sure reminds me of myself at that age.*

How long would it be, she wondered, before Mac demanded to know the truth? She couldn't go on lying to him forever. How long could she stand to go on like this, expecting the blow to come at any minute? The tension was becoming unbearable, the anxiety robbing her of sleep.

To make matters worse, her body ached for his touch whenever she was close to him. How long could she go on hiding that from him? It seemed as if all three of them, she, Mac and Tim, were heading on a collision course that was destined to meet in disaster sooner or later.

Burying her face in the velvety, fragrant blossoms, she carried them into the kitchen. With trembling fingers she filled a vase with cold water. She must have been a fool, she thought, to expect this arrangement to work. She would have to think of an excuse to get rid of Mac. She would have to let him go. She just couldn't stand the strain anymore.

She jammed a rose into the vase and yelped when a thorn pricked her thumb. She sucked the puncture and picked up the rest of the roses, thrusting them into the vase. She would have to arrange them later, she told herself. Now was not the time to try to be creative.

Carrying the arrangement into the living room, she heard the front door slam and Tim's footsteps rushing into the den.

"Hey, Mom?"

"I'm in here," she called out as she stood the vase on the coffee table.

"Guess what!" Tim barged into the room, his face alight with excitement. "I got the saddle on the bronc in record time. Mac said I did a great job."

"So he tells me." She managed a genuine smile.

"Not only once, but three times. The first time wasn't too good, but after that it was dead simple."

"That's great, honey," Sharon murmured. "Now you'd better go and wash up, it's almost suppertime."

"He says I'm not ready to ride yet, but I know I am. If he'd just give me a chance, I could show him what I can do."

She lifted her chin at that. "If Mac says you're not ready, you're not ready," she said firmly. "And I don't want you bugging him about it, okay? He agrees with me that it will take time before you're ready to try riding a bronc."

"But it's a saddle bronc," Tim said, his voice turning belligerent. "It's not as if it's bareback."

"It's still going to buck, saddle or not. You know that."

"But—"

"I don't want any more argument, Tim." In spite of her best efforts, her voice had risen.

Tim gave her a look of pure defiance. "When are you going to stop smothering me?" he muttered.

"When you can prove you are mature enough to handle things on your own." She dusted her hands on her jeans. "I don't want to talk about it anymore. Now, please, go wash up for supper."

"I'm not hungry."

"Tim—"

As usual, her plea fell on deaf ears. He turned his back on her and stomped out of the room, his face growing dark with resentment.

She watched him go, the sinking feeling in her stomach telling her that she had made a big mistake. Far from satisfying Tim, the lesson that afternoon had only whetted his appetite for new thrills.

She was losing her hold on everything around her, she thought as she walked back to the kitchen. She felt as if she were on a roller coaster, soaring up to the sky one minute, hurtling back to earth the next.

Where it was all going to end, she couldn't bear to imagine.

Heedless of the damp grass beneath his knees, Mac knelt in silence by the grave of his old friend. He had visited the churchyard twice before with Sharon, but then there had been only one headstone in the plot. Now there were two, reminding him poignantly of the gruff, big-hearted man who had picked him off the street and given him a home.

"Look," he whispered, "I know I should have written you and told you why I left like that. I couldn't do it, though, without telling you about Sharon and me. I figured you'd kill us both if you knew. And I wasn't about to lie about the reason I left. There just wasn't any way I could say anything without hurting both of you."

He swallowed and dug his thumbs into the pockets of his jeans. He wondered if Sharon had told the old man, though he seriously doubted it. There was only one man Sharon Douglass feared and respected, and that was her father.

Randall Douglass had given his tough little daughter more freedom than was wise, but he'd come down hard on her when she messed up.

No, Mac thought, she wouldn't have told him. Her pride wouldn't have let her admit how much she'd given up for a man who'd taken off the very next day.

He sank back on his heels, and stared at the white stone until the black engraving on it began to blur. Now that he was here, at the side of the man who'd been better than a father to him, the enormity of what he'd done was coming back to him.

"I was just a kid," he said softly. "I didn't know what else to do. It seemed right at the time."

He'd lost so much. Watching Tim that afternoon, he'd been reminded vividly of just how much. Once he'd been like that—ambitious, a little wild and very determined. Once he'd had the promise of the world at his feet if he'd wanted it.

He'd lost all that the night he'd lost control of his emotions. In one blind moment of passion, he'd lost everything. And he'd paid.

"I'm trying to make it up to you," he whispered, leaning forward to touch the grassy mound beneath the headstone. "I'm doing my damnedest to turn things around for the Double S. I want to be sure Sharon will be okay before I leave again."

He bowed his head and briefly closed his eyes. "She misses you, old friend. So does Tim. I guess I miss you, too. I wish..."

His throat closed and he got to his feet, unable to take much more. He couldn't go back to the house yet. He couldn't risk being that close to Sharon, feeling the way he did right then.

Lifting his hand in a gesture of farewell, he turned away and strode back to the pickup. The engine started on the first turn, and he gunned it, taking a small measure of comfort in that small fragment of control as the engine roared.

Then he took off, faster than he should, and didn't slow down until he reached the tavern.

Sharon tried not to look at the clock again. She'd been glancing up at it every five minutes for the last hour, unsure whether she was more concerned about Tim or Mac. Neither one of them had turned up for supper.

She couldn't help thinking about the incident with the stampeding horses, and the attack on Tim's car. The more she thought about it, the more concerned she became. Anyone could be lurking out there somewhere, ready to strike at an unsuspecting victim.

It wasn't unusual for Tim to miss a meal, but it wasn't like Mac to miss supper without telling her he wouldn't be back.

She wondered if he'd been upset by the visit to her father's grave. It didn't seem likely he'd be affected too much. After all, he'd left without a word to Randall Douglass, so he couldn't have been as fond of her father as he'd led her to believe.

Nevertheless, she couldn't help feeling uneasy. She eyed the phone, wondering if she should call Mike's house to see if Tim was there. Though if he were there, he'd probably be furious with her for checking up on him.

She would just have to wait until he got home, she decided. As for Mac, he was big enough to take care of himself.

Telling herself that she needed to get out of the house for a while, she headed for the stables, intent on taking

Windsong out for a short run. A few minutes later she was racing across the meadows toward the rise.

In a small corner of her mind she nursed the hope that Mac had decided to work late with the bronc in the far corral. As she topped the rise, for a moment she thought that hope had been realized.

Squinting into the setting sun, she could make out a horse tied to a tree, and the silhouette of a man with the bronc in the corral. She urged Windsong forward, and raced across the grass.

Drawing closer, she shaded her eyes and stared hard at the shadowy figure circling the skittish bronc with a rope in his hand.

It wasn't Mac after all. It was Tim.

Furious now, Sharon thundered toward the corral. Tim glanced over his shoulder and saw her just before she reached the gate. He lowered the rope and waited for her, his expression defiant as he stood with his back to the horse.

"What the hell are you doing?" Sharon demanded, keeping her voice low so as not to spook the unpredictable bronc.

"Just taking a closer look at him."

Tim's look of innocence didn't deceive her for one minute. "You were trying to halter him, weren't you?" she snapped.

"No, I wasn't. I just wanted to see how close he'd let me get to him."

Without warning, the bronc's head jerked up, his ears flattened against his head. His dark pupils looked black against the expansive whites of his eyes as he reared up on his hind legs and, with a loud whinny, indignantly pawed the air.

Sharon yelled a warning, and Tim obediently ducked out of the way. In seconds she had the gate open and slipped through, closing it again behind her. "Get out of the corral," she said quietly, her eyes on the fidgety animal.

"Why won't you let me try and put a rope on him?" Tim demanded. "I'm sure I can do it if you just let me try."

"Don't argue with me, Tim," Sharon said, sending him a dark look that meant business. "If you don't know enough never to turn your back on an unbroken horse, you don't know enough to halter him. Now do what I say and leave the corral before we both get hurt."

"For gosh sakes, Mom, I just forgot. Anybody can forget sometimes. How am I ever going to ride rodeo if you won't let me learn anything?"

Her eyes still fixed on the bronc, Sharon said in a low, fierce voice, "That's enough. I've had it up to here with your whining about the rodeo. You get back to the house this minute. You can't be trusted, so from now on you stay away from the broncs. And don't you ever mention a word about the rodeo to me again."

Losing his temper, Tim flung the rope to the ground, accidently flipping the horse's nose.

Incensed now, the bronc reared up again, his eyes rolling back as he flailed the air with his hooves. His shrill whinny seemed to echo across the valley as his forefeet slammed the ground then rose again, aiming for Tim's head.

Sharon's mouth went dry as she watched her son freeze in the enraged animal's path. Slapping the bronc smartly on the rump, she yelled, "Get out, Tim. *Now!*"

Snuffling with rage, the bronc turned to face this new irritation, and to Sharon's relief she saw Tim run for the fence and scramble over it.

Backing away from the stomping horse, she reached the fence and climbed up just as the bronc rushed her. His hooves thrashed at the top railing seconds after she dropped to the ground.

Tim was already halfway across the meadow on the back of his roan. By the time she arrived back at the house, his car was gone. No doubt he was over at Mike's house, she thought ruefully, complaining about his mean mother.

Aware of a dull ache in the back of her head, she walked into the den and dropped onto the couch. She would have to tell Mac what happened. Surely he would agree with her this time that Tim couldn't be trusted to keep his word. There was no doubt in her mind that her son had not only intended to halter the bronc, but he was also going to attempt to ride it.

He wouldn't have stayed on the animal for longer than a second. The horse had never been ridden. Even if he had, it was doubtful Tim could have stayed on his back. Not without extensive training, which included the essential lesson of how to fall so as to minimize the chance of injury.

Letting out a sigh, Sharon glanced at the photo of her grandfather on the writing desk. In spite of all her efforts to teach him restraint, Tim was just as headstrong and stubborn as she'd been at that age. And given the fact that Mac was his father, no wonder she had trouble with her son.

She sat there in the den, trying to ignore her headache as the night crept in through the window. It was ironic, she thought, that she should feel so sleepy sitting there, yet the minute she got into bed she was wide-awake.

Opening her eyes again with a start, she realized she must have dozed off. A glance at the clock told her it was almost midnight.

She sat up, her heart skipping a beat. Tim was supposed to be home by ten-thirty on school nights. She hadn't heard him come back. It was possible he'd crept in without disturbing her, she thought, trying to reassure herself.

Doing her best not to panic, she hurried out to the porch to see if his car was parked out in front. Her stomach plummeted when she saw the empty driveway.

Cursing under her breath, she rushed back into the house and picked up the phone. It rang several times before a sleepy voice answered.

"Oh, Mike, I'm sorry to wake you up," Sharon said quickly. "I was just wondering if Tim has been over there tonight."

"He was here, Mrs. Carlson," Mike said, sounding a little wary. "He left around ten, I guess."

Sharon could feel the tension creeping up her neck as her head throbbed painfully. "Did he say if he was going anywhere?"

"No, ma'am. I figured he was going straight home."

Don't panic, she ordered herself. Somehow managing to sound unconcerned, she said pleasantly, "Thanks, Mike. I'm so sorry to have bothered you."

"Is something wrong? Tim's okay, isn't he?"

"Tim's fine," Sharon assured him, praying that was the truth. "He's most likely around here somewhere. I just haven't seen him come in, I guess. Go back to sleep, Mike. I'm sorry I woke you up."

"S'okay," Mike mumbled. "Good night, Mrs. Carlson."

"Good night, Mike." She replaced the receiver, her heart racing. Where could he be? She refused to think about the terrible morning she'd discovered Mac had left. Tim wasn't Mac. He wouldn't just leave home without saying a word to her. Not her only son.

If only Mac were there. He'd know what to do. But he was missing, too. Panic tore at her, scattering her thoughts. Should she call the police? Not yet. Tim would never forgive her if he was simply late getting home. It wouldn't be the first time he'd been late.

He'd always called before. Stop it, she told herself. He'd been mad at her earlier. He was just getting his own back. He wanted her to worry about him. She'd have a long talk with him when he got home. *If he got home.*

Unable to stay another minute in the den, she hurried once more to the porch. The car was still missing. She could see lights on in the bunkhouse, so at least someone was there. Maybe Tim had gone over there to talk to the men. Maybe Mac was there. Sometimes he played cards with the men in the evenings.

She started down the steps, trying to think of a plausible excuse why she should visit the bunkhouse at that time of night. Something caught her eye, and she paused, staring across the meadow at the skyline above the buildings.

She hadn't imagined it. She could see a faint glow just below the roofline of the stables.

Without wasting another second, she flew down the steps and across the grass to the bunkhouse. Pounding on the door, she yelled at the top of her voice. "Fire! Hurry! The stables are on fire."

After several agonizing seconds of slamming her fists against the door, it opened suddenly, and to her immense relief she saw Mac standing in the doorway. He was buttoning his shirt, and before he could speak she grabbed his sleeve and tugged.

"The stables are on fire," she cried, jerking her thumb over her shoulder. "Call the fire department. We have to get the horses out."

Mac uttered a muffled exclamation. Turning his head, he yelled out, "Let's go, guys! We've got a fire!"

Sharon didn't wait to see if he was following her. She set off at a run for the stables, refusing to let her mind dwell on the horrifying visions conjured up by her imagination.

Racing across the yard, she could hear now the shrill cries of the terrified horses. Smoke billowed from the open doorway, lit by an ominous glow from inside.

At least she couldn't see any flames yet, she thought as she darted through the doorway. Smoke swirled all around her, choking her, making it difficult to see. She whirled around and flung both doors wide open. As she did so, she saw the figure huddled on the ground in front of one of the stalls.

Her heart seemed to stop beating. Coughing and spluttering, she rushed outside to fill her lungs with clean air, and saw to her relief, Mac and Barney sprinting toward her. Then, taking a deep breath, she ran back inside.

Tim lay on his side, his face buried in his arm. Desperately she felt for a pulse, and her breath came out in rush when she found one. He was unconscious, but at least he was still alive.

Mac reached her side and swore. "Leave him to me," he said, giving her arm a little shake. "I'll get him outside. Barney will need a hand with the horses."

She nodded and, with a last look at Tim, scrambled to her feet. The smoke was getting thicker, and the horses had begun kicking the sides of the stalls.

Opening the door of Windsong's stall, she put out a hand and stroked the frightened animal, murmuring words of reassurance as she worked a halter over his head. She tried not to think about Tim as she struggled to control the horse. She needed all her strength and concentration just to guide Windsong out of the stall.

At last he was heading in the right direction, and she got him outside into the blessedly clean air. Mac was striding toward her, his face smudged with smoke. "The fire department is on the way," he told her, "and I sent Nick back to make sure they send an ambulance."

She was shivering almost uncontrollably. "How is he?"

"He's got a nasty bump on the head, but he's breathing pretty good. I reckon he got hit by something, maybe one of the horses. He's over there on the grass. I covered him with a horse blanket. He'll be all right for a while."

She nodded, resisting the urge to rush over there and be with him. "We have to get the mares out fast, or they could lose their foals."

She turned back to the stable, but Mac stopped her with his hand on her arm. His grim expression frightened her, but the firm grip of his fingers was somehow reassuring. She even managed a shaky smile.

"Try not to worry, Sharon," Mac said gruffly. "He's going to be all right, I promise."

Unsteadily she nodded, trying to hold the smile through the stinging tears. "I know. He just has to be."

He hesitated, as if he wanted to say something else, then with a shake of his head he let her go and raced off toward the smoke-filled barn. Now she could see the flames shooting out of the top window. The horses would have to take priority right now.

She made herself wait until all the animals were safely herded into an empty corral, and then at last she was free to go to her son. The faint wail of sirens reassured her, as did Tim's steady breathing, though his eyes remained closed in his stark, white face.

Hearing footsteps across the yard, she looked up and saw Mac striding toward her. He was covered in soot, and his hair hung in bedraggled locks across his forehead.

"How's he doing?" he demanded, his voice hoarse from the smoke.

"I wish I knew." She swallowed, afraid to say more in case she burst into tears.

She felt his hand on her shoulder, gently squeezing. "I'd better get back," he said quietly. "Hang in there, Sharon."

She nodded, her gaze glued to her son's still face. She didn't see Mac leave.

Within minutes the fire engines were racing up the driveway and across the yard. The ambulance pulled in seconds later, and two paramedics jumped out, one of them stopping to grab a stretcher while the other knelt at Tim's side.

Sharon waited, hardly able to breathe, while the young man quickly examined Tim, talking all the time into a radio at his side. Red lights blinked and swung around the yard, making her feel dizzy.

The smell of burning wood and hay was almost unbearable, and she couldn't seem to stop shivering. Barney came and stood by her side, asking quietly, "How's the boy?"

"I don't know. He doesn't look good. I'll feel better when he's in the hospital and they can tell me more."

"You okay? Want me to come with you?"

She shook her head, rubbing her arms in an effort to keep from shaking. "Thanks, Barney, but I'll be okay. You'll all need to stay here to help clean up this mess."

He seemed relieved to hear that. "They've got it under control, they think. Not too much damage to the stables, except for the water soaking the hay. The worst of it is in the loft and roof."

She managed a shaky grin. "Well, I guess the floor needed working on up there anyway. Now the insurance company can pay for it."

Barney's face brightened. "Every cloud has a silver lining, I reckon."

"I guess so."

He cleared his throat, then erupted into a fit of coughing. Finally getting his breath back, he croaked, "Well, I'd better get back and help the others."

"Barney..." She hesitated, then as he stood waiting, she added quickly, "Is Mac all right?"

"He was the last time I saw him. He was up in the loft with the firemen."

"Tell him—" she paused for a moment "—tell him I'll be at the hospital."

Barney nodded. "Sure thing, ma'am. We'll all be rooting for the boy. He's gonna be okay, you'll see."

She managed a smile. "Thanks, Barney. I'll let you know how he is."

Barney nodded, then shuffled off, his shoulders hunched in weariness. She watched him go, wondering if Mac would interpret her message and meet her at the hospital. Right now she needed him. In a way she'd never needed him before.

Chapter 8

Gritting her teeth, Sharon watched the medics pick up her son and lay him on the stretcher. Politely they asked her to follow in her own car, rather than ride in the ambulance, and reluctantly she agreed.

Following the white vehicle with the flashing lights down the driveway, she was reminded vividly of another ambulance just a few short months ago.

Please, she prayed, *not Tim. Please don't take Tim, too. I couldn't bear it.*

The drive to the hospital seemed interminable, and she was exhausted, both physically and emotionally, by the time she drove into the parking lot. Somehow she remembered to lock the car and take note where she'd left it before hurrying to the emergency ward.

After filling out the admittance forms, she sat in the deserted waiting room for what seemed like hours, until a friendly-looking young man in a white coat hurried in.

"Mrs. Carlson? I'm Dr. Reynolds. You're Tim's mother, right?"

She rose, feeling as if she would never be able to draw breath again. "Yes, I am. How is he?"

"He's going to be all right. Tough kid, and he's in pretty good health generally. That always helps."

He peered closer at her, his eyes narrowing. "In fact, Tim looks a good deal better than you do at the moment. Can I get you a cup of coffee?"

She shook her head. "Can I see him?"

"Sure. He has a slight concussion, but he's awake at the moment. He doesn't seem to have suffered any ill effects from the smoke, which is helpful. I want to keep him in overnight, though, just for observation. If all goes well, he should be able go home tomorrow."

She fought to hold back tears of relief. "Where is he?"

"Come on, I'll take you to him." The doctor grasped her arm and began leading her to the door. "Are you sure you don't want a cup of coffee? Tea? A soda? Personally I think a good shot of brandy would be better, but I'm not allowed to offer that, of course."

She even managed a smile. "Thank you, Doctor, but I'll be fine just as soon as I can see my son."

An hour later she sat at Tim's bedside, her chin dropping down every now and again as sleep overwhelmed her determination to stay alert.

Tim lay sleeping peacefully, but she couldn't seem to rest, even though she knew there wasn't much she could do. She wanted to stay awake in case he opened his eyes. Even so, she found it more and more difficult to keep her own eyes open.

She must have dozed after all, for the sound of the door opening startled her awake. Her rush of raw emotion at the sight of Mac standing in the doorway, his hat in his hand and anxiety lining his face, almost destroyed the last elements of her composure.

"Hi," he said softly. He had showered and changed and looked terribly tired. His face was strained as he moved quietly into the shaded room and closed the door behind him. "How is he?"

She swallowed, afraid for a moment that she was going to burst into a flood of tears. "He's going to be all right. A slight concussion, that's all. He talked to me awhile, then the doctor gave him something to help him sleep. The nurses are checking on him every hour."

Mac's face cleared, and he crept over to the bed.

Sharon watched him as he bent over Tim. The soft light fell across his harsh features, and for an instant she saw such a look of compassion and concern on his face she almost cried out.

Clenching her hands, she heard him whisper, "You're gonna be okay, big guy. It's takes more than a bump or two on the head to put a Douglass down."

"I always knew he was a hardhead," Sharon said, trying desperately for a touch of humor. She was afraid that she was going to break down and bawl like a baby any second now.

Mac straightened, his face once more impassive, and she wondered if she'd imagined his expression earlier.

"Want to tell me what happened?" he asked, "or would you rather I left you alone? I didn't give Barney time to tell me the whole story."

"No, stay." She ran her tongue over her dry lips. "I want to stay awake, and it will help to talk."

She waited until he'd pulled a chair forward and sat down on it. After a moment she said quietly, "I caught Tim trying to get a halter on the Sage City bronc this afternoon."

Mac looked startled. "Who told him to do that?"

"No one." She tightened her mouth. "I guess he wanted to show you how well he could handle a wild bronc."

Mac shook his head. "Fool kid, he could have had his neck broken. You can't mess with a mean one like that."

"I got pretty mad at him," Sharon went on, feeling her nerves tightening again at the memory. "He took off in his car, and when he didn't come back, I went out to the porch to look for him."

Mac watched her, his face expressionless. Apparently he'd regretted his momentary show of emotion earlier. It was as if those brief moments had never happened.

He had rarely ever revealed cracks in that damn wall of his. Where was his heart, she wondered, that he could be so damn indifferent toward her at a time like this? Why couldn't he look at her the way he'd looked at her son?

"Tim told me that after he left Mike's house," she went on when Mac failed to comment, "he went back to the stables to get a harness. He was going to try and ride the saddle bronc, to prove once and for all that he was capable of handling the rough stock."

"He's a Douglass all right." Mac looked over at the sleeping boy. "Stubborn as all get-out."

"The fire started in the loft, apparently," Sharon said, holding on to her own fragile control. "Tim saw it smoldering and went to let out the horses before going for help. One of the beams must have fallen from the roof and caught him a glancing blow on the head. It knocked him out cold."

"Poor kid," Mac murmured. "He's had his share of bad luck lately."

"Bad luck?" Striving to keep her voice low, Sharon said fiercely, "Tim has deliberately gone out of his way lately to endanger his life, all because of the damn rodeo business. He could have been burned to death tonight."

Finally losing her frail hold on her control, she lashed out at the only person close enough at hand. "You promised me that you would do your best to discourage him. It seems to me that all you've managed to do is make matters worse."

Mac looked at her for a long moment, and she could see the tiny pulse beating in his throat. "I did the best I could with the authority I had," he said at last. "I can't tell him what to do. He's not my son." Her stomach dropped like a stone when he leaned forward and fixed his intent stare on her face. "Or is he?"

Somewhere down the corridor a bell rang insistently. The sounds of hurrying feet rushed by the door, then faded. "I told you..." Sharon stammered.

"I know what you told me. I also know what I see. Dammit, Sharon, I want the truth. I'm entitled to know."

She was too tired to fight it anymore. She had very nearly lost Tim tonight. He might have died not knowing about his father. She owed them both the truth.

"I'm sorry, Mac," she said wearily. "I should have told you the truth before this. You are right. Tim is your son."

The silence went on for so long that for a crazy second, she hoped he hadn't heard her. Yet part of her wanted him to know... had always wanted him to know.

It was only her concern about Tim's reaction that had kept her from telling him sooner. Now she could only wait, her breath stilled, her body tensed.

It seemed an eternity until he spoke. When he did, his voice sounded different as if he had trouble forming the words. "Why didn't you tell me you were carrying my child?"

She lifted her hands helplessly, then let them drop into her lap. She felt lifeless, drained of all energy. She no longer cared what happened to her. She had lived a lie for so long. Now it was time to tell the truth.

"You would have felt obligated to marry me," she said dully. "I couldn't let you do that. Neither one of us would have been happy. You would have been saddled with a wife and child you didn't want, and I would have had to live with that for the rest of my life."

"Didn't you at least feel that you owed me the opportunity to make my own decisions?" He swore quietly. "No, of course you didn't. You always make decisions for everyone else, don't you? You always know what's best for everyone."

She closed her eyes against his bitterness. She could expect nothing less.

"Why didn't Randall let me know?" Mac demanded, his voice harsher now. "He could easily have contacted me. I should have thought he'd want me to take care of my...obligations."

He'd spoken the last word as if it were something ugly. She lifted her chin, making herself look at him. She would not...could not cry in front of him.

"He wanted to tell you. I told him that if he did, I would leave and he would never see me again. I told him that you had left, without a word to either of us as to why or where you were going, which proved you didn't care."

She paused, then added deliberately, "What I didn't tell him was that I'd thrown myself at you that night, and by leaving, you had made it crystal clear that you regretted what I had made you do."

"Dammit, Sharon, I didn't do anything I didn't want to do. Don't you think I haven't condemned myself over and over again for what I did to you?"

As if remembering the sleeping boy, he dropped his voice again. "We were both to blame that night. We lost our heads, and I should have had more sense."

He buried his head in his hands, and she fought the urge to reach out and stroke his hair. His voice sounded weary when he added, "Why do you think I left without a word to you or Randall? I was so damn ashamed of what I'd done. I'd betrayed you both, the only two people in the world who meant anything to me."

She stared at him, joy mixing with despair at his words. He had cared for her after all. And now it was too late.

"I should have had more control," Mac muttered. "The one night I really needed it, I lost it."

"I'm sorry," she whispered.

"So am I." He lifted his head and looked at her, his eyes bleak with pain. "Does Tim know?"

"I...couldn't tell him. He thinks Will is his father." She shot a nervous glance at her son, reassuring herself that he was still asleep.

"What about Will? Did he know?"

She nodded, unable now to meet his accusing gaze. "I was pretty far along when he married me. Everyone assumed it was his baby, and we agreed to let them go on thinking that."

"That was generous of him, under the circumstances," Mac said, his voice tight.

"Yes, it was. Unfortunately it didn't work out." Once more she glanced over at Tim to make sure he was asleep. "I guess Will never could forgive me for what I'd done. He did his best to hide it, but he bitterly resented Tim. Especially since we never had any children of our own."

A light tap on the door disturbed them just then. The slim, dark-haired nurse who entered smiled at them. "I just came in to check his blood pressure," she said softly.

"I'll wait outside." Mac got to his feet and strode to the door, while Sharon watched him go, feeling as if her lifeblood was draining from her body.

"He didn't have to leave," the nurse said, slipping the end of a thermometer into Tim's ear.

"Yes, he did," Sharon said quietly.

She got to her feet as Tim murmured a protest and blinked his eyes open.

"Hi," she said softly, as his gaze focused. "How're you feeling?"

"Okay." He managed a weak grin. "You still here?"

"Yes. I didn't want to leave you alone."

"I'll be okay." Already his eyelids were drooping again. "You go on home and get some sleep," he murmured. "I'll be fine."

"He's right, you know," the nurse said, unwrapping the blood-pressure gauge from his arm. "You look exhausted. You won't be able to take care of him if you don't take care of yourself first."

She gathered up her instruments and smiled at Sharon. "He's going to be perfectly all right. We're monitoring him, and there's nothing you can do for him tonight. Come back tomorrow when you're more rested, and you'll probably be able to take him home."

Sharon nodded, not fully convinced, yet aching to crawl into bed and escape this nightmare for a little while. She watched the nurse leave the room, then turned back to Tim, who had drifted back to sleep.

Reaching for his hand, she covered it with her own. She had come so close to losing him. She knew now what it would do to her. How could she tell him the truth about his father now?

Sadly she watched the boyish face of her son in sleep. She had already given up so much for him. She couldn't risk losing him now. If it came to a choice between Tim and Mac, she had no question in her mind. She could not risk losing her son. Even though the consequences of her decision threatened to tear her apart.

Mac paced back and forth in the corridor, unable to come to terms with what he'd just heard. Although he'd suspected that Tim could be his child, he hadn't truly believed it until now. At first he'd been furious, feeling he'd been denied a significant and irreplaceable part of his life.

Now that he'd had time to think about it, part of him could understand how Sharon must have felt at the time. With her alone and afraid, it must have been so hard to tell her father she was pregnant.

How she must have hated him for what he'd done. He found it hard to understand now, why she had agreed to hire him back. She must have been terrified he'd find out.

The door of Tim's room opened, shattering his thoughts. The pretty nurse smiled at him, pausing to say, "I think you should take your wife home, Mr. Carlson. She is exhausted, and badly needs a rest."

"I'm not her husband," Mac said, doing his best not to sound bitter. "I'm only a friend."

"Oh." The nurse uttered an embarrassed laugh. "Sorry. Sometimes we tend to take these things for granted, I'm afraid. But in any case, Mrs. Carlson should go home. She's in no fit state to drive, though. Could you take her home?"

He nodded. "Sure. I'll see that she gets home safely."

"Thank you." She gave him another smile. "She might be a little hard to persuade," she said as she hurried off. "But do your best."

"Yes, ma'am," Mac muttered under his breath. "I always try to do my best."

He waited another moment or two to calm his thoughts before pushing the door open.

Sharon sat by Tim's bedside, her hand over his, her head leaning on her arm. Her eyes were closed, and for a moment he thought she might be asleep. But then she opened her eyes and looked at him with a look of such despair he longed to fold her in his arms and comfort her.

"Hi," she said wearily. "I thought you'd gone home."

"Nope." He crossed the room and looked down at Tim's face. He couldn't see any likeness in the peaceful features. Tim took after Randall more than anyone. But now that he came to think about it, he and Tim had the same eyes. That's why Tim's eyes had seemed so familiar. And the boy sure had a way with horses. That couldn't be denied.

It hit him all at once—the full implication of what had happened there tonight. He felt his breath catch as a lump formed in his throat. Dear God, he was a father.

He had a son.

For a long, heartrending moment he could neither move nor speak. When he could finally trust his voice again, he moved around to the other side of the bed and grasped Sharon's arm. "Come on," he said gruffly. "You're going home."

To his surprise and relief, she took one last, long look at Tim, then bent over and kissed him gently on the forehead. Without once looking at Mac, she gathered up her purse and walked out of the room.

He followed her, his mind bombarded with questions. *What happens next? Will she want him to leave without acknowledging his rights as a father? Did he have any rights as a father? What would be best for Tim?*

At the door she paused and looked back at him. "My car is outside," she said, her voice barely above a whisper. "I'll see you back at the house."

"No, you won't." He took hold of her arm and guided her though the door. "The nurse informed me you were in no fit state to drive. I'm taking you home."

"I'm all right—"

"I don't care what you think you are." He let the door swing to behind him and marched her out to the parking lot. "This time you do as I say. And I say I'm taking you home."

She was either too shocked or too tired to argue. He really didn't care. For once he was going to decide what was best for her.

He led her firmly to the pickup and helped her into the passenger seat, then strode around to the other side and climbed in next to her.

"I'll bring you back in the morning, and you can drive Tim home," he said as he let in the clutch. "We'll talk after that and decide what's best to do."

She nodded, her eyes half-closed. Before he was out of the parking lot, she was asleep, her head lolling against his shoulder.

Once he was out on the road, he settled himself more comfortably, supporting her with an arm around her shoulders. Her hair tickled his cheek, and her summery fragrance brought back sharply the image of a young girl racing Whitefire across the meadows.

He tried not to think about the consequences of his attraction to her back then. It was way too late to change things now. Sooner or later he would have to face the issue, but right now he needed sleep.

The lights were out in the bunkhouse when he pulled up in front of the house. It seemed that the men must have gone to bed.

No one was going to get much sleep that night, he thought ruefully as he cut the engine. Carefully he eased his arm from around Sharon's shoulders and settled her back against the seat.

His footsteps echoed on the hard driveway as he walked around to the passenger side. Already the first streaks of dawn were creeping across the dark sky. The cool, damp air smelled fresh and earthy, mixing with the unforgettable fragrance of the firs. Somewhere in the branches above his head, the first early birds chirped quietly as he opened the door of the pickup. Sharon stirred and opened her eyes. "I slept all the way home?"

She sounded shocked and he smiled. "Yep. You didn't twitch a muscle."

She looked a little confused as she scrambled down from the truck. Her hair was mussed, her face still smudged from the smoke-filled stable.

At the door he took the key from her and fitted it into the lock. The door opened easily under his touch. "You going to be all right?" he asked gently.

"Yes ... I ... no." She turned away from him, but not before he caught the rare sight of tears glistening on her lashes in the porch light. "I'm scared, " she whispered, so low he barely heard her.

"Don't worry about Tim," he said gruffly. "He's going to be all right."

"It's not Tim so much."

She stepped through the door, but he caught her arm. "Then what are you scared about?"

"I don't know." She tried for a trembling smile, but didn't quite pull it off. "I guess ... it's everything. The attack on Tim's car, the horses stampeding ... and now this."

He could feel her shivering in the crisp morning breeze. "I'm afraid that someone might have set the fire in the stables," she said. "The person who's trying to hurt Tim. He could be here ... waiting."

"Tomorrow we go talk to the sheriff," Mac said firmly. "If someone is threatening Tim, they'll know how best to deal with it."

She nodded, and his heart turned over when he saw her bottom lip trembling.

"It's just ... this house is so big ... and now that it's empty, it seems ..." She uttered an awkward laugh and turned away from him. "Listen to me, I sound like a nervous teenager instead of a grown woman."

He could no more let her go into that empty house alone like that than he could walk on water. "I'll come in and fix you a nightcap," he said, stepping in through the door. "It will help you sleep."

She looked as if she wanted to refuse, but then she caught her lower lip between her teeth and nodded. Turning away from him, she left him to close the door as she switched on the lights in the hallway.

"I have a bottle of brandy and some Scotch in the cupboard," she said, leading the way to the kitchen. "Dad was the only one who drank it. It's been there since he died."

Mac pretended not to notice the slight crack in her voice. "Brandy will do just fine."

He followed her into the kitchen and sat her down at the table. "Which cupboard?"

She pointed to it and he opened the door, reaching for the bottle of brandy. Opening another door, he peered inside the cupboard and found a glass. He set it down on the table and poured her a generous measure.

"Aren't you going to have some?" she asked as she took it from him.

He shook his head. "I've already had my share down at the tavern."

She lifted the glass, and carefully sipped on the rim. Making a face, she shuddered and set the glass down in front of her. "I never could understand how anyone could drink that stuff for pleasure."

"You soon develop a taste for it, believe me." He glanced up at the clock. It was almost five. "You sit here and drink that," he said, moving toward the door. "I'm going to take a look around the house, just to make sure everything's secure before I leave."

She gave him a grateful look that warmed him inside and out. "Thanks, Mac. I have to admit, I would feel much better if I was sure there's no one in the house."

His heart seemed to be jumping all over the place. He'd never seen her like this. She was always so damn independent. No one ever told her what to do or how to do it. She was always so confident of where she was going and what she was doing.

This was a different woman, a soft, vulnerable, exposed woman who needed him. No one had ever needed him before. Especially Sharon. The fact that he knew how strong she really was made her dependence on him all the more appealing.

He made himself turn around and walk out of the kitchen before he gave in to the temptation to haul her into his arms. He wanted to smother her with kisses and drive all those worries out of her mind, until all she could think about was his mouth...his hands...his body...his touch.

Inwardly cursing himself, he left her alone.

Sharon watched the door close behind him, and pulled in a shaky breath. The brandy warmed her, in spite of the terrible taste and the burning sensation in her throat.

She stared at the amber liquid shimmering in the glass, and tried to relax the tension gripping her body. *We'll talk after that and decide what's best to do.*

How could they possibly know what was best to do? Up until now she hadn't even considered the fact that Mac might want Tim to know the truth. She would have to face it now. It wasn't just her and her son anymore. There was a third person involved, with his own rights and needs.

He'd cared once, she told herself. But that was a long time ago. She wasn't sure he was capable of a deep, lasting commitment. She could accept nothing less.

She wasn't even sure how she really felt about him. Maybe her reactions now were simply adolescent memories, nothing more. They had both changed; they weren't the same people they had been back then. Maybe there was nothing left between them now.

So what then? Let Tim finally know his father, only to watch Mac walk away? Expose her son to the kind of pain that she'd gone through the last time Mac had left?

Her thoughts splintered into tiny fragments as the door opened and Mac walked into the kitchen.

"I've checked every room in the house," he said, dropping onto a chair. "You're safe for tonight, at least. Tomorrow we'll talk to the sheriff."

She nodded, afraid to speak. Tears were perilously close but she wasn't about to let them spill now.

She avoided his gaze as he said, after an awkward pause, "I guess I'd better get back to the bunkhouse."

Locking her jaw, she rose and took the half-empty glass over to the sink. "Thanks, Mac," she said, unable to avoid the small quaver in her voice.

She heard him get up, and she closed her eyes, praying he would leave before she broke down.

"You okay?"

Again she nodded, but the concern in his voice proved too much. The tears spilled over and ran down her cheeks. Impatiently she dashed at them with the back of her hand.

Behind her she heard him mutter a curse, then his hands locked on her arms. "No, you're not," he said gruffly, and turned her around to face him.

"I'm just tired . . ." The sob escaped, and with it more tears. "I'm sorry. . . ." She waved her hand helplessly in the air, trying desperately to halt the flow of tears.

She heard the harsh anguish in his voice as he muttered her name. "Sharon . . ."

"I'm fine." She gulped and tried again. "Please, go to bed, Mac. I'll be okay as soon as I've had some sleep."

She looked up at him, and through the haze of tears saw his eyes burning with a look in them she'd never seen before. Her breath caught, and her tears ceased as if the heat radiating between them had dried them on her face.

"Maybe you'll be okay," Mac muttered, "but I damn well won't be if I leave now."

Once more his hands gripped her arms. She lost her breath completely as he pulled her hard against his chest and covered her mouth in a savage kiss.

For a moment she froze, afraid of her own escalating excitement. She had done this before, and had paid dearly for her reckless emotions. She'd be a fool to give in to them again.

But then his kiss seared her mind, setting her body on fire, inflaming her soul. She didn't know how or why, but this time it seemed different. She could sense the raw power, barely leashed, that drove his emotions. But this time she could respond, with a new, intense force of her own.

A small moan escaped her lips as his hands moved over her body, searching, impatient with the buttons of her shirt. His fingers, warm and gentle on her bare breast, shocked her reeling senses.

She drew in a sharp breath, and he paused, his mouth drawing delicious little paths over her neck. "You want me to stop?" he whispered against her sensitive skin.

"No, damn you," she muttered. "I don't want you to stop."

"Good." Once more he drew his mouth down her neck, his fingers tightening on her breast. "Because I sure as hell don't want to stop."

Just to convince her, he drew her hand down below his belt. A shudder of excitement shook her body as she touched him. Raising both hands, she tore at the buttons on his shirt and dragged it open.

His sharp murmur of pleasure as she flicked his hard nipple with her tongue sent a thrill through her. She raised her head and looked at him, all her weariness long forgotten as her body throbbed beneath his touch.

"I like that," he said softly.

"So do I."

His gaze lowered to her breasts, freed from her bra by his impatient hands. "I'd like to return the favor."

"So what are you waiting for?"

"I was hoping you'd invite me upstairs where we can be more comfortable."

She managed a grin. "That's an offer I can't refuse."

A very small part of her mind questioned her sanity as she led him up the stairs. She was opening herself up to more pain, more disappointment, more heartache. She wasn't a teenager anymore. She was a grown woman. She should have more sense.

For just an instant she paused at the door to her bedroom.

Mac paused, too, his gaze questioning as his hands moved inside her shirt once more. "Second thoughts?" he asked lightly.

She felt his warm fingers cup her breast, and shivered. "No," she whispered. "How about you?"

For answer he lowered his head to her breast.

She cried out as the intense, sweet pull of desire rocketed through her body. It had never been like this before. Not even with him, that first time, had she felt such a potent awakening of her innermost senses.

"If you think I'm leaving now, lady," Mac murmured, his lips moving up her throat to her ear, "you're not getting the message."

"Oh, I'm getting the message loud and clear." She moved her hand down to touch him, thrilling again at his sharp hiss of breath. "I'm more than willing to exchange favors with you."

"Then what are we waiting for?"

He pushed the door open and guided her through, then closed it firmly behind them, shutting out the world. "Where's the light?" he murmured. "I want to see what I'm doing."

She felt for the switch and flicked it on. The subdued light from her bedside lamp bathed the room in a soft, warm glow. She watched him glance around the room, his gaze wandering over the pale rose-and-green comforter and pillow shams to the apple green blinds at the windows.

"Nice," he murmured.

"Thank you." She felt awkward now, the tension once more creeping over her body. She had felt no pain with

Will. But she had felt nothing else, either. At first she had derived comfort from the contact, then boredom and finally repulsion.

Some wild sense hammering inside her told her it would be different this time with Mac. She hoped with all her heart that she could respond the way she wanted to so badly.

As if sensing her thoughts, he drew her close again and once more covered her mouth. This time his kiss was gentle, lightly probing with his tongue until the heat once more eased her tension.

He undressed her slowly, as if savoring each moment, touching, tasting until she was trembling with anticipation. At last she was naked, and swiftly he pulled the covers back and laid her on the bed.

She watched him take off his clothes, his eyes never leaving her face. She had never seen him fully naked before. There hadn't been time for that the first time.

She liked what she saw—a strong, firm chest, flat stomach and long muscled legs sprinkled with a dark fuzz of hair. He seemed to relish her inspection, taking his time before moving toward the bed.

Her heart began to pound once more as he leaned over her. "You are a beautiful woman," he murmured, his gaze moving slowly down her naked body.

"You are a beautiful man."

He smiled. "A beat-up cowboy like me?"

She reached out and drew her fingers down his chest to his belly. "You are beautiful to me."

He caught her hand and lifted it to his lips, then lowered his body beside her. "I don't know what you find so beautiful, but I'm sure as hell not going to waste any time arguing about it."

His slow, burning kisses stunned her. The sensation of his bare flesh sliding over her skin, the feel of his tongue on the most vulnerable parts of her body, the touch of his skillful fingers gently exploring unfamiliar and erotic territory aroused agonizing pleasure such as she'd never imagined.

Gradually, as the sensations overtook her mind, she became aware of a different kind of tension taking hold. Her body seemed alive, reaching, striving for something she didn't quite understand.

It was as if she had become one person with him, drowning together in the pleasures both given and taken. She wanted more, needed more…no…*craved* more. She dug her fingers into his smooth shoulders and cried out as the tide swept her up, driving her relentlessly onward like a leaf helplessly caught in a racing current.

"Easy, honey," Mac murmured, his voice hushed in the swirls of misted passion. "Go with it, don't fight it. Trust me. Let go."

Trust me. Let go. Her mind screamed the words, and she gave up her hold on the last vestige of her will. It was like letting go of a life belt, knowing she would be carried away to inconceivable depths by the thundering tide.

Trust. That's what it took. Complete, unconditional trust. The joy of it seemed to burst in her mind like a blaze of fireworks as she arched under the sheer ecstasy of his fingers.

An overwhelming sensation shuddered through her body, and once more she cried out, this time in wonder and immeasurable pleasure.

Then she was floating, more relaxed than she'd ever been in her life, aching with love for the man who had finally led her into the mysteries of total fulfillment.

She was not allowed to rest for long, however. Mac's kisses became more urgent, spurring her on once more. This time she followed his lead, exploring his body, learning with each new fascinating discovery how to please him and excite him.

Up until now he had been the one in control. Now she wanted to see him as she remembered him the last time, wild with passion and driven helpless by his desire.

This time she felt no fear, no pain. This time she welcomed the fierce, ruthless power of his body as he entered her. She rejoiced in the feel of him moving urgently inside her, until once more the torrent swept her up and flung her again into the erotic whirlpool of intense pleasure.

This time she strove with him, clinging to him as his body thrust, arched, until, with a final shudder, he sought and found the ultimate release.

They slept, their arms around each other, while the world moved on, creating a new day. When Sharon finally opened her eyes again, sunlight filtered through the upward slats of the blinds.

She lay for a moment, soaking in the sheer joy of the morning. Tim was safe for the moment, and she was alone with the man she loved more than life itself. Although the word wasn't mentioned between them, she felt sure he shared her feelings. How could he have done the things he had last night if he didn't truly love her?

She pushed away the tiny shred of doubt with an impatient move of her head. *Trust me,* he'd said. And she did. With all her heart and soul. As she'd never trusted before.

Chapter 9

She dozed again, finally awakening an hour or so later. Mac still slept soundly at her side, and she snuggled close to his warm body, secure in the knowledge that the doubts of the night had been swept away in the tumult of their lovemaking. Everything was going to be all right after all.

Tim adored Mac, she thought, reassuring herself that she was making the right decision. Her son had never shown much interest in the man he'd thought was his father. He would be thrilled to know he was Mac McAllister's son.

And now that Mac was there to support and defend her, between them they would be able to persuade Tim to give up his dream of the rodeo.

Hearing a slight movement, she turned her head and found Mac watching her, a smile playing around the firm, hard lines of his mouth. Her heart seemed to melt as she looked at him.

"Hi," she said softly.

"Hi, yourself." He propped his head up on his elbow and regarded her with the intent expression she knew so well. "What were you thinking about?"

"I was wondering what Tim will say when he finds out you are his father."

His eyes widened in surprise. "You're going to tell him?"

A faint chill touched her heart. "Yes, of course. Don't you want me to?"

"Well, yes, of course I do." He dropped a light kiss on her mouth. "It's going to come as a big shock to him, though. It might be as well to wait until he's recovered from his trip to the hospital."

"I want to tell him now." She lifted a hand to trace the faint stubble on his jaw with her palm. "Any time we tell him will be a shock to him. It might as well be now. Besides, he's bound to notice that things are different between us now."

Mac's expression was grave as he looked down at her. "Have you considered the fact that it might turn Tim against both of us? He might not forgive you for lying about his father. Or me for running out on you. It could make things even worse between you than they are now."

"That's a risk we'll have to take," Sharon said firmly. "You have a right to claim your son, just as Tim has a right to know his real father. I've lived this lie long enough. It's time it was all out in the open."

"How do you think the other men will take it?" Mac asked soberly.

"I really don't care about the other men. As far as they are concerned, nothing has changed. You are still the foreman and head trainer."

"And the father of the boss's son."

She took his face between her hands and kissed his mouth long and lovingly. "I thought I was the one who always worried too much," she said when she finally let him go.

"Hmm." He looked thoughtfully at her. "It's worth worrying a bit if you're gonna kiss me like that."

"Oh, I can kiss you a lot better than that." Throwing off the covers, she rolled over on top of him. She flattened her body on top of his, and looked deep into his eyes. "Now where would you like me to start?"

He uttered a low growl deep in his throat. Sliding his hands over her buttocks, he pulled her down hard against his hips. "Just about anywhere you want, ma'am."

"Mighty happy to oblige," she murmured, and set to work.

"One thing I have to admit," Mac said later as they faced each other across the kitchen table, "all that exercise sure gives a man an appetite."

"You're going to need plenty of exercise if you eat too many more of those pancakes," Sharon observed, eyeing his empty plate.

"Yeah? Well, fill my plate up, ma'am. I'll take any excuse I can for that kind of exercise."

She wrinkled her nose at him. "You don't need an excuse. All you have to do is show me that big, beautiful body of yours, and I'll give you all the exercise you can handle."

Mac rolled his eyes. "All she wants is my body."

And your name, she added silently. That was something she couldn't say to him. That would have to come from him.

She got up from her chair to refill his plate, and heard him yawn. "I can't imagine why you're tired," she teased. "You just got out of bed."

"After about two hours' sleep. How come you look so sprightly? All you had was that little doze on the way back from the hospital."

She carried the plate back to the table and set it down in front of him. "Women can handle lack of sleep better than men. It's a scientific fact."

"Is that right?"

"That's right." She glanced up at the clock. "Speaking of sleep, I imagine Tim is awake by now. I think I'll call the hospital and see if we can bring him home."

Mac nodded, his mouth full of pancake.

She rose and went over to the wall phone. It took a moment to find the number, and as she dialed, Mac said quietly, "You're sure you want to tell him today?"

"I want us both to tell him. As soon as possible." She looked away as a voice answered the ring.

"Yes," she said, "this is Mrs. Carlson. I was wondering if my son Tim is ready to come home?"

"Just a minute."

During the long pause that followed, Sharon smiled at Mac. "Don't worry, Tim will take it well. I'm sure he'll be thrilled."

She felt a cold finger of doubt as Mac shook his head. "It's going to be an awful shock to him to find out after all this time that you lied to him about his father."

"I know. But—" She turned back to the phone. "He is? Oh, that's wonderful. Yes, we'll be there to pick him up in about an hour. Give him my love and tell him we're looking forward to bringing him home."

She replaced the receiver, feeling a rush of warmth at being able to use *we* instead of *I*.

She went back to her seat at the table, and picked up her coffee. "We'll wait until we get him home before we tell him," she said, and took a sip of the hot liquid.

"Whatever you say."

She frowned at him over the rim of her cup. "You don't sound too sure yourself," she said, lowering the cup. "I thought you wanted him to know."

"I do." Mac passed a hand across his eyes. "I just don't want to make matters worse for you and the boy. I guess I'm worried he'll be real angry with both of us for messing up his life."

"That's ridiculous," Sharon said sharply. "How have we messed up his life? If you hadn't left, we might have got married, and he would have grown up right here on the ranch anyway."

"Exactly," Mac said dryly.

She shook her head. "I must be missing the point somewhere."

"All I meant—" Mac broke off as the doorbell pealed throughout the house.

Sharon jumped up. "I wonder who that could be this early in the morning." Her heart skipped a beat when she saw Mac's expression.

"Want me to go?" he asked, getting slowly to his feet.

"No, it's okay." She smiled at him as she crossed the room to the door. "I can't go on forever running scared of everything. Besides, I doubt if any intruder is going to ring my doorbell at nine o'clock in the morning."

He nodded, but his uneasy expression put a dampener on her joy as she hurried to the front door.

Pulling it open, she was surprised to see a uniformed officer on the doorstep.

"Mrs. Carlson?" he asked, touching the brim of his hat with his fingers. "I'm Officer Tom Larkins and I'm with the Oregon State Sheriff's Department. I want to talk to you about the fire in your stables last night. May I come in, ma'am?"

She stood back to let him in, a gnawing feeling of anxiety eating at her stomach. For some reason she had the distinct impression that she wasn't going to like what she was about to hear.

Ushering the deputy into the kitchen, she saw Mac raise his eyebrows. She gave him a quick shrug, then turned to the police officer. "Would you like a cup of coffee?"

The officer shook his head. "No, thank you, ma'am. I won't keep you long."

Mac rose, and reached for his hat. "I'll leave you alone," he said, moving toward the door.

"I'd like you to stay." Sharon glanced at the police officer. "That's if you have no objection."

The officer shook his head. "No, ma'am. I only came to tell you that we've had a report from the fire department. The cause of the fire last night has been located."

Sharon's stomach seemed to flip over as Mac paused at the door.

"Apparently," the deputy went on, seemingly unaware of the apprehension his words were creating, "someone was smoking up in your loft. I guess whoever it was failed to put the butt out before he dropped it."

For a long moment nobody spoke, then Sharon said carefully, "Thank you, Officer. I appreciate you coming to tell me."

The deputy nodded and moved toward the door. "Reckon it will save the insurance folks a visit."

"Indeed it will."

She saw him out, then returned to the kitchen, where Mac was refilling the coffee cups.

"So what do you make of that?" he said as she sat down at the table and took the cup he offered her.

"I don't know." She took a sip of coffee. "Do you think it could be Jerry? He could have started the fire with a cigarette, trying to make it look like an accident."

Mac shook his head. "I think if Jerry had wanted to burn down the stables, he would have done a proper job of it. Leaving a lighted cigarette butt around on the off chance it will catch doesn't seem like Jerry to me. I think it's more likely the way the deputy said. Someone was smoking and didn't put out the butt.''

Sharon stared at the black liquid steaming in her cup. She couldn't avoid the obvious any longer. ''There's only one person I can think of who might go up to the loft to smoke.'' She looked up at Mac, and met his cautious gaze. ''Tim.''

''Yep. That's the way I had it figured.''

''I guess we'd better ask him,'' she said unhappily.

Arriving at the hospital an hour later, she was relieved to see Tim sitting up in bed, apparently none the worse for his ordeal, except for a very large bruise on his forehead.

''I can go home,'' he announced as soon as she and Mac walked into his room.

''I hope you realize how lucky you are,'' Sharon said, handing over the clean clothes she'd brought with her. ''The doctor told me that things could have been a lot worse. He said that you could have died from the blow on your head, or from smoke inhalation if you hadn't been found when you were. Not to mention the fact that you could have burned to death if I hadn't happened to see the fire from the porch.''

Looking suitably intimidated, Tim muttered, ''I know.'' He climbed out of bed and started pulling on his clothes.

''Tim,'' Sharon said, determined to get to the bottom of the matter as soon as possible, ''have you been smoking up in the loft?''

Tim's flushed face clearly registered guilt as he struggled into his jeans.

When it became apparent that he wasn't going to answer, Sharon sent Mac a pleading look.

He gave her a slight shake of his head, warning her not to say any more.

This obviously was not the time to bring up the sensitive subject of his real father, Sharon decided as Tim finished dressing in silence. She would just have to wait until they got home.

Driving back to the house with Mac a few minutes later, she kept up a meaningless conversation, ignoring her son sulking in the back seat. Mac seemed preoccupied, and answered her with a vague word or two that told her he was listening with only half an ear.

They arrived back at the house, and the minute Tim was out of the car he headed for the house.

"I'd better get over to the bunkhouse," Mac said, glancing at his watch. "The men will want to know what's going on."

"The men can wait," Sharon said quickly. "I'd really like you to be with me when I talk to Tim."

Mac hesitated, then shrugged. "If you're sure that's what you want."

"I'm sure. But first I'm going to lecture him on the hazards of smoking, if you don't mind."

"No, ma'am. That's one thing you and I do agree on."

She led the way to the house, wondering if there was something he disagreed about.

Tim was in his room, and answered in a low voice when Sharon tapped on the door.

"We'd like to talk to you," she announced as she opened the door. Tim made no comment, and she motioned for Mac to follow her in.

Seating herself on the edge of the bed, she said quietly, "I want you to understand the terrible risks you took by smoking last night. After everything you've heard about the dangers of smoking, I'm shocked and surprised that you are willing to risk your health in that way."

Tim started jiggling his knee, a sure sign he was rattled.

Sharon decided to take advantage of his reaction and hammer home her point. "You not only took a risk with your life last night by smoking in the stables, you risked the entire family business. The horses could have been killed,

the outbuildings burned to the ground and everything that
your grandfather and I have worked so hard for could have
been lost. All because of your thoughtless and careless attitude.''

Tim looked stubbornly at his knee bouncing up and
down.

"The men worked hard to get the horses out last night,"
Sharon said deliberately. "Any one of them could have
been injured, just like you were, by a falling beam. I hope
you understand how irresponsibly you have behaved."

Tim's chin shot up, his eyes blazing. "It's all your
fault," he muttered. "If you'd paid more attention to me
and listened to what I wanted, I wouldn't have had to go
around doing all those things to get you to notice me."

Stunned, Sharon stared at him.

After a moment he dropped his gaze and once more
stared defiantly at his knees.

Slowly Sharon shifted her gaze to Mac. He was watching her, a strange, thoughtful expression on his face. He
seemed to know what she was thinking.

She felt a chill touch her heart as she turned back to
Tim. "Just what exactly do you mean by that?" she asked
quietly.

For painful seconds the silence hung heavy in the room.
Tim's bed squeaked as he continued to jiggle his knee, the
nervous habit that she thought he'd long outgrown.

She was about to question him again when he muttered, "I smashed the mirrors on my car."

She bit back her cry of dismay and waited, guessing
what was coming.

"I didn't mean anything by it at the time," Tim said,
beginning to sound more confident. "I was angry. You
wouldn't listen to anything I said, and I didn't know what
to do about it. And then that night, when I told you about
it, you felt sorry for me. You took me out to dinner and

you actually took the time to talk about Mac, and about the rodeo.''

Out of the corner of her eye Sharon saw Mac look at her. He must be wondering what they'd said about him, she thought, then forgot her momentary discomfort as Tim went on talking.

"I figured that a good way to get your attention was to make you feel sorry for me again,'' he said. "So I stampeded the horses. I was going to pretend to get knocked down, but I didn't get out of the way fast enough, and one of them caught me in the head.''

Sharon hugged herself to ward off the cold feeling in the pit of her stomach. "Go on,'' she said grimly.

"Well, it worked, didn't it? You listened to me again. You even agreed to let me learn to saddle the broncs. But then you got mad at me and you said you didn't trust me with the rough stock. You said you weren't going to listen to me about the rodeo again.''

"So you set fire to the barn,'' Sharon said, feeling sick.

"Not on purpose.'' Tim's voice sounded close to tears now as he stumbled on. "I was upset. Mike gave me a couple of cigarettes. I was pretty fed up so after I got back from his house I took them up into the loft to smoke. It was the first time I'd tried it.''

He lifted his face and looked at her with an expression of abject misery. "Honest.''

"I hope it will be the last,'' Sharon said a little more gently.

"It sure will.'' Tim pulled a face. "It tasted like the pits. I dropped it, and then put it out. But I must have not done a good job because I fell asleep, and when I woke up the straw was on fire. It was only a small fire, and I guess I could have put it out, but I started thinking about how you always listen to me when something bad happens to me, so I figured I'd let it burn.''

Sharon closed her eyes. "Oh, Tim.''

"I tried to get the horses out," Tim said, beginning to cry, "I wouldn't have left them in there. But something came down on my head. The next thing I remember is waking up in the ambulance on the way to the hospital. I'm sorry, Mom. I only wanted you to listen to me."

Sharon buried her face in her hands. She felt Mac's strong arm around her shoulders, but for once the contact failed to comfort her.

"I'll wait for you outside," he said softly, and left the room.

Tim sniffed. "I'm sorry," he whispered again.

She raised her head and took a deep breath. "No," she said unsteadily, "I'm sorry."

Shifting closer to her son, she put her arm around his shoulders. "I guess I didn't realize just how much this dream means to you," she said, steadying her voice. "You were willing to risk your life to get what you wanted."

"I just wanted you to listen to me and at least talk about it."

Sharon drew a shaky breath. "What you did was terribly wrong, Tim. I hope you understand that. You will have to make up for that in some way. You have to learn that there are consequences for everything that you do."

She paused, sorting out her thoughts while Tim looked miserably down at his knees, which were now still.

"I'll put you in charge of the repairs to the stables," she said after a while. "You'll spend all your spare time working on it until it's finished. You'll be out of school in a couple of weeks, so you'll have plenty of time. Barney will help you, but you'll have to do the major portion of the work. Is that agreed?"

Tim nodded, looking even more miserable.

Sharon struggled for another moment or two with her conscience, then said abruptly, "As for the rodeo, if you want to do it that bad, I guess I can at least discuss it with you. Perhaps we'll be able to work something out. We'll talk about it tomorrow. Today you need plenty of rest. I want you to stay in your room, okay?''

The blaze of hope in Tim's eyes at her words helped ease the ache in her heart as she left the room.

Mac was waiting for her in the den, and to her dismay his expression seemed once more remote for some reason. "How'd it go?" he asked, and she gave him a weary smile.

"Okay. I told him he'll have to work on the repairs to the stables. Barney can help him, but I'd appreciate it if you'd keep an eye on him, too."

He gave her a brief nod. "I'll be sure and do that."

"Thanks." She studied him for a moment, then said gently, "Is something wrong?"

She felt a cold, sinking feeling in her stomach when he shrugged and moved away from her toward the window. He seemed to stare at the meadows for a long moment, then he said quietly, "I've been thinking things over."

The tight feeling spread across her chest. "Oh? What things?"

"I don't think we should tell Tim the truth about me."

Now her throat felt tight, and she found it difficult to swallow. "Not yet, perhaps," she said carefully. "I agree, the shock might be too much on top of everything else right now. But later..." She let her voice trail off, waiting, praying he wouldn't say what she thought he was going to say.

When he turned to look at her, his face was as bleak as the winter plains. "I mean we shouldn't tell him at all," he said flatly. "I think it's best we leave things the way they are."

She fought to suppress the anger boiling up inside her. Once more he was running away. "In other words, you don't want to be a father to him."

His eyes blazed for a second, then cooled to frosty ice. "If that's what you want to think."

Keeping her voice low for fear Tim would hear, she demanded fiercely, "What else am I supposed to think?"

He muttered something she couldn't hear and strode to the door. "It didn't occur to you, I suppose, that I might just be concerned about upsetting your relationship with your son?"

"Our son," she corrected bitterly. "But of course, that's something you'd rather forget."

He looked at her for a long moment while she stared back without flinching, then with a muttered oath, he flung himself out of the door. A moment later she heard the front door slam. The sound seemed to hit her like a physical blow. He had withdrawn from her again. Only this time the pain was far deeper than any she ever remembered.

The next morning, after a sleepless night, Sharon resolved to ignore her differences with Mac. She didn't need Tim asking awkward questions about their sudden animosity. After all, she told herself as she pulled on jeans and a dark blue shirt, maybe Mac was right, and Tim would be better off not knowing the truth.

She couldn't ignore the ache in her heart, though. Not only was Mac rejecting his son, but he was also rejecting her, too. Again. The pain of that would always be there. She cornered Mac on the porch after breakfast as he was leaving to return to the corrals.

"I have a favor to ask," she said as he paused on the step below her.

His eyes seemed wary, and didn't quite meet hers as he nodded. "Okay, shoot."

"I was wondering if you'd mind giving Tim some lessons after school is out. After he's put in his share of work on the stables, of course."

Mac raised his eyebrows. "Lessons?"

Sharon nodded. "Everything he needs to know to compete in rodeo."

He looked at her for a long moment, as if considering the request. "Well, when you change your mind, you really do a turnaround," he said finally.

She shrugged. "You know what they say. If you can't beat 'em, give in with a grin."

He smiled faintly at that. "What did Tim say to that? I'm surprised I haven't heard him hollering all the way out to the mountains."

"I haven't told him yet." She looked past his shoulder to where a pair of hawks glided gracefully above the tall pines. "There's a condition, and I'm not sure how he'll take it."

"If he wants to ride rodeo as much as I think he does," Mac said quietly, "he'll agree to pretty much anything."

"I hope so." She looked back at him with a wistful smile. "How are the expectant mothers doing?"

"Just fine. Should be any day now."

She nodded. "I guess I'd better let you get back to work."

He nodded, his expression cool and impersonal.

With a cold, sick feeling in her stomach, she turned away from him, pausing when he said quietly, "Sharon, I really think it's best that we don't tell Tim."

She looked back at him over her shoulder. His expression had softened, but his eyes were still bleak. "So do I," she said briefly.

She left him then, before she could grab his arm and beg him to kiss her again, the way he had two nights ago.

She sat down with Tim in the den that afternoon, happy to see the color returning to her son's face.

"It looks as if you'll be able to finish out the last two weeks at school after all," she said when Tim assured her he was feeling great. "We'll see what the doctor says when he checks you out tomorrow."

"Okay. I'll have to make up some tests, though," Tim said, looking gloomy.

"Yes, you will."

He heaved an exaggerated sigh. "I know. It's what I deserve."

"It's important you keep up your grades." Sharon felt a pang of sympathy for him. It was time to give him her decision. "Especially if you want to do some rodeo work next summer," she added casually.

Tim's chin shot up. "Rodeo? You're kidding!"

She smiled, shaking her head. "No, I talked to Mac this morning. He's willing to give you some lessons, providing you put in at least six hours a day on the stable repairs. If he thinks you are ready, and if you graduate with good grades, I'll agree to you trying out for the rodeo next summer."

"All right!" Tim jumped up and threw his arms around his mother's neck, threatening to strangle her.

"Wait a minute," she protested, her voice smothered in his bony shoulder, "there's a condition, and it's a big one."

Tim sat back, his face flushed with excitement and a wary look in his eyes. "What is it?"

"I want you to promise me you will attend at least two years of college. You can ride in the rodeo during college breaks if you want. After that it will be your decision to do what you want with the rest of your life."

For a bad moment, while he thought about it, she thought he might give her an argument. But then he grinned and nodded. "Sure, why not. Who knows, it might be fun."

"And you might just learn to like it," Sharon said hopefully.

"Miracles do sometimes happen," Tim agreed. He leaned forward, his eyes shining with enthusiasm. "When do the lessons start?'' he asked eagerly. "Can we start to-day?''

Sharon laughed. "No, you can't start today. You have to get a clean bill of health from the doctor for one thing. Then you have all those tests to make up. You can start after school is out, in two weeks."

Tim bounced to his feet again. "Is it okay if I go over to Mike's and tell him about it?''

"All right," Sharon agreed reluctantly. "Just make sure you're home for supper. I don't want you to be out too late until the doctor's had another look at you."

With a wave of his hand Tim rushed from the room, leaving it suddenly quiet.

Sharon rose and walked to the window, smiling a little at the memory of her son's elation. Mac was a good teacher, she reassured herself, and he wouldn't let Tim ride until he was sure he was ready.

With any luck, by the time Tim had completed two years at college, he could have had enough of the rodeo to get it out of his system.

Now that the vague threat of danger that had been hanging over them was resolved, she had nothing more to worry about. The ranch was beginning to turn around, thanks to the efforts of Mac and the rest of the men.

The damage to the stables was a small setback, but with the insurance money and Tim working on it, the building would be in good shape by the end of summer, she assured herself.

The mares were about to foal any day now, and the new colts were ready to begin training in the next few days. Most importantly her long-standing battle with her son seemed to be resolved, as well, stabilizing their relationship at long last.

In fact, Sharon thought as she stared out across the green meadow to where the horses were corralled, she could be very happy indeed, if it were not for Mac's withdrawal.

Reminding herself that she had resolved to live with that, she went out into the kitchen to prepare supper.

Tim didn't stop chattering throughout the entire meal that evening. He bombarded Mac with questions, each one spilling out before Mac had answered the first.

Watching them together, Sharon felt a deep pang of bittersweet regret. If only Mac could accept his role, he would make a wonderful father. Although he seemed somewhat subdued, he patiently answered all of Tim's eager questions, managing to satisfy the boy without actually making any promises.

When Tim asked if Mac would show him how to ride a bull, Sharon felt compelled to put her foot down. "Let Mac eat his dinner," she protested. "If you keep this up, he'll change his mind about giving you lessons."

"Sorry." Tim subsided on his chair, only to bounce back again. "What if I did real good with the broncs, do you think I could ride a bull?"

"Tim—" Sharon began, but Mac held up his hand.

"Okay, Tim, enough. You'll give your mother an ulcer. There'll be no bull riding, at least for the first year."

Tim looked momentarily dashed, but immediately brightened. "That's okay, as long as I can ride the broncs."

Sharon sent Mac a grateful look. She could relax, she told herself; Tim was in good hands.

By the time Tim was out of school for the summer, Mac seemed to have forgotten he'd ever learned the truth about his son. In fact, he went out of his way to avoid the subject.

Conversation at mealtimes had become awkward, each of them weighing every word before speaking.

It was history repeating itself, Sharon told herself. Mac was a loner, and he wasn't capable of making a commitment. Although she was sure he cared for her in his own way, just as he had all those years ago, he wasn't the kind of man who could tie himself down with a wife and family.

In a way she wished he would tell her that himself, and put an end to the persistent hope that would not die. But there was no point in hashing over something she already knew. It would only be painful for them both.

It was better not to say anything, and maybe one day she would stop aching for him every time she looked at him, or dying just a little inside whenever he was close.

At the end of the first week of Tim's lessons, her son announced that Mac wanted to take him to a rodeo. "He also thinks it would be a good idea if you came, too," Tim said when Sharon halfheartedly agreed.

Her first instinct was to turn down the offer. She'd had her fill of rodeos, and she had no desire to go to see another one. But Tim insisted, and in the end she agreed to go with them.

The hot June sun poured down on their heads as they sat in the stands. Tim sat between Mac and his mother, and Sharon preferred it that way. The rising tension between her and Mac was becoming uncomfortable.

Waiting for the show to start, she sat on the hard bench, her eyes hidden behind a pair of oversize sunglasses, and watched a young couple fussing over their baby. The father held the wriggling child while the mother did her best to fasten the strings of a bonnet under the baby's chin.

The task completed, she held out her arms. The father dropped a loving kiss on the baby's forehead and handed the child back to its mother, then leaned across and gave his wife a quick kiss, too.

Sharon felt a pang of envy. She'd never had that kind of relationship with a man. Will had barely acknowledged her son, and had never been affectionate in public. In fact, he had rarely been affectionate in private, either.

Tim broke into her thoughts by asking if she wanted an ice cream. She shook her head, giving him a quick smile. "No thanks, but you go ahead."

"Okay, I won't be long." He slipped out of his seat, leaving her alone with Mac.

Feeling the need to break the heavy silence between them, Sharon said lightly, "Do you know any of the riders here?"

Mac nodded. "As a matter of fact, I thought I'd take Tim back and introduce him, if you don't mind."

"No, of course I don't mind."

He looked at her, his eyes crinkled against the sun beneath the brim of his hat. "You're welcome to come, too, you know."

She managed a smile. "Thanks, but I'll find a shady spot to wait for you."

"Tim will get a kick out of it."

"I imagine he will." She paused, then asked lightly, "How are the lessons coming?"

"Okay. He's impatient to try his first bronc. I think he's getting tired of practicing on a barrel, but he's got to learn how to hold his seat first if he wants to compete."

"I hope he's not giving you any trouble."

"Nope. I'm enjoying it. He's a good kid."

The chill in her heart thawed a little. "Yes, he is," she said softly.

For a long moment they stared at each other, and the sounds of the crowd around them seemed to disappear. Sharon was only vaguely aware of the vendors yelling, the music blaring and the chatter of voices all around her. All that mattered was the face of the man seated just inches away from her.

"Sharon," Mac said, his voice hushed and difficult to hear, "about Tim. I—"

Whatever he was going to say was cut off as Tim scrambled back down the row and plunked himself down between them. Handing an ice cream to Mac, he said urgently, "You'd better lick it now, it's beginning to drip everywhere."

Mac obediently ran his tongue over the ice cream, and Sharon shivered as a vision of him tasting her naked body erupted in her mind.

Tim must have felt the movement, as he looked at her with concern saying, "You can't be cold, Mom. Are you all right?"

"Yes, I'm fine," she said with a nervous little laugh. "I was just thinking of what ice cream does to my teeth."

Her gaze strayed to Mac, who was enjoying his ice cream with all the concentration of a child. Her heart seemed to turn over, and she felt ridiculously like crying. She wondered what he'd been about to say when Tim had interrupted them, and if she would ever know what it was.

"Are you sure you don't want an ice cream?" Tim asked, sounding worried. "I can soon go and get one for you."

"No, thanks. I'll get a soda later on," she assured him.

It was with relief she heard the fanfare that announced the opening event. Determined to put her morbid thoughts out of her mind, she settled back to watch the show.

Chapter 10

Tim sat enthralled throughout the bareback events, shooting questions at Mac every now and again and demanding detailed explanations of the various rules.

Sharon heard Mac pointing out how important the grip was, since it was all the rider had to hold on to. Watching the cowboys fight to stay on the back of the wildly bucking animals, she couldn't help feeling a stab of misgiving.

It was too late now, she told herself. She'd given her promise, and she would have to stick by it. Instead of watching the broncs, she contented herself studying the pickup horse. Beautifully trained, the agile horse and its rider came perilously close to the wildly thrashing hooves of the bronc until the contestant could leap from the plunging back and onto his seat behind the pickup man.

The calf-roping events came next, something Tim wasn't quite so enthusiastic about. Listening to Mac explaining the extent of training a rider and his horse must go through in order to compete in this event, Sharon remembered the nights she used to slip out and try to train Whitefire to back up.

She'd had no idea that Mac had been watching her. How long had he spied on her, she wondered, without her knowing he was there? Had he cared for her then, or had his concern merely been for the young daughter of his boss?

Lost in her thoughts, she was startled when the announcer, informing the crowd it was halftime, followed with the announcement that last year's champion, Mac McAllister, had been spotted in the audience.

"Maybe we can persuade him to come into the arena and take a celebrity ride. Come on, folks, let's give the champ a big hand."

Tim yelped in delight, but Mac looked as if it were the last thing on earth he wanted to do.

Sharon could guess how he felt. This entire afternoon had to be fraught with painful memories for him. To be back in the arena again would only enforce the realization that he would never compete again.

The crowd, however, was not about to let him off the hook. Wildly cheering and clapping, they urged him to come out into the arena. Reluctantly Mac got to his feet, while Tim looked as if he would burst with excitement.

For an instant Mac's eyes met Sharon's above Tim's head. Her heart ached to see the anguish in his face.

"I won't be long," he said quietly, then turned to thread his way down the row amid much backslapping and good-natured comments from the spectators.

While they waited for Mac to reach the chutes, the clowns came out to entertain the crowds, with the help of a very irritated bull.

Sharon barely heard Tim's comments. Her shoulders felt stiff with tension as she waited for Mac to appear. Although his limp had improved considerably, and he appeared to have no trouble riding again, she knew that another fall would probably cripple him for life.

She could only hope he wouldn't be tempted to do something foolish in order to impress the crowd.

A loud burst of applause scattered her thoughts, and her heart turned over once more as Mac rode out on a frisky gray, waving his hat to the crowd as the horse pranced around the arena.

The cheers and whistles were almost deafening. Sharon smiled when she glanced at her son's face. He wore an expression close to adoration as he watched Mac trot past them. She knew he was imagining himself up there, taking a triumphant ride in front of an adoring crowd.

A sudden loud crackling noise snatched her attention back to the arena. What she saw stopped her heart in terror. Someone had thrown a firecracker into the arena almost at the gray's feet. It was on its hind legs, whinnying in fear, while Mac fought desperately to control it.

Sharon jumped to her feet, her eyes glued to the startled horse and its rider. The crowd roared its approval as the horse reared again, but she felt a cold dread as she watched Mac struggling to hold his seat.

Without realizing she'd spoken aloud, she cried out above the noise of the spectators. "Hold on, Mac. For God's sake, please, hold on!"

A clown raced across the arena, trying to make it look as if he was part of the show, while she stood frozen with her hand pressed against her throat.

Before the clown reached Mac, however, he'd finally gotten the spooked horse under control. Amid thunderous applause, he completed the circuit and dismounted, giving his fans a final wave before disappearing behind the chutes.

Sharon sank onto the chair, surprised to find her entire body shaking. She turned to look at Tim, and saw a strange expression on his face as he stared at her.

She gave him a weak grin. "That was close," she said shakily.

Tim slowly nodded his head. "I knew he could handle it, though. He's not champion for nothing, you know."

"I know." Feeling self-conscious now, Sharon uttered a light laugh. "I guess I'm getting overprotective. Ever since your grandfather died, I worry about someone else falling off a horse. I know it's silly." She patted his hand. "Don't worry, I'll get over it."

Tim looked at her, his expression grave. "You like him, don't you?"

Sharon's heart skipped a beat. She waited a moment to compose herself before saying lightly, "Mac? Of course I like him. He's a good worker, and he's nice enough to give you free lessons. I like anyone who saves me money."

Her attempt at humor fell flat as Tim shook his head. "No, I mean you *really* like him." He shrugged his shoulders, looking embarrassed. "You know..."

Sharon sighed. Her son was more observant than she'd given him credit for. "Yes," she said softly, "I really like him."

"Does he know?"

"Oh, I think so." She hesitated, then as Tim continued to watch her, she said quietly, "Tim, just because someone cares for someone else, it doesn't mean that anything's going to come of it."

"You mean he doesn't like you that way."

She smiled, even though the pain threatened to cut her in half. "That's exactly what I mean. And it's nobody's fault. People can't force themselves into feelings they don't have."

Tim looked immeasurably sad. "I know."

Sharon gave him a quick hug. "It's okay, Tim, I really don't mind too much. As long as you and I love each other, that's all that matters to me."

She let him go, and his face brightened.

"Just give him time," he said confidently. "He'll learn to like you, too."

"Maybe." A thought occurred to her. "Please, Tim, promise you won't say anything to Mac. This is our secret, okay?"

Tim looked shocked. "Aw, Mom, I wouldn't say anything to Mac about that stuff."

A stirring of applause as Mac returned to his seat cut off any chance of further conversation. But Sharon couldn't rid herself of the ache beneath her breasts.

For the first time since the night they'd spent together, she'd finally admitted the truth out loud. She didn't know why it should hurt so much, since she'd subconsciously known it all along.

Maybe it was hearing herself say the words that gave them such finality.

Mac didn't care enough for her to give up his freedom. He was never going to make a commitment, either to her or to the son he'd fathered. It was that simple.

Mac stood by the corral railing a few days later and watched Tim go through his exercises on the barrel. Any day now the boy would be ready to take his first ride on a bronc. He had one picked out already. The horse was partially broken, but still frisky enough to give him a good ride.

Mac planned to surprise Tim. He didn't want Sharon to witness her son's first attempt to ride an unbroken horse. She was likely to worry too much, and Mac needed his full concentration on the boy. He didn't want the added distraction of a nervous mother at his side.

The subconscious reminder that he was also Tim's father never failed to give him a jolt. He was doing his best to forget that. There seemed to be so many good reasons why he shouldn't tell Tim the truth and very few why he should.

He couldn't help believing that it would be selfish of him to claim his son. When he thought about the tremendous upheaval the announcement was bound to cause, not to mention the possible repercussions between Tim and his mother, Mac knew he couldn't risk that.

There didn't seem to be any good way to explain why he'd left the Double S, even if he hadn't known about Sharon's pregnancy. And Sharon would have to explain why she had never told her son the truth.

Looking back, Mac thought, he'd been pretty selfish, thinking only about his own shame and guilt, instead of what his leaving would do to the two people he had cared about the most.

He'd done his best to make up for that, even though it had been too late for Randall. He wasn't about to blow it for Sharon now. Not again. If he was the cause of a rift between her and her son, he wouldn't be able to live with himself.

Watching Tim, he felt a sharp ache of regret. Tim had grown up without him, and would manage to live the rest of his life just fine without ever knowing the truth. Better, in fact, if it meant the difference between keeping or losing his relationship with his mother.

Tim's shout broke off his thoughts. "Hey, Mac! How am I doing?"

Mac nodded his approval. "Keep it up, and we'll make a champion of you yet."

Tim swung his foot over the barrel and jumped to the ground. "When am I going to get a chance at the real thing?" he demanded, stomping over to the railing. "I'm getting slivers from that darn barrel."

Mac grinned. "A sliver or two is a heck of a lot better than a broken bone. I don't want to have to explain to your mother why your arm is hanging at a weird angle."

Tim pulled a face. "She always worries too much about me."

"She loves you," Mac said, giving him a friendly slap on the shoulder. "Come on, I guess that's enough for to-day."

Tim climbed over the fence and dropped to the other side. "She's a pretty good mother, I guess, even if she does worry too much."

"You bet she is." Mac glanced at his watch. "We've got about fifteen minutes to wash up before supper."

"She's pretty, too, I guess," Tim said off-handedly.

Mac narrowed his eyes. A little warning bell sounded in the back of his head. "Yep," he said carefully, "I guess she is."

"She's real good at running the ranch, and she knows how to cook and everything."

"Sounds like a good mother to me," Mac said, striving to sound casual. "And she's going to be pretty steamed if we're late for supper, so you'd better get moving."

Tim looked a little frustrated. "Okay. I'll see you at supper."

Mac watched him trot back to the house, his brow creased in a frown. Now, what the heck was that all about? he wondered. Surely Sharon hadn't been saying anything to him?

He dismissed the thought immediately. Sharon seemed every bit as reluctant as he was to discuss the matter.

Not that he could blame her at all. She must be wondering, as he had, just how Tim would've taken the news. She had gone through a pretty bad time with the boy after her father had died, and now finally they seemed to be getting along just fine. It wasn't surprising she agreed with him about not telling Tim the truth.

Cursing under his breath, Mac headed for the bunkhouse. He should have known better than to go into that empty house with her. Knowing how easily she could destroy his control, he should have made her stay outside while he checked out the house.

He'd done his level best not to give in to his emotions again. It was the tears that had finished him. In all the years he had known her, he had never seen her cry.

The sight of those tears glistening on her eyelashes had torn him apart, and he'd been helpless to stop what had followed.

Changing into a clean shirt, Mac let himself dwell on the memory of that night for the first time since it had happened. He hadn't been prepared for the overwhelming intensity of his feelings. He'd never been able to forget the first time he'd made love to her, but the years had clouded his mind, dulling the memory of his response to her touch.

He had no trouble remembering their last night together, however. He had never before experienced that kind of desperation—the hot, throbbing demands of his body, and the raging need to satisfy his raw hunger.

The thrill of her hands on his bare flesh had driven him out of his mind, yet behind it all had been an intense desire to please her, and to bring her to fulfillment.

He couldn't remember if he'd been as considerate the first time. Or even if he'd ever been that caring with any woman. He only knew that this time his need to satisfy and please her had far outweighed his own hunger. The knowledge both surprised and gratified him.

It meant that he had at least kept some measure of control. He didn't want to dwell on what else it meant. It would only lead him down a dangerous path, one he could not allow himself to follow.

He had regained his self-control by the time he joined Sharon and Tim for supper. Tim was chattering as usual about his progress that afternoon, and while Sharon listened and commented now and again, Mac had the feeling that she had something else on her mind.

Tim left the table early that night, intent on going over to Mike's house. After he'd left the room, Mac finished his coffee, trying to think of a good excuse to leave, as well.

"Tim seems to be doing well with the lessons," Sharon remarked in an obvious attempt to break the awkward silence.

Mac nodded. "He'll be ready to ride soon."

Sharon smiled faintly. "I figured it wouldn't be long."

He felt a small stab of sympathy for her. "Don't worry," he said gently, "he'll be fine. I'll go easy on him at first."

"Oh, I'm not worrying anymore." She laughed, a dry sound that held no humor in it. "Not much, anyway. If this is what he wants to do, I'm not going to stand in his way. He would have done it eventually, anyway, with or without my approval. At least this way I know he has a good teacher. The best, in fact, next to my father."

"Thanks," Mac said gruffly. He drained his coffee cup and set it down. He started to get up, but she reached out a hand. The touch of her fingers on his arm was like the stab of a red-hot needle.

"Mac, don't run off just yet."

He sat down again with a dull feeling of resignation. It had to be settled sooner or later. It might as well be now. "Something wrong?" he asked, trying to make his voice sound light.

"I...just wanted to talk to you about...what happened."

He made himself meet her gaze, and felt himself flinch at the impact. Her dark brown eyes looked back at him, filled with pain.

"Okay," he said cautiously. "Shoot."

Her mouth twisted in a wry smile. "I just wanted to say that I understand how you feel. I wanted you to know it's okay. I don't like this tension between us. Even Tim is beginning to notice. He's asking questions."

Mac's mind flew back to Tim's comments earlier. "What kind of questions?"

"He wants to know why we barely speak to each other anymore. He thinks it's his fault. He thinks I resent you for teaching him to ride broncs, and he won't believe me when I say it isn't true.''

He stared at her, searching desperately for something to say.

''I just wanted you to know,'' Sharon said softly, ''that I don't bear any grudges. I wanted what happened as much as you, and I'm a grown woman now. I knew what I was doing.''

He had to get out of there, Mac thought frantically. If he didn't, he was going to reach over there and grab her, and never let go again. ''No hard feelings, then, is that it?''

Her expression reminded him of a doll with a painted smile. ''That's about it. I wanted to clear the air, that's all.''

He nodded and rose to his feet. ''Consider it cleared.'' His own smile felt stiff and unnatural, but he held it until he'd turned his back on her and could escape to his room, where, he promised himself, he'd do his damnedest to blot out all thoughts of Sharon Douglass and try to forget what she could do to his emotions.

The following morning Tim called out to him as he passed the stables. Shading his eyes against the sun, Mac peered up at the roof, where Tim was perched with a hammer in his hand.

''Hold on, I'm coming down.'' Tim dropped the hammer and climbed over to the ladder.

Mac watched him scramble down, wondering what was coming next. He didn't have long to wait. Tim drew him over to the corner of the building and looked around as if making sure no one was within earshot.

''It's Mom's birthday next week,'' he said quietly. ''I want to surprise her.''

Mac's stomach took a nosedive. How could he have forgotten? Seventeen years ago she'd turned eighteen. Almost to the day.

"That sounds like a great idea," he said carefully. "What did you have in mind?"

"I want to take her to her favorite restaurant for dinner," Tim said eagerly. "It's about an hour's drive from here, overlooking the river. It's got great food, great view, candles and dancing, all that stuff that women like."

Mac hid a smile. "I'm sure she'll love it."

"Yeah, well..." Tim hesitated. "There's this girl I know, she's going to be a junior this year, and we kind of got to know each other."

Mac nodded, beginning to see the drift. "And you want her to go, too."

Tim shrugged.

"Well, I was thinking about asking her. She's real interested in the rodeo, and we always have a good time together."

"Well, I reckon your mother won't mind having another woman along," Mac said, laying his arm across Tim's shoulders. "But if you want my advice, mention it to her first. Kind of get her reaction."

"Oh, I was going to do that," Tim said hurriedly. "The problem is, I don't want her to feel left out or anything. I was wondering if you'd come, too. That way it would kind of even things out."

Candlelight dinner and dancing, Mac thought grimly. And Sharon. Just what he needed.

"I know it's not really your thing," Tim said, giving him a pleading look, "but it would really help things out if you'd come."

"Your mom might not want me butting into a family birthday," Mac said, beginning to feel cornered.

"Oh, yes, she would. I know she likes you a lot and..." Tim broke off, looking guilty. "I think she'd like it very much," he added weakly.

Mac hesitated, trying to figure out how he could turn down the invitation without hurting Tim. Somehow he had the feeling that Sharon would not be too thrilled at spending the evening with him. In spite of Tim's insistence that she "liked him a lot."

"Please, Mac," Tim said urgently. "It would really mean a lot to me."

"Well—"

"And Mom," Tim added hurriedly.

Damn, Mac thought irritably. It was impossible to ignore that imploring look in his son's eyes. "Okay," he said gruffly. "If it means that much, I'll go."

Tim swiped the air with a triumphant fist. "Yes!" He rushed back to the ladder, then tore back again. "Just one thing," he said breathlessly. "I want to surprise her, so don't say anything to her, okay?"

"How are you going to do that," Mac asked slowly, "if you're going to ask her about taking your friend?"

"Oh, I'll think of something." Tim gave him the pleading look again. "Please? I don't want to spoil the surprise."

"Okay, okay, I won't say anything. But you'd better make sure she knows before she gets to the restaurant."

"She will, I promise." Tim gave Mac's shoulder a smack that stung. "Thanks, Mac. I knew I could depend on you."

Mac watched him rush off, his heart full of misgivings. Something told him he was making another mistake. It was too late to back out of it now. He would just have to go to Sharon's birthday dinner, and do his damnedest to ignore the mess she made of his good intentions.

Sharon was intrigued that evening when Tim rushed into the kitchen as she was preparing supper, his face brimming with excitement. She hadn't seen him all day, as he'd taken his lunch to eat with the rest of the men at the picnic tables.

"I've got a surprise for you," he announced when she asked him how his day had gone. "I'm going to take you out for your birthday next week."

"Really? That's great! Where are we going?" She watched his face with a pang of bittersweet nostalgia. He'd grown up without her noticing. He was almost a man, and she'd lost the child forever.

"To the Canterbury Inn. For dinner."

"Wow," she said, suitably impressed. "That really is a surprise. And a wonderful one." A fleeting qualm about what she'd wear passed through her mind. This would be the first time she'd had a grown-up date with her son.

"I thought you'd be happy about that." A look of apprehension crept across his face. "There's just one thing—"

"Oh?" She watched warily as he hesitated.

"I'd like to ask Rachel to come, too, that's if you don't mind."

"Rachel?" She wasn't sure if she felt relieved or disappointed. For a moment she'd thought he was going to invite Mac.

"Yeah, she's a girl I met at school. She's real cool, and we like a lot of the same things. I'd really like you to meet her."

"I'd like to meet her, too," Sharon said warmly, feeling immensely pleased. "Of course I don't mind."

"Oh, great. I'll ask her, then." Tim started for the door, then paused, looking back at her. "I might need an advance on my allowance."

Sharon smiled. "No problem. I owe you a salary for fixing up the stables."

"I'm getting paid for that?" Tim's eyes seemed to pop right out of his head.

"Of course. Just because you're paying for a mistake doesn't mean the work goes unrewarded."

"You know something," Tim said, coming back to her to give her a hug, "you are the greatest mom in the world."

"Remember that when I nag you to clean up your room."

He grinned. "I will. And thanks, Mom."

"No, thank *you*. I'm really looking forward to that dinner."

"So am I." He leapt in the air to slap the top of the door frame as he passed underneath it.

Sighing, Sharon put the casserole into the oven. The transition from boy to man could be unpredictable, she thought. But there was no doubt that Tim was maturing. This was the first time he'd wanted her to meet a girl-friend.

Smiling to herself, she rinsed the mixing bowl under the faucet. Things had certainly changed between her and Tim since the fire in the stables. Maybe it was just as well she and Mac had kept quiet about what had happened.

Her smile faded. She couldn't help the little nagging doubt in the back of her mind that Tim deserved to know the truth, no matter what the consequences might be. Shaking off the misgivings, she told herself it was too late now. Nothing would be gained by telling him, since Mac seemed unwilling to acknowledge his son.

A week later she dressed for the dinner with extra care. She wanted her son to be proud of his mom when he introduced her to his girlfriend.

She chose a black silk dress with a short skirt that swirled around her knees. The low, scooped neckline gave her the opportunity to show off the pearls her father had given her when she'd graduated, and she wore matching drops in her ears.

Tiny cap sleeves left her arms bare, and she brushed her hair into a soft, gleaming cloud that settled below her ears. It was the first time in years she'd left her hair untied, and she was pleased with the way the style softened her features. Pale brown eye shadow and a touch of mascara deepened her eyes, and the coral lipstick complemented her light tan. Before leaving the bedroom, she added a dash of her favorite perfume behind her ears, at her wrists and between her breasts.

Her efforts must have been worthwhile, since Tim raised his eyebrows with an appreciative whistle as she walked carefully downstairs on the two-inch-heeled slim black sandals.

"Wow," Tim said, eyeing her outfit, "you look super."

"Thanks. So do you." She grinned at him, her heart turning over with pride at the sight of her son in gray slacks, dark blue sport coat and white shirt. "I hardly recognized you."

Tim's expression changed, and he looked nervously at the clock. "Mom, would you mind if I run over to pick up Rachel? I'll meet you at the restaurant, okay?"

Guessing that Tim wanted to show off his sports car, Sharon smiled. "Sure. I don't mind driving myself."

"Oh, you won't have to." Tim backed hurriedly toward the door. "Mac can drive."

Sharon's heart seemed to leap into her throat. "Mac?"

"Yes." Tim's eyes widened in exaggerated innocence. "Oh, didn't I tell you I'd invited him, too? Sorry, I forgot to mention it. I hope you don't mind."

Sharon's throat felt suddenly dry, and she swallowed. "No," she said faintly. "Of course I don't mind."

"Oh, good." Tim's face flooded with relief. "He should be here any minute, so I'd better get going. We'll meet you at the inn, then."

He'd rushed out of the door and slammed it behind him before she caught her breath. He'd most likely figured she'd put up an argument about Mac being there, she thought, frowning at the door. That's why he hadn't told her until the last minute.

He would have been right. With Mac there she would find it very hard to relax and act naturally.

She would have to try, she told herself as she checked her small black purse to see that she had everything. For one thing Tim had already detected the undercurrent between them. She would be on edge wondering how much he noticed. She could only hope that he would be so wrapped up in Rachel, he wouldn't pay too much attention to his mother.

The worst part would be driving there and back, alone in the car with Mac. It would be the first time they'd really been alone since they had made love a few weeks ago.

Heat surged to her face when she remembered how freely she had explored his body that night. How wild and reckless her response to his touch. For the first time she'd understood what it was like to be so caught up in the throes of passion it was impossible to tame the savage emotions.

Those memories would be uppermost in her mind tonight. She couldn't help wondering if Mac would be thinking about them, too. The doorbell rang sharply, and shock shivered down her spine. He was here.

Slowly she walked down the hallway. She hoped he wouldn't ask her to dance. If he touched her, held her in his arms, she would be lost. Taking a deep breath, she pulled open the door.

She had never seen him dressed up before. His suit was dark gray, and he wore a pearl gray shirt with it. His tie blended in perfectly, in shades of black and gray and a hint of burgundy.

His darkly tanned face was freshly shaven, and she could faintly detect the musky fragrance of his cologne. Somehow he managed to look rugged and sophisticated at the same time, and she had trouble breathing as his appreciative gaze swept over her from head to foot.

His face hardly changed expression at all, but his voice held a slight catch as he said slowly, "You look . . . very nice."

"Thank you." Her own voice didn't sound too natural, and she cleared her throat. "You look quite charming yourself."

His smile was faintly cynical. "Charming? I'm not used to hearing that word applied to me."

"I didn't even know you owned a suit."

"I didn't. I thought I should have something suitable for the occasion. The woman who sold it to me said it made me look debonair."

"I bet she did," Sharon murmured, moving back to let him in.

He stepped inside the hallway. "I don't even know what *debonair* means."

She looked up at him, and caught a gleam of amusement in his eyes. Relief made her feel light-headed. It was going to be all right after all. Whatever feelings he had about his relationship with Tim, he was apparently determined to make the best of the evening. She would take her cue from him, and for Tim's sake, pretend that she was having a wonderful time.

"Shall we go?" she said lightly, and walked out into the cool, fragrant night.

The drive to the restaurant seemed to pass quickly, mostly because the conversation centered around Tim and his progress, both on the work with the stables and with the lessons.

"He'll have to do a lot of the work himself now," Mac remarked, concentrating on the road ahead. "I've taught him about as much as I can. From now on it will be just practice, practice and more practice."

"When will he start riding a bronc?" Sharon asked, trying to keep her attention away from the strong, tanned hands guiding the wheel. It seemed as if everything about him shouted out at her tonight—the line of his thigh resting so close to hers, the touch of his shoulder now and again when they rounded a bend.

Whenever she glanced at his dynamic profile, her pulse quickened and her stomach jiggled with apprehension. She didn't want to dance with him tonight, she told herself. Then in the next breath, *Oh, God, she longed to dance with him tonight.*

"He already has," Mac said calmly.

"What?" Startled, she tried to remember what she'd asked him.

"I guess I should have told you," Mac said, sending her a quick glance. "But I knew you'd worry. You'll be happy to know that he managed to fall off without hurting himself, apart from a bruise or two. I take it he didn't mention it."

Dimly she became aware of what he was talking about. "Tim's been riding a bronc?" she said weakly.

"Yep. He's doing just great. You should be proud of him. He's worked hard."

"Oh, I am," Sharon said quickly. Why hadn't he told her? Why hadn't either of them told her? Were they both so afraid of what she'd say they had to keep it a secret?

Sobered by the thought, she sat back in her seat and stared at the road unwinding in front of them. Dusk was settling over the mountains, and the setting sun had tinged the white peaks with gleaming gold and bronze.

Usually the magnificent sight brought her a special kind of peace, but tonight the turmoil in her heart could not be stilled.

"I'm sorry if I upset you," Mac said quietly. "I thought that was what you wanted."

She made an effort to smile at him. "No, I'm not upset. Just surprised, that's all. I'm happy he's progressing so well."

Mac nodded, but the rest of the drive he seemed preoccupied, and she wondered unhappily if the evening was doomed after all.

Once inside the restaurant, however, Mac seemed to recover his earlier light spirits. Tim and the pretty young girl with him arrived soon after the waiter had shown Sharon and Mac to their seats.

Tim shyly introduced Rachel, who turned out to be a sprightly redhead with a sense of humor and a quick, intelligent mind. Sharon liked her right away.

"I hope you like this," Rachel said, handing a small, carefully wrapped package to Sharon. "They're my favorite."

With an exclamation of pleased surprise, Sharon thanked her and unwrapped the gift. Inside she found a box of candied fruits. "They happen to be my favorite, too," she said, glancing at a grinning Tim. "Thank you, Rachel. I shall enjoy these very much, as long as I can keep them hidden from Tim."

"Aw, Mom," Tim protested.

Rachel laughed and gave Tim a friendly nudge. "Go on, it's your turn."

"Oh, right." Tim opened his jacket and pulled out a long, slim envelope from his inside pocket. "I know you'll like this," he said with another grin.

"I thought the dinner was my gift," Sharon said, taking the envelope from him.

"Well, this is just something extra, for being such a great mom."

Sharon gave him a look that she hoped told him how much his words meant to her. She opened the envelope, and gasped in delight when she pulled out two theater tickets. They were for a local production of her favorite Broadway show.

"Tim, that's wonderful! How did you get them? That show has been sold out for ages."

"I pulled a few strings," Tim said, looking pleased with himself. "You're not the only one with connections, you know."

Thrilled that he'd gone to so much trouble for her, Sharon leaned over and gave him a quick kiss on the cheek. "Thank you, honey. That was a wonderful surprise. You're really spoiling me this year."

Tim shrugged self-consciously. "Well, I figured it's the first birthday without Gramps . . . I wanted to make it perfect."

Sharon looked away quickly before the threatened tear formed.

"I reckon it's my turn now," Mac said, reaching into his pocket. He pulled out a small, square package and handed it to her. "Happy birthday, Sharon."

"Thank you, Mac." She was aware of her fingers trembling as she unwrapped the tiny package. Her breath caught when she opened the lid of the box. Nestled inside lay a pin in the form of a miniature white horse, mane and tail flying as it galloped into the wind.

She could remember, so clearly, the feel of that wind in her hair, the strong muscles moving beneath her as she raced her beloved horse across the meadow with a young, virile Mac thundering behind her.

"Whitefire," she whispered.

She lifted her gaze and met his, questioning, searching for something there that would tell her how he really felt about her.

For a long moment his gaze held hers, and she forgot the other two people at the table. It seemed as if she were there alone with Mac, lost in a love that could not, would not be denied.

Chapter 11

Tim broke the spell by saying, "I've ordered a bottle of champagne. I hope it's okay. I know Rachel and I can't drink it, but I thought you and Mac would probably like to toast your birthday."

Sharon dragged her gaze away from Mac. "Champagne? That's wonderful, Tim."

She and Mac had shared a bottle of champagne once before. Seventeen long years ago. She wondered if he remembered, and found it impossible to look at him again.

When the champagne arrived, Tim made the toast, and he and Rachel raised their glasses of soda. Sharon did her best to keep her hand from shaking as Mac lightly touched her glass with his.

"To many more," he murmured.

She sipped the sparkling wine, while Tim and Rachel echoed the toast. The live band was playing a familiar ballad, and several couples swayed on the minuscule dance floor, barely moving.

"Come on," Tim said, grabbing Rachel's hand, "Let's go and dance."

The two of them left the table and joined the couples on the floor. Sharon lifted her glass and took another sip of champagne.

"She seems like a very nice girl," Mac said, watching the young couple dancing together.

"Yes, she does. I'm so happy Tim has found someone he likes. He never has had much luck with girlfriends."

"Just a late starter, that's all."

She looked up at him, and found him watching her, a quizzical expression on his face. Her heart jumped, and she looked away hurriedly to where Tim was talking animatedly to Rachel. She appeared to be utterly fascinated with what he was saying.

"He's growing up so fast," she said quietly. "I guess it won't be too long before he'll go off somewhere and start his own life."

"You'll miss him."

"Yes." She stared down at the glass in her hands. "All I ask for is that he keep in touch. You know, visit now and again, call me once in a while, spend holidays with me. I keep thinking about that old saying, about a son being a son until he takes a wife."

"He'll keep in touch. You and he have a great relationship now. He won't let that go."

"I hope not." Her heart was pounding again, wondering if he would bring up the subject of Tim's birth. How could he go on ignoring it, she wondered miserably, acting as if it had never happened?

The chance to say anything else at all was lost as Tim and Rachel returned to the table, their faces flushed and slightly bemused. All throughout the meal the two young people seemed absorbed in each other, while Sharon struggled to keep up a conversation with Mac.

At last the dishes were cleared away, and Sharon could look forward to ending the painful evening. Until Tim said suddenly, "I haven't seen you and Mac dancing yet. You can't come out to a nice place like this and not have at least one dance with each other."

Sharon felt a stab of panic. She opened her mouth to make some excuse, but Mac forestalled her.

"I was just about to ask your mother," he said, rising to his feet. He laid his napkin on the table and held out his hand. "Shall we?"

Aware of Tim's eyes on her, Sharon nodded. She couldn't trust her voice to speak.

She led the way to the dance floor, conscious of Mac close behind her. The music seemed to flow over her, soft and sensuous, when he took her in his arms.

"I'm not very good at this," he murmured in her ear as he began to move around the floor.

"Just relax and shuffle," she said, forcing a cheerful note in her voice. "I'll follow."

He smiled down at her, and her heart stopped. She looked away, concentrating on the music. Level with her eyes, his hair curled slightly at his nape. She seemed to be mesmerized by the soft line of it, unable to take her gaze away from his strong, tanned neck.

Her senses sharpened, and she became acutely aware of every sensation—the smooth texture of his jacket beneath her hand, the touch of his thigh against hers, warm and incredibly provoking. There was no longer any sign of a limp. His steps were confident and sure.

His hand clasped hers, palm against palm, and his fingers rested firmly between her shoulder blades. He smelled of soap and cologne, a unique fragrance she couldn't define.

Images raced through her mind—his naked body leaning over her, his voice husky and thick with desire.

She shut her thoughts down, and tried to watch the rest of the couples on the floor.

"You look very beautiful this evening," Mac said softly.

She felt her nerves jump, and looked up at him. "Thank you. It isn't often I get the chance to dress up."

His eyes looked serious as he gazed down at her. "You should do it more often. Get out, I mean."

She seemed unable to breathe again. "I'd like to. Nobody asks me."

He smiled. "Not even Barney?"

Her eyes widened in shock. "Barney?"

"Relax, I'm only joking."

"I certainly hope so. Barney's like a father to me."

"I know." He changed the subject, as if sensing that he'd unsettled her. "I hope you're enjoying Tim's birthday treat."

"Very much." She glanced down to where she'd pinned the little white horse. "And I love your gift. Thank you."

"I saw it when I went to buy the suit. It reminded me of Whitefire, too."

Her heart had begun pounding again. "That was a long time ago."

"But never forgotten."

She smiled wryly. "Certainly not by me."

She felt his body tense, and immediately regretted the thoughtless comment. It was too late now to take it back.

"I'm sorry, Sharon," Mac said quietly. "I know there's not much else I can say."

She felt as if her heart had shattered into a million tiny pieces. There was a lot he could say. He just couldn't bring himself to say it. And she wasn't going to beg. She hadn't then, and she wouldn't now.

"It was over and done with a long time ago," she said briefly. "Let's just forget it."

"I'm not going to forget it, Sharon. I just..." His voice trailed off as the song came to an end.

Unable to take much more, Sharon pulled away from him and hurried off the floor.

"I'm sorry, honey," she said to Tim, "I have a headache. I think I'd like to go home now."

"Oh, that's okay," Tim said, pushing his chair back. "We were thinking of leaving anyway."

Relieved, Sharon said goodbye to Rachel, making her promise to come over to the house for dinner sometime soon. Then, once more she was alone in the car with Mac.

"Have you taken anything?" he asked after they'd traveled some time without speaking.

"What?"

"For the headache."

She shook her head. "I don't like to mix pills with alcohol."

"Good thinking."

She made an effort to pull herself out of the pit of misery she'd slumped into. "I had a wonderful evening, Mac. Thank you for coming."

"I enjoyed it, too. I know Tim and Rachel had a good time."

"Yes." She forced a laugh. "It's hard to remember how it feels to be that young."

"I don't think I was ever that young," Mac said dryly.

Remembering the kind of childhood he'd been subjected to, Sharon felt a sharp pang of sympathy. He'd been Tim's age when he'd first arrived at the ranch. He'd been years older emotionally. It had taken a few more years to soften the hard, bitter edges of that tough, brooding kid.

She settled back in her seat, her heart aching with the memories. How she had adored him. She'd followed him everywhere, copying every word he said, every gesture. Her father had grown tired of correcting her when she'd used the street language that had become Mac's way of communicating.

She had never given up on him. She'd taken his insults, his hurtful remarks, his scorn, his sarcasm, and gradually she'd earned his respect.

She'd wanted more. She'd wanted his love. He'd cared for her then. He'd admitted as much. But that was a far cry from the kind of love she had felt for him. That was something she would never have.

"What are you so busily turning over in your mind?"

She started, unaware that he'd been watching her. "Oh, nothing much. Mostly about Tim, I guess."

The look he gave her was strangely intense, and for a moment her skin tingled. Then he turned his attention back to the road, and she was left to wonder what had been the reason behind that odd stare.

Thinking about it gave her an uncomfortable feeling in the pit of her stomach. There seemed to have been a purpose, an odd sense of finality behind that look. She didn't care to dwell on what it might mean.

A few minutes later Mac pulled up in front of the house and switched off the engine. The sudden silence seemed to numb his thoughts, freezing them in a safe place where they couldn't torture him anymore.

He climbed out of the car and walked around to the passenger side. For the first time in weeks he was conscious of the ache in his leg. He almost gave in to the need to limp again.

Sharon didn't wait for him to open the door for her. She was out of the car and heading for the steps before he reached her. He followed her up to the porch, feeling more tired than he'd ever felt in his life.

"Will you be all right?" he asked as she fitted her key into the lock.

She sent him a quick, nervous smile. "I'll be fine, thanks. I don't have to worry now about someone lurking around the house. Besides, I'm sure Tim will be home soon."

He nodded. "In that case, I'll say good-night."

She didn't look at him again. Instead, she stepped inside the hallway, sent a muffled "Good night, Mac" over her shoulder and gently closed the door.

He felt as if the world had suddenly shut him out. He stood for a long moment, staring at the door that remained firmly closed between them, then he turned and made his way slowly down the steps.

His footsteps on the driveway seemed to echo in the branches of the pines as he trudged toward the bunkhouse. Halfway there he paused, his gaze on the shadowy outline of his pickup. He hesitated for a moment, then headed for the vehicle, unbuttoning his jacket on the way.

Reaching the truck, he dragged off the coat and threw it onto the seat. Then he climbed inside, tugging on his tie until it was free of his neck.

His keys were in his pocket. He pulled them out and fitted one into the ignition. The sound of the engine exploded across the meadow like a blaze of gunfire.

Dragging open the top two buttons of his shirt, he gunned the motor and shifted into gear. The pickup rolled forward, and he headed down the driveway to the open road.

He passed Tim's sports car on the way, but didn't look to see if Tim had recognized him. He didn't want to think about Tim.

He needed to be where there were people, loud music and a smoke-filled haze of lights. A place where he could hide from the painful thoughts that wouldn't let him alone.

He arrived at the tavern and parked in the back. He could hear the thump and wail of the latest country tune as he crossed the parking lot, his feet keeping in time with the persistent beat.

The door opened before he reached it, and a group of young people spilled out—laughing, shouting, bumping into each other as they hit the darkness of the cool night air.

He pushed past them, into the choking, warm atmosphere of the bar. The shrill laughter of a skinny woman with black-rimmed eyes screeched in his ear as he shouldered his way to the counter.

She eyed him up and down while he waited for the barman. "Hi, honey," she purred as he let his glance flick over her.

He deliberately turned his back on her, leaning an elbow on the counter while he looked wearily around the room. What he saw only depressed him more.

The dim yellow lamps hanging low over the tables wore a halo of smoke. The men and women who sat there gazed at each other with a lustful sentimentality that would disappear like morning mist once the effects of the beer wore off.

It was a game that lonely people played—all of them looking for something that would always be just out of reach. Each of them hoping to find the elusive answer in the face of the stranger who sat opposite them.

"What'd you want, fella?" the barman's hoarse voice demanded behind him.

"Forget it," Mac muttered. "I've changed my mind." He left the bar and climbed back into his pickup, then headed out of town until he could breathe clean air again.

He sat on an outcrop of rock under a carpet of stars with the valley spread out below him. He was looking down on Douglass land, and it looked small and defenseless from his perch on the ridge.

Although it wasn't a big spread, it brought in a good living. Now that things were beginning to turn around again, it should be fairly easy for Sharon to keep the Double S working on schedule.

He flicked a small pebble off the edge of the ridge and listened to it scattering dust as it tumbled down below. Tim would probably pull his weight more now that he had the prospect of competing in rodeo.

Mac spread his feet in front of him and studied his boots. That's the way it should be, mother and son working together. They didn't need anybody coming along to mess that up.

If Tim learned the truth, he could resent it enough to put a rift between him and his mother that would never be mended. It was easy to see how much her son meant to Sharon. Tim had been her whole world ever since he was born.

It wasn't as if the boy would lose anything by not knowing the truth. He'd grown up without ever knowing his father.

Mac swore and flipped another pebble over the edge. It would be better to let things be. Now that Sharon had resolved her differences with Tim, he couldn't risk coming between mother and son and maybe messing up everyone's lives again. He'd already done that once. And the longer he stayed around, the bigger the chance of Tim finding out about him.

Pain knifed through him as he contemplated his future. Maybe he was always meant to go it alone, free of any commitments or responsibilities. Maybe Sharon had done him a favor by showing him how impossible it was for him to be a part of any family.

Getting to his feet, Mac paused long enough to gaze down for the last time on the Double S. Deep in his subconscious, he'd always reckoned on coming back some day. Even though he'd left, he'd never really cut himself off from that.

Now he was leaving for good, and the pain went deep. This had been his first real home. And probably his last.

Turning his back on the memories, he climbed into the pickup and headed out.

* * *

Sharon slept fitfully, her sleep disturbed by shadowy dreams where she danced with Mac, only to find herself alone in an empty ballroom, dancing with empty arms amid the sound of jeering voices laughing at her.

She awoke with a start in the early hours of the morning, and couldn't go back to sleep again. After a while she gave up, and got up to make some coffee.

The morning paper was on the doorstep, and she picked it up, hoping that the headlines wouldn't depress her any more than she was already. As she turned to go back inside, something caught her eye.

A white envelope had been tucked inside the framework of the porch, close to the front door. Frowning, Sharon plucked it out and looked at it.

Her name was scrawled on the front in a hand she instantly recognized. The letter was from Mac.

At first she wanted to tear it open right there, but the fear of what it might contain held her back. Instead, she carried it into the house, and left it lying on the writing desk while she went back to the kitchen to pour herself a cup of coffee.

She stood at the kitchen window for a few moments, staring out at the eastern sky. As she watched, the sun broke through the clouds and sent golden shafts of sunlight in all directions. After a minute or two the clouds closed again, obliterating that brief moment of glory.

She closed her eyes, and prayed for the strength she knew she would need. Then she made herself carry her coffee back to the den and sit down at the writing desk.

The hot liquid scalded her throat as she swallowed the first mouthful, but she was scarcely aware of the pain. The ache beneath her ribs hurt a lot more.

Carefully she set the steaming mug down on the desk and picked up the envelope. Sliding her thumbnail under the flap, she lifted it, then drew out the sheet of notepaper. She held it in hands that were unnaturally still, and started to read.

I couldn't leave this time without saying goodbye. Although I couldn't find the courage to face you with this. I guess I was afraid you'd look at me with those beautiful, sad brown eyes and change my mind. It's not going to work, Sharon. I'm not cut out to be a family man. I never learned how to be a father, and I'm too old to start learning now. Just be glad we didn't tell Tim the truth. At least he won't know that his real father ran out on him twice.

There was more, words she could hardly see for the tears that stung her eyes. He'd left a list of instructions for the men, and a recommendation that Barney be promoted to foreman.

Reaching the bottom of the letter, she dashed a hand across her eyes to wipe away the tears.

Tell Tim to keep his head up and his shoulders back, and never let the bronc forget who's boss. I hope he won't hate me too much for leaving without saying goodbye. Tell him I'll watch for him on the circuit. Thanks, Sharon, for taking in a beat-up cowboy for the second time. It was more than I deserved. Sorry it had to be this way.

So long, Mac.

As daylight slowly filled the room, she folded the sheet of paper and tucked it into the pocket of her robe. She didn't know yet if she could bear to keep it or bear to part with it. One thing she did know. Tim must never see it. He must never know. The pain would be twice as hard to bear if he found out that Mac had left before he'd had the chance to acknowledge him as his father.

Somehow, she thought as she watched the clouds drifting across the sky, she would have to tell Tim that Mac was gone. But not right now. This was her time to grieve, and when she was done, she would not open up that part of her heart ever again.

Laying her arms on the desk, she leaned her forehead on them and gave in to the tears.

By the time Tim came clattering down the stairs, she had composed herself. A shower had helped revive her, and makeup had managed to disguise the worst of the ravages caused by her weeping.

She even managed to smile as Tim rushed into the kitchen and threw himself down at the table. "What did you think of Rachel?" he asked eagerly as she planted a plate of pancakes in front of him.

"I like her." Sharon turned back to the stove and poured the warm syrup into a jug. "She's bright, funny and very well mannered."

"She loves horses, too," Tim said, munching on a mouthful of pancake. He chewed for a minute, then swallowed. "I was thinking about inviting her over to see me ride the bronc. Do you think Mac will mind?"

Sharon put the syrup down on the table. "Tim—"

"He seemed to like her, didn't he?" Tim grabbed the syrup and poured it over his plate. "He was being real nice to her."

Sharon took a deep breath. "Tim, I've got something to tell you."

He glanced up at her, his face changing when he saw her expression. "You and Mac had a good time, didn't you? I mean, you were dancing and everything...." His voice trailed off, and he put down his fork with a clatter. "Mom? What's the matter? Something hasn't happened to Mac, has it?"

Sharon sat down on the chair and reached for Tim's hand. "I'm sorry, honey. I'm afraid Mac has left."

Tim snatched his hand back as if he'd been burned. "Left? What do you mean?"

"I mean he's gone. Packed his bags in the night and left."

Tim looked back at her, full of accusation. "Why didn't you tell me he was planning on leaving?"

"I didn't know," Sharon said, praying her voice wouldn't break. "He didn't say anything to anyone. He just left."

How she hated to see the disillusion in her son's eyes. He stared at her for a long time as disbelief and anguish swiftly gave way to resentment.

"He seems to make a habit of doing that," he said, his voice flat and expressionless. "I guess we should have expected it."

Swallowing her own pain, Sharon said softly, "Honey, I'm so sorry. I know how much you liked him."

Tim shrugged, pushing his half-eaten breakfast away from him. "It's not so much me, it's you I feel bad about. I really thought he liked you."

From somewhere Sharon conjured up a smile. "Men like Mac aren't capable of feeling deeply for anyone. He was hurt very badly when he was a child, and he's never learned how to love. Mac belongs to a very different breed of men, Tim. They are loners, drifters, always moving on and leaving nothing behind but the memories. I guess no one ever truly owns the heart of a cowboy."

"Well, I'm not going to be like that," Tim said defiantly. "Even if I joined the rodeo circuit, I wouldn't be like that. I'd still want a wife and a home some day, and maybe a dog and kids—" He broke off, looking embarrassed. "Well, you know what I mean."

"Yes," Sharon said gently. "I know. Just don't be in too much of a hurry, okay?"

"Oh, I won't." Tim got up from the table. "I've got too much to do first. I've got college, and decisions to make.

I have to decide what I want to do with my life first. Maybe then I'll think about marriage.''

Once more the tears stung her eyes. But now they were tears of relief. *I have to decide what I want to do with my life first.* Apparently, now that the obstacles to his dream had been removed, he didn't seem so anxious to pursue it. She had a lot to be thankful for, she thought, smiling at her son.

"I've got to get out here and see to the livestock," Tim said, eyeing the clock on the wall. He paused, then put his arms around her, giving her a swift hug. "Don't worry, Mom," he said gruffly. "You've still got me and all the other guys out there."

She hugged him back, feeling some of the pain ease just a little. "I know," she said, fighting more tears. "I love you, Tim."

"Love you, too." He let her go and rushed out the door, calling out over his shoulder, "I'll be back for lunch."

She watched him pound across the grass to the bunk-house, her heart aching for what might have been.

Today, she decided, she would allow herself to grieve. Tomorrow she would be strong again. Tomorrow she would begin the difficult path back to the way things had been, before a tall, blue-eyed cowboy had drifted into her life and shattered it for the second time.

Tomorrow she would start forgetting, and put the past behind her forever. Tomorrow.

The following days were difficult to get through—the nights impossible. After a week of lying awake, tossing from side to side in a rumpled bed, Sharon decided she had to get tough with herself. She needed something new in her life, a new direction to take her mind off her problem.

The idea hit her in the early hours of the morning. At first she rejected it completely, but the more she thought about it, the more sense it made.

Tim had no real interest in the ranch, except for learning how to ride the rough stock. He didn't need to live on a ranch to do that. In any case, the way he'd been talking lately, it seemed as if his interest in the rodeo was waning. He hadn't mentioned it in several days.

The repairs were finished on the stables, all the mares had foaled and the older colts were just about ready to be shipped to the broker.

Sharon sat up, her heart beginning to pound. She would sell the ranch. They could buy a house in town, closer to Portland, even. She would be closer to Tim when he went to college, and she would begin a whole new life for herself. There were plenty of things she could do; maybe she could even start a small business somewhere.

She could meet people, and have a social life instead of burying herself on a ranch in the middle of nowhere.

An image of Mac's face formed in her mind, and for a moment her heart twisted in pain. Then she shut him out, and concentrated on everything she would have to do.

Unable to go back to sleep, she slipped out of bed and went down to the kitchen. With swift, unconscious movements, she filled the coffee machine and measured the coffee into the basket. Her mind raced with decisions, questions and calculations as she reached in the cupboard for a mug.

The voice behind her startled her out of her wits. "Mom? What are you doing up in the middle of the night?"

She swung around to face Tim, who was staring at her with a dazed, worried look on his face. "I'm sorry, honey," she said quickly. "I couldn't sleep. I didn't mean to wake you."

"I wondered who was down here." Tim slumped down on a chair, looking half-asleep. "I thought we had a burglar."

Sharon smiled at him. "If we had, the dogs would have barked."

"Yeah, I guess. I didn't think of that." He peered sleepily up at her. "You okay? You're not sick or anything, are you?"

"No, I'm not sick." She opened up the fridge door. "You want a soda?"

He nodded and she took one out, pouring it for him into a glass. "Here. My coffee will be ready in a minute.

Tim sipped the dark liquid, and put the glass down. "So tell me why you can't sleep. Are you upset about something?" He narrowed his eyes and stared at her. "Is it Mac? Are you still upset about Mac leaving?"

She looked at him, uncertain how to answer. "I'm thinking about selling the ranch," she said quietly.

Tim's jaw dropped open. "Why? I thought we were doing great again."

"We're doing all right. But I'm getting tired of living here alone. You'll be in college soon, and now that Gramps has gone, there's really nothing to keep me here any longer."

He stared at her, his eyes full of disbelief and confusion. "It *is* Mac, isn't it?" he said roughly. "If he hadn't left, you'd have been perfectly happy to stay here. Damn him. I wish he'd never come back. I hate him."

Surprised by his vehemence, Sharon said quickly, "I don't want you hating anyone, Tim. Mac cared for you very much. He was proud of all you'd achieved. He told me to tell you he'd be watching for you on the circuit."

Tim's eyes widened. "When did he tell you that?"

For several moments Sharon was at a loss for words. The silence seemed to go on forever, while Tim continued to stare at her with growing suspicion in his face.

It was no use, Sharon thought. She would have to tell him the truth. He deserved to know the truth about his father. And the best way to learn it was from Mac himself.

"I have something to show you," she said. "It will explain everything."

She left Tim sitting at the table, his face a mask of confusion, and hurried to the den. Her hand shook as she pulled down the lid of the writing desk and opened the small drawer in the back.

Taking out Mac's letter, she unfolded it and read it one more time. Then, with a heart full of apprehension, she walked slowly back to the kitchen.

Tim looked up expectantly when she walked into the room. "I want you to read this," she said. "Mac left it for me the night he went away. I didn't show it to you before, and I think you'll understand why when you read it. Before you do, though, there's something I want to say first."

Tim's glance drifted down to the letter, then back up to her face. "All right," he said, sounding skeptical.

"I want you to know, Tim," Sharon said steadily, "that whatever I have done in the past, I did because I felt it was best for everyone concerned. I'm sure Mac felt the same way."

Tim's frown deepened. "I don't understand."

Taking a deep breath, she handed him the letter. "Read this," she said quietly. "Then you'll understand."

She waited, her gaze intent on Tim's face, as he read the letter. She saw his eyes widen, and a deep red flush stained his face.

He read the letter through twice, then slowly lifted his head. "My father?" he whispered.

Sharon nodded and sat down heavily at the table. "I know I should have told you the truth a long time ago," she said, covering his hand with hers. "At first I didn't because I didn't think it would be fair to Will. He might not have been much of a father to you, but he did help raise you for the first seven years."

"I never did feel that close to him," Tim said slowly.

"I know. I guess I should have told you the truth after we left, but you were seven years old, it was hard to explain a thing like that to a little boy. I guess I was afraid to add more confusion on top of all the upheaval of leaving Will. In any case I never expected to see Mac again."

"You could have told me when Mac came back," Tim said.

He was looking at her as if she'd struck him, and her heart ached. She let go of his hand and silently pleaded with him to understand.

"I was going to tell you," she said, "but when Mac first came back, he didn't know the truth, either. I never told him."

"Why not?"

The harshness in his voice seemed to knife through her heart. She was silent for a moment, thinking through her words before speaking them. "He would have insisted on doing the right thing and marrying me," she said at last. "I didn't want him on those terms. I wanted him to marry me because he loved me. Not because he was forced into it by his own sense of decency. None of us would have been happy that way."

"It wasn't too decent of him to run out on you, either," Tim said in disgust.

"I guess he was afraid of getting too deeply into something he couldn't handle." She took a quivering breath, knowing she couldn't take too much more.

"What did he say when you did tell him?"

"He was shocked, of course." Sharon closed her eyes briefly, remembering those painful moments. "But when he'd had time to absorb the news, I could tell he was thrilled. It was while you were in the hospital. You were sleeping and he came and looked down at you."

She smiled at the bittersweet memory. "I wish you could have seen the look on his face. He looked as if he'd just discovered a miracle."

"Is that why he ran out on me? Because he was thrilled to know I was his son?"

The pain in his voice matched the ache in her heart. Desperately Sharon wished there was something she could say to take away the hurt in his eyes. "It had nothing to do with you, Tim. You must believe that. Mac left because he isn't able to settle down. He just couldn't face the responsibilities."

"Why are you making excuses for him?" Tim demanded, shoving back his chair. "He ran out on you, after all you did for him. I know how much he meant to you. I could see it in your face every time you looked at him."

"Please, Tim, don't get upset on my account." Sharon got up, too, and laid a hand on her son's arm. "I've always known what Mac is, and it's not his fault."

"You're right," Tim said coldly. "He's not worth getting upset about. If he can walk away from both of us that easily, he's just not worth it."

Watching him charge out of the room, Sharon wished she could agree with him. For no matter what Mac had done or how much he had hurt her, she could not make herself stop loving him.

Maybe in time she could stop hurting quite so much, but the kind of love she felt for Mac was the kind of love that could not die. As long as she lived, she would love him, as she always had, ever since that first night she'd seen him standing rebellious and defiant in her father's den.

Face it, she told herself as she cleared away the breakfast dishes. Whether he wanted her or not, she was Mac McAllister's woman.

Mac hadn't been able to leave town after all. He'd found a quiet motel a mile or so down the road and decided to hole up for a while until he could get his head on straight. He needed time to think, to decide what he was going to do next.

He couldn't go back to the rodeo; that much was certain. He could no longer compete, and he couldn't face the thought of taking one of the menial jobs available after being top dog. God knows he had little enough pride left. He had to hang on to whatever tiny piece of it remained.

He spent the next week or two combing the ads in the daily paper. Nothing appealed to him. The only thing he knew was horses, and there wasn't too much call for a ranch hand in this neck of the woods. Most of the local ranches were small and family run. He would have to go out to eastern Oregon or Washington if he wanted ranch work.

Yet something held him back. A persistent, stubborn part of him that would not let him leave. He wasn't even sure what he was waiting for or why he was hanging around. Both Sharon and Tim probably hated him by now. The only good thing about it was that Tim didn't know he'd lost a father again.

God, how he missed them. He'd lie awake at night, fighting the urge to relive over and over again that night he'd spent in Sharon's bed. No matter how hard he tried, he couldn't forget.

Tossing around in the tangled covers, he cursed himself for his weakness.

He missed Tim, too. He kept imagining he could hear his son's voice, the whoops and yells as he rode the plunging back of the bronco, his back arched and his free arm thrashing the air.

He would not let himself dwell for long on the memories. Each time they invaded his mind, he shut them out, hiding behind the invisible shield that had always served him so well in the past. Nothing could get past that formidable barrier. He'd made very sure of that.

One night, as he walked the solitary path that led to a field behind the hotel, he hit upon an idea. He didn't need to work for anyone. He had enough put away to buy some land . . . not much, but enough to make a living, if he did things right.

Not that he wanted to be in competition with Sharon, even if he could. He couldn't afford a spread that size, anyway. But the way things were going, there'd certainly be enough business for both of them. He didn't need a lot of money, just enough to get by.

Feeling the first stirring of interest that he'd had since he'd left the Double S, Mac took his nightly stroll across the field to think about it.

The night was clear, allowing the stars to sparkle in a velvet sky. The moon rode low over the distant mountains. It looked a little hazy, promising more hot weather for the next day.

The night scents of the woods wafted on the gentle breeze, and the sudden sharp fragrance of fir knotted his stomach. Deliberately he made himself forget the Double S.

He concentrated instead on his plans for a new ranch, when he found the land. He couldn't decide what to call it, and after a while gave up trying to think of something. There would be plenty of time for that once he'd bought the land.

Suddenly impatient now, he turned back to the motel, anxious to look at the latest ads. The machine outside the motel often had the Sunday paper on Saturday evening.

As he rounded the corner of the building he saw a red sports car, a lot like Tim's. For a minute his heart stopped, then he shook his head. He had to stop seeing reminders of Sharon in everything he saw.

Cursing himself, he dropped the coins into the machine and took out the paper. He was halfway back to his room when he saw a shadow move in front of his door. Again his pulse leapt, and this time he couldn't dismiss the illusion. For there, coming out into the light, was the tall, lanky figure of his son.

Chapter 12

Mac waited, delight mixing with apprehension as he watched Tim walk slowly toward him. Something about the set of the boy's shoulders warned him that this was not a joyous reunion.

Tim halted in front of him, and in the shadowy reflection of the street lamp his face seemed to have aged. "Hi," he said in a tone Mac had never heard him use before. "I saw your pickup. I figured you weren't too far away."

Mac winced, wondering if he'd subconsciously parked his truck so it could be seen from the street. "It's good to see you, Tim."

"You might change your mind about that when you hear me out."

Mac sighed. It was obvious now that Tim wasn't there to chat about the rodeo. For a treacherous moment he wondered if Sharon had sent him. "Look," he said, "I know how you must feel—"

"No, I don't think you do." Tim backed away as Mac attempted to lay a friendly hand on his shoulder.

Mac shrugged. "Well, at least come inside. If you've got something to say, I'll listen."

"I don't want to come inside." He looked around the darkened parking lot, as if making sure they were alone. "I just came to tell you that I know you are my father."

He'd said it so matter-of-factly that Mac wasn't sure he'd heard right. Then he was left in no doubt as Tim added quietly, "I just wanted you to know that I don't need you. I never have. And neither does my mother. She's doing fine without you. It might have been nice to have you in our lives, but we don't *need* you."

Mac's heart seemed to turn to ice as he watched his son march steadily over to his car and climb inside. The sound of the engine ripped the silence of the parking lot, and then roared away down the street and out of his life.

He walked slowly back to his room, went inside and closed the door behind him. Sinking onto the bed, he held his head between his hands, trying to stop the overpowering thoughts tumbling through his brain.

He'd lost Sharon. He'd never fully realized that until now. Memory after memory assaulted his mind until he thought he would go crazy. The ache spread rapidly throughout his body, a crippling, haunting physical pain that was like no other he'd ever felt before.

This was what he'd been afraid of all of his life—this tearing, agonizing pain of loss. He'd fought it all before...when his brother had died, and the first time he'd left the Double S.

This was what he'd struggled to avoid during the savage beatings he'd received from his father. The physical pain he could endure, and eventually recover from the scars it left on his body. The mental anguish was something else. Something he would not allow himself to feel.

Control...that's what made him a man instead of the sniveling animal his father had wanted him to be.

Only now he seemed to be losing the fight. Now it was real, far more terrible than he'd ever imagined. So fierce he moaned out loud. Putting his head down on the pillow, he finally gave up the battle and let the agony wash over him, until at last he fell into an exhausted sleep.

"Have you had any bites on the ad?" Tim asked as Sharon dished up the linguine for supper one night.

"A couple." She set the plates down on the table and returned to the stove for the bread rolls. "I talked to the agent on the phone today. He's got someone coming out at the weekend to take a look."

Tim nodded, his concentration on the food on his plate. "How soon do you reckon they'll want to take over?"

"I don't know." She felt the same sharp pang of apprehension that had bothered her every time she thought about leaving the ranch. "I hadn't really thought about it." She set the rolls down on the table and sat down.

"Don't you think we should start thinking about it?" Tim attacked a roll with the butter knife. "I mean, we must have somewhere to go when we move out."

Again the sharp little pain hit her. "I suppose we should. I thought we might sell most of the furniture, maybe to whoever buys the ranch, and then move into an apartment until we decide where we want to go."

"I really don't want to go anywhere," Tim mumbled. "I'm happy here."

"Don't talk with your mouth full," Sharon murmured absently. She hated to admit it, but she was beginning to have serious second thoughts herself. In the next instant she chided herself for her cowardice. How was she going to make a new life for herself if she was buried at the ranch? The loneliness would be enough to drive her insane.

Throughout the rest of the week she found herself repeating that question more and more often. The closer it got to the weekend, the more sure she was that she'd be making a mistake to move. The Double S was her life. How would she survive in the city, she wondered, when all she'd ever done was work with horses?

By Friday morning she'd come to a decision. Maybe one day she'd sell the ranch, she told herself, but not now. Tim still had another year of high school. She'd wait until he was in college and see how she felt then.

With a tremendous rush of relief, she eagerly dialed the agent's number and gave him her decision. Then smiling, she replaced the phone. Now, she thought, to tell Tim.

He was in the corral when she found him, and he reacted pretty much as she'd guessed he would when she told him the news. With a wild whoop of relief, he swung her off her feet. "I was hoping you'd change your mind. I like breaking in the horses. I think I'd rather do that here at the Double S than travel all over the place next summer with the rodeo."

Sharon laughed out loud. "That decision wouldn't have anything to do with a certain pretty redhead, would it?"

He grinned. "It might. Then again, I am the man of the house now. I should be pulling my weight around here. Besides, Barney is a bit sloppy as a foreman. He doesn't notice things too well. He needs me behind him all the time to show him what needs doing."

"I really don't think he likes being foreman," Sharon admitted. "He doesn't seem to have the right temperament for it."

Tim nodded. "Yeah, I noticed. It's like he's afraid to tell the men what to do in case they get mad at him."

"Well, give him as much help as you can," Sharon said, giving him an affectionate pat on the shoulder. "By the time you're back in school in the fall, I should be able to find us a new foreman."

The familiar pain was just as sharp and as prolonged as that first morning when she'd read Mac's farewell letter.

It had taken her a long time to heal after the first time he'd left. This time it seemed as if the pain was getting worse instead of better.

Shaking off her sudden depression, she watched Tim for a moment as he expertly slipped a halter over a shying bay. He seemed to have grown up overnight. If there was one thing Mac had done for him, it was to teach him how to be a man.

Sadly she turned and headed back to the house. It was too bad the two of them had never had any time together as father and son. They would have been so good for each other.

Deciding once again that there was no point in dwelling on what might have been, Sharon headed back to the house, her mind full of plans to spruce up the place now that she had decided to keep it.

New curtains, she thought, and maybe wallpaper in the living room and den to brighten things up. She could even move Tim to the large bedroom at the end of the house, once she'd cleared out her father's things.

Feeling more positive with every step, she tried to forget the past and concentrate once more on tomorrow.

It wasn't so easy to forget, though, when night fell and she was alone in her room with only the shadows for company. Once more the memories invaded her mind, giving her yet another restless night.

The next morning she was still tormented by Mac's lingering image that had kept her awake the night before. After clearing away the breakfast things, she watched Tim take off in his sports car, on his way to spend the day with Rachel at the lake.

Feeling somewhat abandoned, Sharon decided to take out Windsong for a ride. She didn't bother with a saddle; it had been a long time since she had ridden bareback and she wanted the special feeling of being one with the horse.

Windsong seemed happy to be free of the binding girths, though he accepted the bridle with his usual patience. Slipping onto his back, Sharon gathered in the reins and clicked her tongue at him.

Immediately he moved off, and she urged him into a trot and then a gallop once she was past the corrals. She rode for an hour, taking the trail along the creek.

She paused every now and then to watch blue heron fish in the water, and listen for the slap of a beaver's tail warning of her approach. Soon she began to feel the peace again, as she usually did when alone with nature.

At last she was ready to go back to the house. She paused at the top of the rise to gaze across the meadows where she had grown up. They spread out before her, green and gold under the hot summer sun.

To her surprise, instead of the quiet, serene empty space she usually saw, a horse and rider appeared, speeding toward the rise.

Her heart jerked in apprehension, and she narrowed her gaze, shading her eyes against the sun. It couldn't be Tim; he was gone for the day. And it surely couldn't be any of the ranch hands. Unless something was wrong.

She held her breath, anxiously worrying at her bottom lip as the rider drew closer. Windsong jerked his head, stepping sideways as the thunder of hooves echoed across the valley. For a moment her gaze was distracted as she turned the horse back. When she looked up again, her breath seemed to slam into her throat.

She recognized the rider now. Her heart began to pound, and her fingers curled on the reins as she watched Mac racing toward her.

She waited, hardly daring to breathe, until he pulled up in front of her, reining in his snorting horse.

"Barney told me you were here," he said, steadying the restless animal with his strong, expert hands. "I want to talk to you."

She couldn't seem to speak. He looked the same, yet different somehow. He wore a tan work shirt, open at the neck, and jeans tucked into Western boots. His black hat sat low over his eyes, and as always she couldn't tell anything from his expression.

She had visualized his face so many times in the past weeks. Looking at him now, at the familiar rugged features, his mouth looked softer than she remembered, his jaw more relaxed.

"I won't keep you long," he said as if he'd taken her silence as a protest, "but there's something I want to say. I know how you must feel about me now, but I couldn't get out of your life without saying it."

She could feel the tiny flutter of apprehension swelling into a feeling almost of terror. She had nursed the hope before, and watched it die an agonizing death. She would not let him hurt her again.

"Don't," she said sharply. "I don't want to listen to anything you have to say."

"I don't blame you." He shifted his position on the horse, moving the animal with a subtle ease until he was between her and the trail back to the ranch. "I know I have no right to ask you to listen, but I'm going to anyway. I need to talk to you."

Yes! her mind screamed silently. *Listen to what he has to say!*

She tightened her hold on the reins. No matter what he wanted to say, it couldn't be what she wanted to hear. He'd probably decided he was better off working on the ranch than trying to find a job elsewhere.

He probably wanted his job back, and if she listened to him, she might just be stupid enough to give it to him. He seemed to have that effect on her. He could always cloud her mind with confusion just by looking at her.

Then she would have to face the prospect of seeing him every day, and dying a little inside every time she set eyes n him. No matter how much the ranch needed him, she ure as hell didn't need him. She didn't need the heartache or the disruption his presence always caused.

And there was Tim to consider. How would he take having his father around, after Mac had made it clear he didn't want to acknowledge his son?

"Leave me alone," she said abruptly before Mac could mesmerize her once more with his compelling gaze. "I don't want to talk to you. In fact, I never want to see you again."

She thought she saw a flash of pain in his eyes, but she couldn't be sure. In any case, she wasn't going to wait around to find out. The thought that he might care enough to hurt was enough to sway her judgment. She had to get out of there before she succumbed to whatever hold he always seemed to have on her emotions.

Gathering up the reins, she made herself look into his eyes with all the indifference she could command. "As far as I'm concerned, you are through with the Double S, Mr. McAllister. I'll thank you to get off my horse and off my land. And please do me the favor of staying off it."

He gave her a long, hard look while she steeled herself to return it, then without another word he wheeled the horse around and urged it into a furious gallop toward the ranch.

She was shaking, trembling so hard Windsong kept shifting beneath her. She couldn't go back to the house. Not yet. She needed to be alone, somewhere where she could cry and no one could hear her.

Turning Windsong's head, she nudged him forward, breaking into a trot and then a fast gallop. Head down, she urged the powerful horse into the trees and the narrow trail that would take her to the clearing.

There she could be alone, except for the birds and the squirrels, and maybe an inquisitive deer. None of them would care if she laughed or cried. No one but herself, and her broken heart.

She barely remembered the ride. Leaves and twigs brushed her hair as she ducked beneath the branches, and now and again one clipped her face. She scarcely felt the sting. Her emotional anguish was far too intense to care about a scratch or two.

Reaching the clearing, she slid off Windsong's back and tied him to a tree. Then she flung herself down in the damp, cool grass and cried with the abandon of a child.

She never heard him coming. She was either too over-wrought, or making too much noise herself. He'd left the bay somewhere in the woods and walked the rest of the way, his feet making little sound on the soft earth.

The first indication she had of him being there was his voice, quietly speaking her name.

"Sharon," he said softly. "Please...don't cry. You never cry."

Immediately she caught the next sob and held her breath. Lying flat on her stomach, her head buried in her arms, she waited until she could trust herself to speak. "Go away," she muttered. "I told you, I don't want to talk to you."

"Sharon..." He paused, and the silence was so deep even the birds appeared to have stopped singing. The thundering of her heartbeat in her ears seemed to be the only sound in the quiet, shaded circle of trees.

"I love you, Sharon," Mac said quietly.

At first she couldn't trust herself to believe she'd heard the words. She held her body stiff and tense, afraid to let go of the defense she wore like a suit of armor.

"Dammit, Sharon, did you hear what I said?"

"I heard," she said bitterly, her voice muffled by her arms. "It's a little late, isn't it?"

He was silent so long she was afraid he'd left. Then he spoke in a low voice raw with emotion. "I don't blame you

>r being bitter. If it's any consolation, I have a pretty low
>pinion of myself right now. I don't expect you to come
unning back into my arms. I don't deserve you, and I
now it. But dammit, I can't leave without telling you how
feel.''

"What about how I feel?" she turned over and sat up,
rushing her hair back from her eyes. "When did you ever
onsider that?"

For the first time since the night she'd first laid eyes on
im, she saw misery in his eyes. Her pulse leapt, but her
ride and her skepticism wouldn't allow her to accept what
e was saying.

"I thought I was doing the right thing. I didn't know
ow much you meant to me until I knew I'd lost you."
lowly he lowered himself to the ground beside her. "All
y life I've been terrified of losing someone I love. I was
kid when I lost my brother, the only person I loved and
usted in the world. I couldn't bear to go through that hell
gain. I guess I wouldn't let myself love anyone... until
ou."

She couldn't look at him. If she did, she'd fall into his
ms and forget all the pain he'd caused her. She waited,
the almost unbearable silence, for him to go on.

"Sharon, I loved you from the moment you faced me
cross Whitefire's back and made me realize you had be-
ome a woman. I wouldn't admit it to myself, and when I
ok the most precious gift a woman can give a man, I
uldn't live with myself. I thought I couldn't give you
hat you wanted and needed. I took the easy way out. It
as the biggest mistake of my life."

"And then you did it again." She looked at him then,
er heart wanting desperately to believe him, her head
arning her not to listen.

"I know," he whispered.

She had never seen such pain in his eyes before. In all the
ne she had known him, she had never seen him display

such emotion. If she didn't know him better, she would have said he was close to tears.

"I don't know how to say I'm sorry," he said, reaching for her hand. "I was afraid of so many things. Of disappointing Tim. Worried that he'd reject me as his father, guess. Then I was worried that knowing the truth might put a wedge between the two of you. You'd worked so hard on improving your relationship with him. I know how much that meant to you."

"I can't live my life for my son," Sharon said gently. "He has his own life to live. I must have mine. That took me a while to figure out, I admit, but it's clear enough now."

He turned her palm over, holding it as if afraid of hurting her. "That wasn't all of it. I figured that what I'd done to you in the past would be too tough for you to forgive. couldn't see how you could possibly love me after that. guess I was afraid to find out for sure. It was easier to walk away."

"It always is. I've done some of that myself."

Very slowly he lifted her hand to his mouth and pressed his lips to her palm. "Would you believe me if I swear to you that I'll never walk away from you again?"

All at once her heart seemed to melt. "Can I have that in writing?" she asked unsteadily.

The blaze of hope in his eyes was beautiful to see. "I'd take a plane up and write it across the sky if it would help."

"You can't fly a plane."

His mouth hovered on a smile. "I could learn."

"I think a Valentine's card every year would be safer."

"You got it." His gaze raked her face, as if still searching for something. "I meant what I said, Sharon. I do love you. I've never admitted needing anyone in my life, but need you as I need the air to breathe. I'm only a shell without you."

At last she could believe him. With joy bursting in her heart, she placed a hand behind his neck and pulled him toward her. "Prove it," she whispered.

He raised his eyebrows at her. "Here? Isn't this a little primitive?"

"Can you think of a better place? After all, we were under the open sky the first time we made love."

"We were a lot younger then."

She lowered her hands and began unbuttoning his shirt. "What's age got to do with it?" she murmured.

His breath caught, and he shuddered as she slipped her hand inside his shirt. "Not a damn thing," he muttered thickly. "Come here, woman. Let's find out how primitive we can be."

She gave herself up to him, heart and soul, as his skillful fingers brought her again and again to the brink of fulfillment. She was on the point of begging when he finally obeyed her urgent demands and slid into her, filling her with the hot expectation of a rapture long denied.

As his plunging body brought her back to the point of exquisite pleasure, she cried out, her voice blending with the song of the birds. Then, at long last, she reached the summit, and together with him sailed through the barriers of misgivings and doubt, into the golden promise of a deep and everlasting love.

"How did you know where I was?" she asked as he sat beside her later, picking leaves out of her hair.

"You always used to come here when you were a kid if you were angry at your father for something. Remember the time I looked all afternoon for you and finally found you here?"

She nodded. "I remember. I was angry at first, angry that someone else had discovered my special hideaway. But then I was glad it was you."

"You were real angry." His smile was rueful. "You chewed me out for invading your privacy. It was almost more than I dared to come here again."

"I was a little brat, wasn't I?" she plucked a fat blade of grass and smoothed it out between her fingers.

"A cute little brat. I used to think you'd have been a lot better off if your father hadn't tried to raise you as a boy."

She looked up at him quizzically. "Used to?"

"Not anymore. I like the way you are. Even if you are stubborn as all get-out."

"No more stubborn than you are."

"True." He gave her a wry grin. "It only took me seventeen years to admit that I love you."

"Is that what you came back to tell me?"

She watched his face as he nodded. He did seem different. More at peace with himself, and so much more relaxed than she'd ever seen him.

"I tried to tell you up on the rise," he said, "but you wouldn't listen."

"I thought you'd come back to ask for your job back. I wasn't about to give it to you, and go through hell every time I saw you."

"You always were quick to jump to conclusions. You didn't give me a chance to explain."

"I was afraid you'd look at me with those gorgeous blue eyes and change my mind."

He winced at the quote from his own letter. "I'm sorry, Sharon. Is Tim very angry with me?"

She lifted her shoulders. "At the moment, yes."

"I can't say I blame him."

Her heart began pounding uncomfortably as she watched his face. "I told him," she said quietly.

She felt a jolt of surprise when he said briefly, "I know. He came to see me."

"He did? When? He never told me."

"A few days ago. He told me he knew I was his father and that he didn't need me. And neither did you."

Her heart ached for him. "He was wrong. We both need you."

He looked up, his eyes searching her face once more. "Need?"

She smiled, knowing what he was waiting for. "Need, and love," she said gently.

He still looked unconvinced.

She reached for his hands and held them against her breasts. "Surely you know that I love you, Mac. I've always loved you. Ever since the moment I first set eyes on you in my father's den."

His face brightened like the sunrise of a new day. "That's all I need to hear." He leaned forward and gave her a long, lingering kiss. When he finally let up, she was breathless.

"I just hope that Tim can be as forgiving," he muttered as she pulled back.

She smoothed the frown lines between his brows with her fingers. "Let's go find out," she said softly.

Tim came home late that night. Waiting in the living room with Mac by her side, Sharon had to admit to strong misgivings about how their son would react to seeing his father again.

By the time the sports car roared up the driveway, she could feel her stomach tying itself up in knots. Even Mac looked apprehensive as the front door slammed and Tim's footsteps sounded in the hall.

He halted in the doorway, a worried look on his face. "Hi! I saw the lights on. Are you...?" His voice died away as he caught sight of Mac.

Sharon's heart skipped nervously as a closed look crept over her son's face. "What's he doing back?" he demanded shortly.

"Tim—" Sharon began, but Mac stopped her with a hand on her arm.

"No. I'll handle this." He got up from the couch, but stayed where he was facing Tim across the room. "I know this will be a shock to you, Tim, but I've asked your mother to marry me and she's accepted. I love you both very much, and I want to be a real part of this family. I hope you'll allow me to try and make up for all the time I lost as your father. I know it will take time for you to accept me, but I'm willing to wait as long as it takes."

Tim's astonished face turned toward his mother. "You're going to marry him?"

Sharon nodded, giving her son a hopeful smile. "I love him," she said simply.

Tim's eyes, so like his father's, stared at her for a long moment. Then he shrugged. "Well, if it's okay with you, it's okay with me, I guess."

Glancing up at Mac, she saw his eyes glinting bright in the light from the lamp. "Want to shake on that?" he asked gruffly, and held out his hand.

Tim looked a little taken aback, but he nodded and came forward to shake Mac's hand. "I don't know if I can get used to calling you Dad," he mumbled.

Mac's laugh sounded unsteady. "That's okay. 'Mac' will do just fine."

Tim leaned down and planted a kiss on his mother's cheek. "Congratulations. When's the wedding?"

"We haven't decided." She caught his hand. "I'm very happy, Tim. I want you to know that."

He nodded, looking embarrassed. "That's okay, then. I'm going to bed now. I'll see you guys in the morning." He reached the door and looked back at Mac. "I guess we won't need to look for a new foreman now."

Mac grinned. "I guess not. You'll have a permanent one around here from now on."

"Sounds good to me." Tim gave his mother the ghost of a smile and disappeared through the door.

"He didn't have much to say," Mac said warily.

"Give him time to get used to it." Sharon caught his hand and pulled him down beside her. "After all, it's not every day a young man acquires a new father."

"It's not every day a beat-up old cowboy gets a son. And a wife." He heaved an exaggerated sigh. "I just hope I'm up to it."

She pulled his head down to hers. "You'll do just fine."

He gave her a long, satisfying kiss, and she sighed with pleasure when he finally lifted his head.

"There's something I have to tell Tim in the morning," she murmured as she settled her head against his shoulder. "I have to tell him I was wrong about not being able to own the heart of a cowboy."

* * * * *

COMING NEXT MONTH

**#709 MADDY LAWRENCE'S BIG ADVENTURE —
Linda Turner**
Heartbreakers
He was the hero of her dreams…as if he were straight from the pages
of a book! But to prim-and-proper librarian Maddy Lawrence,
Ace MacKenzie was all too real and way too dangerous. Because shel-
tered Maddy now found herself on the adventure of a lifetime…
and falling fast for one too-good-to-be-true man.

#710 HUNTING HOUSTON—Sandy Steen
Abby Douglass knew all about men like Houston Sinclair: risk-taker,
pleasure-seeker…*possible killer*. And now her job—her very life—
depended on how well she learned this man's secrets. But in hunting
Houston, Abby found one very frightening truth: she was in love with
a wanted man.

#711 UNDERCOVER COWBOY—Beverly Bird
If single mom Carly Castagne had learned anything, it was that men
couldn't be trusted! And that included Jack Fain, the brooding cowboy
who'd arrived at her ranch full of questions and long on charm. But
what exactly did this man want, and how far would he go to get it?

#712 CHILD OF THE NIGHT—Lee Karr
Tyla Templeton knew Clay Archer was dangerous—she just didn't
realize how dangerous until after she fell in love with him. But could
she trust a man whose own daughter was afraid of him? Somehow
Tyla had to discover the secrets hidden in the Archer family…or lose
the man she loved.

#713 THE ONE WORTH WAITING FOR—Alicia Scott
The Guiness Gang
She hadn't seen him in years, but Suzanne Montgomery would never
refuse Garret Guiness anything—especially after he collapsed on her
doorstep from a gunshot wound! Now town spinster Suzanne found
herself awakening to the only man worth waiting—or dying—for.

#714 THE HONEYMOON ASSIGNMENT—Cathryn Clare
Assignment: Romance
Newlyweds? That was the last role investigators Kelley Landis and
Sam Cotter wanted to play. They'd come close once, but a tragedy had
driven them apart, confirming their single status. That is, until their
honeymoon assignment had them hearing wedding bells…for real!

"Motherhood is full of love, laughter
and sweet surprises. Silhouette's collection
is every bit as much fun!"
—Bestselling author Ann Major

This May, treat yourself to...

WANTED:
MOTHER

Silhouette's annual tribute to motherhood takes a
new twist in '96 as three sexy single men prepare for
fatherhood—and saying "I Do!" This collection makes
the perfect gift, not just for moms but for all romance
fiction lovers! Written by these captivating authors:

Annette Broadrick
Ginna Gray
Raye Morgan

"The Mother's Day anthology from Silhouette is the
highlight of any romance lover's spring!"
—Award-winning author **Dallas Schulze**

by Beverly Barton

Trained to protect, ready to lay their lives on the line, but unprepared for the power of love.

Award-winning author Beverly Barton brings you
Ashe McLaughlin, Sam Dundee and J. T. Blackwood...
three rugged, sexy ex-government agents—each with a
special woman to protect.

J.T. Blackwood is six feet four inches of whipcord-lean man.
And in April, in BLACKWOOD'S WOMAN (IM #707), the
former secret service agent returns to his New Mexico ranch
for a well-deserved vacation, and finds his most dangerous
assignment yet—Joanna Beaumont. The terror Joanna fled
from five years ago has suddenly found her. Now only J.T.
stands between his beautiful tenant's deadly past and her
future...a future he is determined to share with her.

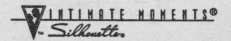

BBPROT3

Alicia Scott's

Elizabeth, Mitch, Cagney, Garret and Jake:

Four brothers and a sister—though miles separated
them, they would always be a family.

Don't miss a single, suspenseful—sexy—tale in
Alicia Scott's family-based series, which features four
rugged, untamable brothers and their spitfire sister:

THE QUIET ONE...IM #701, March 1996

THE ONE WORTH WAITING FOR...IM #713, May 1996

THE ONE WHO ALMOST GOT AWAY...IM #723, July 1996

"The Guiness Gang," found only in—

by
Cathryn Clare

The Cotter brothers—two private detectives and an
FBI agent—go wherever danger leads them...except
in matters of the heart!

But now they've just gotten the toughest assignments of
their lives....

Wiley Cotter has...
THE WEDDING ASSIGNMENT: March 1996
Intimate Moments #702

Sam Cotter takes on...
THE HONEYMOON ASSIGNMENT: May 1996
Intimate Moments #714

Jack Cotter is surprised by...
THE BABY ASSIGNMENT: July 1996
Intimate Moments #726

From Cathryn Clare—and only where
Silhouette Books are sold!

CCAR1

STEP

INTO

THE

A collection of award-winning books
by award-winning authors!
From Harlequin and Silhouette.

Available this May

A Human Touch
by Glenda Sanders

VOTED BEST SHORT CONTEMPORARY
ROMANCE—*RITA AWARD WINNER*

When dire circumstances force together a single mother with
an adorable one-month-old baby and an arrogant lawyer,
emotions start to get out of control as *A Human Touch* proves
to have a powerful effect on their lives.

"Glenda Sanders weaves a masterful spell..."
—*Inside Romance*

Available this May wherever Harlequin books are sold.